PRAISE FOR GEORGE PELECANOS'S
SHOEDOG

"James M. Cain established the drifter as a dark knight of American crime fiction. Pelecanos continues that tradition here....All sinners, none saints, the small-time hoods in this authentic world are crisply limned here in their fallible humanity." —*Publishers Weekly*

"In the best tradition of hardboiled fiction, Pelecanos's haunting, gritty story works its way deep into his readers' collective psyches, simultaneously shocking, attracting, and repelling us with its unvarnished, unbeautiful realism and its explosive, stomach-churning violence. An exceptional, memorable book from a fine writer who is also the author of the equally impressive Nick Stefanos series, which includes *Nick's Trip*." —Emily Melton, *Booklist*

"Don't skip a page of the book...or you'll miss a canny portrait of the shoe salesman (a stripped-down echo of Nick Stefanos in *A Firing Offense*, 1992, and *Nick's Trip*, 1993) who teaches Constantine about Life, or a late-blooming noir retrospect that's so dead-eyed that the sentiment takes on a comic edge. More fun than a Late Show marathon—starting with *The Asphalt Jungle*." —*Kirkus Reviews*

"A hardboiled classic. Thrilling, brilliant.... Pelecanos seems incapable of writing badly, always on top of his form.... An excursion into looming noir territories—a world in which everyone seems doomed."   *—Uncut*

"A model exercise in dysfunction and doomed American cool."   *— The Guardian* (UK)

"*Shoedog* packs an unmistakable Pelecanos punch; a murky tale from a muddled world where honor is a rare thing— especially among thieves."   *—Crime Time*

"Pelecanos aims straight and truly into the abyss with his noirish *Shoedog*."   *—Washington Post Book World*

"*Shoedog* is one of the best examples of noir I've come across in a long while...ranking right up there alongside the works of Jim Thompson and Cornell Woolrich."
                                              —Mike Baker, author of *Cemetery Dance*

"The ending left me reeling. Fans of hardboiled fiction are well advised to check this out."   *—Armchair Detective*

SHOEDOG

SHOEDOG

A NOVEL

GEORGE PELECANOS

BACK BAY BOOKS
Little, Brown and Company
New York   Boston   London

Copyright © 1994 by George P. Pelecanos
Reading group guide copyright © 2013 by George P. Pelecanos and Little, Brown and Company
Excerpt from *The Double* copyright © 2013 by George P. Pelecanos

Back Bay Books / Little, Brown and Company
Hachette Book Group
237 Park Avenue, New York, NY 10017
littlebrown.com

Originally published in hardcover by St. Martin's Press, May 1994
First Back Bay paperback edition, August 2013

Back Bay Books is an imprint of Little, Brown and Company, a division of Hachette Book Group, Inc. The Back Bay Books name and logo are trademarks of Hachette Book Group, Inc.

ISBN 978-0-316-24656-9

Library of Congress Control Number 2013942253

10 9 8 7 6 5 4 3 2 1

RRD-C

Printed in the United States of America

To my parents

SHOEDOG

CHAPTER 1

THE FIRST thing Constantine noticed, as the car pulled over and slowed to a stop, was the bumblebee emblem on the grille. The car had been repainted, twice at least, and the paint now covered the stripes and graphics that had originally wrapped the rear quarter panels and trunk. Constantine listened to the big engine idle, checked the dual scoops on the hood. Stripes or no, this was a '69 Super Bee. He had not seen one of those on the road since high school.

The second thing he noticed was the guy driving the car. From what Constantine could make out, a gray flattop and below that a creased forehead barely clearing the top of the wheel, the guy looked small and a little old to be driving a sixties muscle car.

The car appeared to be sound, though, and a ride was always just a ride. Constantine dropped his thumb and lifted the padded strap of his JanSport pack, easing it onto his shoulder, and walked toward the Dodge that was stopped on the berm. He bent forward and leaned his forearm on the lip of the open passenger window.

"Thanks for stopping," Constantine said.

"Sure," the old man said. "Hop in."

Constantine tossed his pack on the backseat and dropped into the passenger seat, shutting the door. The old man threw the Hurst shifter into first, gave the Dodge some gas. The car spit gravel, moved off the shoulder, and accelerated onto the two-lane.

They drove northwest on 260, the interstate densely lined by oak and scrub pine, broken occasionally by odd, isolated residences, sprawling ramblers of brick and stone. The radio was off, but the old man was moving his head rhythmically, a slight, childish smile on his face as he pointed at the low, white-flowering trees that dotted the interior of the woods.

"Wild dogwoods," he said, turning his head briefly to Constantine. The old man's eyes looked blue as the spring sky, his smile broad and genuine, though it was not a smile to cause worry. Constantine looked at the eyes and the tough hands grasping the wheel, and decided at once that these were not the eyes or the hands of a chicken hawk. "Maryland's beautiful this time of year. Beautiful."

Constantine nodded. "Today was a nice one. I was down at Chesapeake Beach this morning, looking out at the bay." He had sat there on a bench, in fact, for several hours, staring out at the sun-whitened water, the bay at that point expansive as the ocean.

"You from down this way?" the old man said.

"No."

"Where you coming from?"

Constantine stretched his legs, watched the trees blur by. "I was in Annapolis for a couple of days. Had a line on a job there."

"What kind of work?"

"Driving a man around town. A man who had money. A little bit of caretaking, too. That sort of thing."

"A driver, huh?" The old man looked Constantine over, then returned his eyes to the road. "Didn't work out?"

Constantine checked the old man's windbreaker, his worn Wranglers. "Let's just say the guy wore pants with whales on 'em, wore his sweaters tied around his neck. The old-money-and-marina crowd. It wasn't my stick." He sighed, squinted, and drummed the dash with his fingers. "Hitched out of Annapolis this morning, ended up in Chesapeake. I picked up a map there and saw that I was headed into a dead end. Here I am, looking to get out."

The old man took one hand off the wheel and stretched it to the right. Constantine shook it.

"My name's Polk."

"Constantine."

"Just Constantine?"

"That's right."

"I knew a Constantine once. A Greek."

"I'm not Greek."

Polk kept on: "Course his own people never called him Constantine. They called him Dean, some of 'em called him Dino. But I always called him Connie, and he didn't seem to mind. You don't mind if I call you Connie, do you?"

Constantine said, "I don't mind."

Polk barked a cough into his hand, then rubbed phlegm off along the leg of his Wranglers. "You wouldn't happen to have a smoke on you, would you, Connie?"

Constantine reached into the breast pocket of his denim shirt and retrieved a thin pack. He pulled out a Marlboro, handed it to Polk, and crushed the empty pack in his fist.

Polk waved. "I don't want to take your last one."

"I can get more," Constantine said. "Take it."

Polk shrugged and flipped the filter between his teeth as he pushed the lighter into the dash. The lighter popped half a minute later and Polk fired the smoke. "You like the car?" he said.

"Yeah," Constantine said. "I like it."

"It's not the quickest one Dodge made. They had a six-pack version that year—"

"I know. Four-forty Magnum V-eight with three Holley carbs. The big scoop on the hood, though, it attracted too much heat. Anyway, this three eighty-three—it'll do."

"That it will." Polk gave Constantine an admiring glance. He dragged deeply on the cigarette and said through the exhale, "So, where you headed?"

"South."

Polk chuckled. "South's a direction, son. I mean, where you *headed?*"

Constantine said, "Just south."

For a minute or so there was only the sound of the big engine, and the wind jetting into the car. Polk tried again: "I didn't mean to pry. But the reason I was asking, see, it happens that I'm heading south as well. Florida to be exact. Thought maybe we'd head that way together."

Constantine looked over at Polk. The old man talked too damned much, but he was all right. Constantine liked him a little bit; at least he liked him enough to share the ride. "That would be good," he said, pushing his hair behind his ear, settling into the bench seat.

Later, when Constantine walked toward the big brick house, the Beat in his head, the grip of the .45 warm in his hand, the siren wailing in the night at his back, he would think that the whole thing started on that road, with the car stopping for his upturned thumb. He would think that the things that happened to a man were put in motion by something just that small, that random. He would think about that, and he would laugh. But he would keep walking.

"I've got to make one stop, Connie," Polk said, "just above Dunkirk. A man there owes me some dough, and I want to collect. Okay?"

Constantine nodded lazily and closed his eyes. He was listening to the purr of the 383, and thinking of the fine free feel of the wind.

CHAPTER 2

SOMEWHERE NORTH of Dunkirk Polk turned off Route 4 and drove down a two-lane blacktop heavily wooded on both sides. The woods broke on the right to an open field bordered by a split-rail fence. Constantine noticed a stable with one black horse grazing just outside its entrance. The field ended and then there were more woods, though the fence continued along the road. After a while the woods ended again to another stretch of open land, where a large brick colonial sat back a hundred yards at the end of a long asphalt drive. Polk slowed the Dodge and pulled off, stopping in front of a black iron gate bookended by two brick columns. He killed the engine and turned to Constantine.

"This shouldn't take long," Polk said. "Want to get out?"

"Okay," Constantine said. "I gotta take a piss."

They opened the doors and exited the car. Constantine unzipped his jeans and urinated into the gravel of the berm, watching Polk walk toward the gate. The old man had a deep limp, and Constantine noticed the creased toe area of his left shoe. It flapped sloppily with each step, as if it had been filled with something less substantial than bones and flesh. Constantine zipped his fly, adjusted his denim shirt, and walked onto the asphalt drive where he joined Polk at the gate.

Polk pressed a buzzer set beneath a speaker on the left brick column, keeping his eyes on the house. Constantine noticed a broad figure move into the frame of the wide second-story window that was centered above the front door and its stone portico. The figure held a pair of binoculars to its face, then disappeared. Some time passed and then a voice came from the box above the buzzer.

"Yeah?" the voice crackled.

The old man looked into the box. "Polk, here to see Grimes."

"What can I do for you, Polk?"

"I'm here to see Grimes, Valdez. Tell him, and open the gate."

"He's not in."

"Tell him, Valdez."

There was no reply. Constantine listened to the wind rustle the leaves on the trees across the road.

The Latin-tinged voice came back, its inflection stirring a faint recollection in Constantine of the Mexicans he had known in the kitchens and bars south of Los Angeles.

"Wait there, Pops."

Some chuckling on the other end, and then the box went dead. Polk's face, his jaw set hard during the entire conversation, did not change.

Constantine patted his breast pocket where his pack of smokes should have been. He looked down the road at the split-rail fence that fell from view at the next curve, and he looked back at the squat brick pillars and the electronic gate. He wondered, Why the gate, when you could just hop the low wooden fence, or drive through it if you had some weight beneath the hood? He stopped wondering when he heard the front door of the house open and shut.

Two men in black suits walked slowly out toward three black cars—a Mercedes, an Olds 98, and a Cadillac—that were parked at the circular end of the asphalt drive. One of the men was tall and heavy. The other looked to be of average height, and skinny. They got into the Cadillac, the skinny man slipping in on the driver's side. He started the car but let it run for a couple of minutes before he slopped the trans into reverse. Constantine thought that they could have walked quicker down the driveway. He shifted his feet as the Caddy rolled slowly toward the gate.

The driver stopped the car ten feet shy of the gate and touched his hand to the visor. The gate opened in, just clearing the front bumper. The engine continued to idle as the heavy one and the driver got out of the car.

Polk did not move up to meet them. They stopped walking two feet shy of Constantine and Polk, keeping their eyes on Polk. Both of them wore black ties tightly knotted into white button-down collars, with scuffed black oxfords on their feet. The heavy one had a wide brown face and a black mustache, the hairs long and thin, like the whiskers of a cat. His shirt gapped at the belly, and his neck rolled like chicken fat off both sides of his collar. But it would be a mistake to judge him as soft in any sense of the word—Constantine could see the hard bow in his chest, the callused solidity of his meaty hands, and the lazy, uncentered look of his black eyes.

The heavy one said, "It's three o'clock in the afternoon, Pops. You know what that means?"

Polk didn't answer or nod. Constantine figured from the accent that the one doing the talking had been the voice on the box, the one Polk had called Valdez.

"'A Lifetime of Love,'" Valdez said. "Every day I forget all the shit and I sit down in front of the TV set and watch this show. Today is a special show, see, one I been waiting for. This guy they call Taurus, he's the international spy, for a month now he's been trying to nail this brunette, a real piece of ass by the way, like all the ones they get to fall in love with Taurus, before they leave the show to make it in the movies. Personally I figure the guy likes it up the ass in real life, on account of he's an actor, but I root for him to get laid anyway, and today I figure he's gonna nail the brunette. And I been waiting for this to happen, like I say, for a month."

Polk said, "So?"

The skinny one laughed through his nose, the lines deepening on his long, gray face. A gust of wind caught the lapels of his jacket then, blowing them back to reveal the black butt of an automatic wedged into a loosely hung, brown leather shoulder holster. Constantine tried to remember if any cars had passed on the road since they had stopped at the gate.

"So," Valdez said, "I'm a little pissed off with you right now, Pops. You're making me miss my show, all because now we gotta do this dance, even after I told you over the radio box here that Grimes ain't in."

Polk nodded toward the two remaining cars parked in front of the house. "His Ninety-Eight's in. He's in."

"So I'm a liar, then," Valdez said, his eyes getting small. "Is that it?"

"Yes," Polk said evenly. "You're a liar."

Valdez whipped his right hand out and struck Polk's chest with the flat of his palm. Polk went down into the gravel of the shoulder, dust stirring into a cloud around him.

Constantine did not move toward Valdez or the skinny one, and he did not move to help the old man. Whatever this was about, it was Polk's affair. Constantine had taken bad rides before, from drunks, zipperheads, and old homosexuals, and he knew now that he had caught a bad ride today. But the bad parts of those other rides had always passed, and if he stayed where he was, cool and alone, then this bad thing would pass as well.

Polk put his weight on his good foot and stood up straight. He brushed gravel and dust off his windbreaker and Wranglers and walked back toward Valdez without emotion. Through all of it the skinny man had not moved, and neither he nor Valdez had looked directly at Constantine.

"You can keep pushing me," Polk said, "but I'm going to see Grimes. He owes me money."

Valdez laughed shortly as he flicked some loose skin off the bridge of his blunt nose. "You were right, Pops. I lied. And Mr. Grimes told me you wouldn't go away. So he said for you to come back early tomorrow. We'll have a big meeting, talk about your money and maybe a lot more. Ten o'clock. Okay?"

Polk said, "Tell him to have the twenty grand ready, ten A.M."

Polk turned and limped back toward the Dodge. Constantine followed, heading for the passenger side.

Valdez spoke to their backs: "By the way, who's your sidekick?"

Polk answered, kept walking. "My friend's name is Constantine."

The skinny man said, "Some friend."

Constantine slid into the car, their laughter trailing him like a dead leg. Polk got in and fired the engine, reversing the Dodge onto the two-lane without a word. He threw it in drive and headed down the road.

Valdez and the skinny man, who was called Gorman, watched the Dodge take the curve and disappear. They walked to the Caddy and got in, Gorman closing the gate with a touch to the gadget clipped onto the visor. He turned the car around without going off the asphalt and drove slowly back toward the house.

Valdez said, "Step on it, man. I want to catch the end of 'A Lifetime of Love.' I swear to Christ, I been waiting all month for Taurus to nail that brunette. Fuckin' Polk."

Gorman gave the Cadillac some gas. "What's with the twenty grand?"

"Ancient history," Valdez said. "A job we did six years ago. The old man, he's a hard dick, he comes by every coupla years for this money he says Grimes owes him. We always send him on his way."

"What about tomorrow?"

"Grimes wants to put him on the Uptown job. He's a gimp, but he's a good gun."

"What if he don't wanna go out on the Uptown job?"

"I don't know," Valdez said. "Grimes is getting tired of him. I think maybe this time, the old man pushes it too far, Grimes is gonna have me kill him."

Gorman yawned, then rubbed his cheek. "His friend's got weird eyes, like he don't give two shits about nothin'. You notice?"

Valdez said, "I noticed."

"What are you gonna do about him?" Gorman said.

Valdez shrugged. "If he makes me," he said, "I guess I kill him too."

POLK RETURNED to Route 4 and headed northwest. Constantine glanced at the old man, who was grinning now, humming something through his teeth, as if he had not been threatened, as if fifteen minutes earlier he had not been pushed down into the dirt.

"Listen, Polk, about that back there—"

"Don't sweat it," Polk said. "That was acting. We're all a bunch of actors, understand? Anyway, you played it right."

Constantine watched the signs as they approached 301. He could take that south across the Potomac River Bridge into Virginia, maybe down into the Carolinas, maybe back to Murrells Inlet. He could do that and get away from this, right now.

"I'll get out up ahead," he said.

Polk smiled. "Don't give up on me yet, Connie. We'll swing back and pick up that money tomorrow morning, then shoot south. In the meantime, we'll just head on into D.C. for the night. I've got a girl-friend we can stay with, a swell girl by the name of Charlotte." Polk turned his head and winked at Constantine. "She's got girlfriends, too."

Constantine drummed his fingers on the dash as they passed across 301. The traffic had thickened, and the air had lost its green smell. "Washington—I don't think so, Polk."

Polk looked at Constantine's dour expression, his slightly pale face. "What the hell's wrong with you, son? We drive into town, we spend the night, we're gone in the morning. You can count on it."

"It's no big deal," Constantine said without conviction.

"So what's the problem?"

"There isn't any, I guess. It's just"—Constantine cleared his throat—"I was raised in D.C., understand? And I haven't been back in seventeen years."

Polk and Constantine drove in silence for the next few miles. Finally Polk looked across the bench. "We don't have to go in," Polk said. "Not if you don't want."

Constantine squirmed in his seat, pushed hair away from his face. "Fuck it, Polk," he said. "Just drive."

Polk grinned. "No big deal, right, Connie? We pick up the money in the morning, and then we drift south. That okay by you?"

"Sure," said Constantine. "Long as we keep drifting."

CHAPTER 3

LONG AS *we keep drifting.*

That had been Constantine's sole conviction for the past seventeen years.

He had left home at eighteen, a summer graduate of a military high school academy, enlisting immediately for a four-year stint in the Marine Corps. He loathed both the order and the ridiculous concept of uniformed teenagers that marked his high school years, and had in fact possessed both the grades and the SAT scores for entrance into a moderately respectable liberal arts college. But he had enlisted in the corps partly because it was a free, stringless ticket out of the neighborhood, and specifically because it was against his father's wishes.

His father had said, in a rare display of emotion, that "only trash go into the service these days," and Constantine had said, "Is that all you've got to say about it? How about 'good luck'?" His father's only reply was, "You disgust me."

On the last night before he shipped out, Constantine stayed with his girlfriend, Katherine, whom he had met at the Catholic sister school dance the previous fall. They smoked from a bag of Colombian, drank cherry wine, and made love throughout the night on the hill that led to the woods bordering the neighborhood's elementary school. At dawn, Katherine promised to write every week. Constantine kissed her one last time and walked back to his house to get his gear.

His father was up in his own bedroom dressing for work. Constantine retrieved his duffel bag and sat in the dark stillness of the living room, waiting for his father to come downstairs and say goodbye. But his father did not come down the stairs, and after a while Constantine put the strap of the duffel bag across his shoulder and walked out into the street.

Later that day, his friends Mal and Gary, a couple of spent-heads, drove him to the airport in Mal's '68 Firebird, in part because Constantine said they could finish the rest of his weed before he got on the plane. This they did, and in what was to become an informal pattern, Constantine would desensitize himself with drugs and alcohol before departing for new pastures.

At the airport that day, Constantine bought a magazine from the newsstand. It was the month of October in 1975, and Constantine could always peg the date of his matriculation into boot camp, as at the time he was a mild Springsteen fan ("Kitty's Back" was his and Katherine's song), and Bruce was on the cover of both *Time* and *Newsweek* on the rack. Mal and Gary were Bachman-Turner Overdrive freaks, and they teased Constantine about "waxing off" on Bruce's photo in the plane's head. That was their way of saying good-bye, along with a weak promise to write. Of course, they did not write. As for Katherine, she wrote twice, and that was that.

Boot camp was Parris Island. Constantine felt mentally prepared for it—the sterility, the regimentation, even the waxen, brush-cut DIs—and the whole business was a bit of a relief from the morguish, airless atmosphere that had dominated his father's house. Vietnam had "ended" the previous April, so there was little danger of seeing any action, lending an unspoken element of relaxation to the proceedings.

The truth was, Constantine enjoyed that time. He learned to handle firearms and found he was something of a natural marksman. The drills made him hard and lean, and there was seldom time for thought. His relative contentment was not universal—often he would be awakened in the barracks by young men who talked achingly in their sleep, mostly to their mothers. But Constantine's mother had died long ago, and he neither thought nor dreamed of her. In fact, he never dreamed of anything at all.

For the most part, Constantine kept to himself, both at Parris Island and then at Camp Lejeune in North Carolina. He was not disliked, though at first his rather laconic presence was interpreted as snobbery by his fellow marines. Later, when Constantine began to box (a personal challenge for him that held no reward beyond the challenge itself), his quiet and sometimes terse demeanor would be seen as a kind of post-Beat cool. This newfound respect reached its apex when Constantine fought a young man named Montoya, a reputed middleweight with a steel forehead and a steel jaw. The fight was bet heavily on base, particularly by officers, and Constantine was later surprised to find that the bets were split fairly evenly. In the ring, the bout was active and bloody, and the stories about it circulated for months. He lost to Montoya (that steel forehead) but went the distance; it was his last fight in the service.

Constantine experienced the Beat the first time while stationed at Lejeune. He had gotten a weekend pass, and taken it with a friend named Stewart to Morehead City on the Carolina coast. The two of them had a mutual interest in cars—Stewart was a motorhead and a cracker, and looked the part of both—and that interest had brought them together. Once in Morehead, they found themselves drunk and womanless. Even in civilian clothes, they looked like soldiers, in a time when being a soldier was the least hip thing to be.

Somehow the two of them wound up walking in a residential district at three o'clock in the morning. Stewart had modestly walked to the side of a split-level house to urinate, and then they were both in the backyard of the house looking up at the lit second-story bedroom window, and minutes later one of them had turned the knob on the unlocked back door, and finally they were standing in the pitch-black basement of the house. Later, neither of them could explain or admit why they had walked into a random occupied house in a strange town and stood for fifteen minutes, without attempting to steal one thing, in its basement.

It was in the dark of that basement that Constantine felt what he would call the Beat. At first it had been a weakness of the knees, and then it had been the conscious counter-effort to control the adrenaline that told him to run. Stewart had succumbed to that part of it, tugging at Constantine's shirt, whispering urgently as they both heard the muffled voices above, the tentative steps of the home's residents padding toward their phone. But Constantine stayed in the house well after Stewart had left, and the adrenaline turned into a warm calm, a wash of power, and a distinct awareness of his sex. The Beat was knowing he was into something wrong, and the fear of it, and the point when the fear was no longer there. It was a hot buzz; it was in his jeans and his chest, and it was white hot in his head.

Constantine left the house calmly, walked down the street, and met Stewart at the corner. The cop cars came soon after that, siren-less and without cherries, but Constantine and Stewart were out of sight by then, lying beneath parked cars. Constantine felt the Beat once more as a searchlight passed across his folded arms, and then the cops were gone, and so was the Beat.

That was the most memorable night of Constantine's stay in the service. He had enlisted as an act of rebellion against the old man, and after four years he had learned to use a gun and he had learned to fight with his hands. Those were the very elements that defined manhood to his father; at the time, the irony eluded Constantine.

He stayed in the South, taking advantage of his Marine Corps benefits, and enrolled in an arm of the University of South Carolina called Coastal Carolina, in Conway, just outside of Myrtle Beach. Constantine studied French because the sound of the language intrigued him, and because the prettiest coeds hung out at the Foreign

Languages building, though he had no intention of turning the knowledge or the degree into a career. He was not interested then, nor would he ever be, in a career of any kind.

Occasionally Constantine would split a joint with one of those co-eds after class, and once or twice the joint led to something sweaty and momentarily satisfying at his place, a trailer he rented on the cheap at Murrells Inlet. The trailer came with a fourteen-foot Boston Whaler, and when the tide was up on hot, slow afternoons Constantine could take the Whaler and a cooler filled with Pabst Blue Ribbon through the wetlands to Garden City. Sometimes he would fish the black waters of the Waccamaw River, and he would bring the fish back, clean it, and pan-fry it as the sun went down behind his place.

To pay the bills, Constantine worked as a line cook and expediter at a Tex-Mex joint in Myrtle Beach. At twenty-seven he was the grand old man of the mostly college-age staff, and he was afforded the accompanying respect. The waitresses were uniformly blond and brown-skinned, in full bloom, and Constantine partook when the opportunities arose. After the dinner rush he would take his Marl-boros and a cold pitcher of draft beer and sit on a log in the back of the restaurant, and he would smoke and drink as he looked up at the stars, and he would smell the pleasant summer green of South Carolina. He liked working at the restaurant and living in Murrells Inlet as much as anything he had ever done.

Only once in that time did Constantine feel the Beat. He had been dropped off late one night on the highway after a drinking game at a bar in Myrtle, and he had tried to hitchhike back toward the Inlet. Before he could get a ride, he walked by a house where an unlocked Plymouth Duster sat shining under a blue light in the driveway. Constantine hot-wired the ignition, and as it sparked and the lights came on inside the house, he began to feel the Beat. He gunned the Plymouth onto the interstate as the screaming occupants of the house chased him on foot, and the rush inside him faded as they disappeared from the glow of his taillights. He parked the car a block from his trailer and walked to his bed, where he quickly fell to sleep. The next morning he lit a Marlboro as he casually walked by the police, who were dusting the car for prints. He knew that his prints were not on file, and he knew that no one had seen his face behind the wheel of the Plymouth.

The incident was typical, as in those years few bad things touched Constantine. One morning, when he was turning over his boat at the waterline, a moccasin as black and fat as a tire slithered out across his feet, and early on he caught the clap from an orange-haired waitress at a pool hall and bar called Magasto's, in South Myrtle. But these were things that affected him only mildly, and if he learned anything at all it was to keep a sharp eye out for snakes and women who used cheap dye to color their hair.

Constantine left South Carolina three years after receiving his degree. He was nearly thirty, and he had ten thousand restaurant dollars rolled in a shoe box beneath his bed. He sold everything he could not fit into a backpack, bought an old ragtop Barracuda, and headed southwest.

He drove slowly through the South, stopping for a few months in Baton Rouge, where he worked briefly in the kitchen of a bar on the Mississippi River. The bar had a wooden floor filmed with sawdust, and the jukebox played Jimmie Rodgers, Big Joe Turner, and Carl Perkins. Willie Hall, the proprietor, was a bald man with a square head and small green eyes, and he took a liking to Constantine. Hall had inherited the bar from a childless uncle, but his real love was horses. He bred them on a small ranch he owned just outside of town. Before Constantine left, Willie Hall told him to look up his brother, Richard Hall, south of Los Angeles, if he was ever in need of work.

For the next few months, Constantine made his way north and then southwest to California. During this time he met few people. The solitude did not feel odd to him, as Constantine felt that he had always been alone.

The Barracuda threw a rod and died in Pismo Beach, one day

south of San Francisco. Constantine left the car in the lot of the Sea Gypsy Motel, grabbed his JanSport pack, and hitchhiked down the coast to Los Angeles. Once there, he phoned Richard Hall and told him that he needed work. Hall and Constantine agreed to meet.

Hall lived in an airy house in the hills above Newport Beach, overlooking the Pacific. Hall had the same small green eyes as his brother Willie, but the similarity ended there. Richard Hall was solidly built but strangely feminine, with soft, pink hands and smooth, hairless skin. Not gay exactly, but sexless. He wore an open velour robe during the interview and explained to Constantine that he was looking for a driver. Hall owned a high-end Mercedes sedan and a Porsche 911 but he did not drive. He offered Constantine eight hundred a week in under-the-counter dollars and Constantine agreed. Constantine wasn't keen on Hall but the setup was just too sweet.

He settled into his duties and the Southern California lifestyle quickly. His days were spent as a caretaker of the grounds and as a chauffeur and errand runner for Richard Hall. At night he mostly hung out at the marina bars in Newport, where he became friendly with the waitstaff and tenders. He drank moderately and used marijuana infrequently, and cocaine only as a ticket to bed. Time passed like that and Constantine simply grew one year older and acquired a deeper tan.

One autumn night Richard Hall asked Constantine in for a drink. They had hardly spoken, and never about personal issues. Hall appeared to be half in the bag already, but Constantine considered him to be harmless, and admittedly he was a bit curious about this man, who seemed neither to work nor to have hobbies or interests. The two of them sat in Hall's living room, where a large fire set in a marble hearth gave off the only light.

Richard Hall began to talk about his past. He had made his fortune ten years earlier as a crew chief on a sloop that ferried groups of rich people down to Mexico. On one such trip, a very wealthy woman asked him to hold onto "hundreds of thousands" of dollars, in broad daylight and in full view of several seedy characters, while she went ashore. That night, there was a full-blown, machete-wielding assault on their boat. Hall and his partners killed the assailants using the arsenal of automatic weapons they kept on board, and then, without the wealthy woman but with her money, set out to sea. Hall punctuated this section of the story with a toothy grin and a strange, hearty laugh: "Ah-ha...ha, *ha!*"

Hall continued: once out to sea, the crew was followed by a black cloud, beneath which trailed a huge waterspout with three smaller spouts orbiting around it. In the ensuing hurricane the wind sent a fuel-loaded pontoon boat careening toward Hall (he had by now "lashed" himself to the mast), which sheared off the bottom half of one leg. Constantine at this point in the story glanced at the hairless, intact legs of Richard Hall and decided it was time to leave. But Hall kept on, his face ghoulishly lit by firelight. There was an awful lot of talk about his dreams, ancient Indians hiding in the hills above Newport, the lost library of Montezuma, and an octogenarian couple that kayaked from San Diego to Panama during the Great Depression. All ending with that grin and Richard Hall's obscenely frightening laugh. Constantine excused himself and headed for his room.

He packed his bag, walked quietly across the grounds, and spent that night in the bed of a waitress from the Southside Marina bar. In the morning he caught a ride to LAX, where he booked a flight to New Zealand. He had picked New Zealand because of its distance, because he felt that he had seen the States, and because the country reportedly had no snakes. Constantine sat in the airport bar and drank vodka over ice for eight hours, eating 10mg Valiums at regular intervals (a gift from his waitress friend), then stumbled onto the plane and fell asleep before take-off. He awoke once in Honolulu (the baggy-eyed stewards and stewardesses were all wearing leis) and once more to urinate, and the next time he opened his eyes he was touching down in a strange country on the other side of the world.

Constantine bought a map at the tourist information desk from a cute blonde with crooked teeth, and hitched out of Christchurch. He was picked up quickly by an older couple who drove him through hours of green hills dotted with sheep. They dropped him that evening at a campground on Lake Tekapo, where they told him to "bust off." He guessed they meant to wish him a safe trip.

In the morning Constantine drank coffee on the gravelly shore of Tekapo and listened to the honks of geese as the morning sun blazed off the lake against the rise of brown, snow-capped Southern Alps. The mood was shattered by the crack of .22 rounds coming off the opposite shore and the sudden flutter of geese. Constantine grabbed his pack and hit the road.

He stopped at the sportsman's paradise Queenstown, nestled beneath the splendor of the aptly named mountain range, the Remarkables. Constantine pitched his tent on a hilltop campground at sundown and walked down to town, which was colorfully lit by Christmas lights below. He talked to a man walking a Newfoundland pup on the way down. The man said, "Check you later, hear?" as they parted, and Constantine headed for the nearest bar.

He found a stool at a pub named Eichard's by Lake Wakatipu, and slowly drank a couple of tall dark Steinlagers. Next to him sat a man named Neville, who remarked that he was glad to be drinking with a "Euro" instead of another "fuckin' Japanese." New Zealand was a beautiful country, and its people very friendly, but Constantine had long ago decided that ignorance was everywhere, even in paradise. After a while he tuned out Neville and focused on the bartender, a big-boned brunette named Joey with wet brown eyes. She seemed to have a hearing problem, as she constantly had to retake the patrons' orders (one young man said, "Read my fuckin' lips, Joey," to the laughter of his friends), but she took it in stride. Constantine liked her and told her so before he left for the walk in the cool night air up the hill to his tent.

The next morning Constantine took a gondola up to the top of the mountain and stood with his hands in his pockets amid a group of gawking tourists. On the trip down he rode with a man on a holiday from his western Australian sheep station, and two giggly, unrelated girls from Auckland who called themselves the Smith sisters. He lunched on grilled hupaki with marmalade sauce and green Indonesian mussels, then found himself back in Eichard's, thinking of Steinlagers. Joey put one on the bar as soon as he walked in. She seemed glad to see him.

At dusk the two of them took a walk on the wooded trail that wound around the lake. Joey stopped Constantine in a grove of birch trees to listen to the song of a bellbird and then she kissed him on the lips for a long time as the lake flowed almost inaudibly near. They said good-bye after their walk and Constantine slept alone at the top of the hill under what seemed to be thousands of stars. He had been with plenty of women, though the number was not an issue with him, but for some reason he would not forget that kiss.

He was picked up hitchhiking the next morning by a young Auckland college student named Chris and his girlfriend, Julie. They drove a small camper van loaded with gear and Dead tapes, which they played the whole day. Constantine could see that they were loaded on something, and when the endearing Chris offered him some mushrooms, he shrugged and chewed a fistful, choking it down with a DB beer from the cooler.

They drove on one dirt lane, cliffside around Lake Wanaka, then headed into Mount Aspiring National Park, whose snowy peaks, waterfalls, and massive evergreens surpassed everything Constantine had seen in the American West. It was a fine place to be while doing psilocybin. They picnicked at Davis Flat, then stopped near the Haast Pass, where Constantine slept shirtless in a bed of pine needles in the woods, thinking happily as he drifted off that there was zero chance of snakes. Afterward the road opened up to the Tasman Sea and an expanse of northern California–style coastline, complete with tropical fauna and white beach.

Chris and Julie dropped Constantine at the foot of Mount Tasman and moved on. There was a rainbow coming out of the clouds, reflecting off the mountain and its main attraction, Fox Glacier. Constantine watched it for a while and walked to Fox Glacier Motor Park, a campground in the middle of a meadow. He took a room there on the end of a cinder-block row, and settled in for the night. He could not have known then that he would sleep in that room for an entire year.

What made him stay was hard to determine. He would tell himself that it was the white kitten who adopted him the next day, though he suspected it was the job he landed almost immediately (Constantine could never resist a no-tax restaurant gig) as a cook in the no-name local that sat on the edge of the campground. The pub housed two pool tables, kept a friendly staff, and had Speight's and DB on tap. Most of the talk was about the glacier (the townies called it the "glaah-sheer") and the daily stream of tourists it brought into town. Constantine only went up on the glaah-sheer once, led by a guide he knew named Kevin. He was surprised it wasn't colder, standing on the ice.

Mostly he spent his mornings walking in the woods and the mountains, his days at the local, and his evenings reading popular novels left by travelers in the bar. The white kitten grew to be a slow and heavy cat; beyond that, Constantine noticed little change in himself or his surroundings, though the feeling he had then was in general a wary contentment.

That ended, too, one night behind the pub. Constantine was sweeping the kitchen when he heard a woman's cries through the rear screen door. He walked out the door with the broom in his hand and saw a group of three young men raping a Dutch backpacker in the dirt. After that he recalled swinging the broom handle, and the sound of it as it collapsed the skull of the largest, smiling man. The pub's staff got Constantine under control eventually, but not before he had taken the other two almost completely out, ramming one man's skull flat into the cinder-block wall of the pub. Later, he remembered that the blood smelled like the jar of copper pennies he had kept in his room as a child.

His expulsion from the country was political—one man's father was a prominent landowner—but it was something he did not resist. He never met the Dutch girl, and was never asked to identify her attackers. The authorities told him that the wall-rammed man was critical, and that Constantine was an alien working illegally in their country, and strangely, that they would pay for his ticket of departure. Constantine pictured a map in his head, selected a place at random, and told the men that he would like to go to Thailand. Before they escorted him to the plane that would wing him to Auckland, the one cop who had remained silent throughout the ordeal finally met Constantine's eyes, and thanked him.

Constantine had a night to kill in Auckland. He took a room in the Railton on Queen Street, a temperance hotel run by the Salvation Army that had the smell of old age and decay embedded in its lobby. After a bath he stopped at a place called Real Groovy Records, bought a pulp novel, and walked downtown with the paperback wedged in the back pocket of his jeans. He stopped at the Shakespeare Brewery and had three of the best and most potent ales he had ever tasted, Macbeth's Red. After that it was hot beef salad and chicken larb at a side-street eatery called Mai Thai, where he washed down the fiery dishes with two Singhas, then back to Shakespeare's for five more Macbeth's Reds. He had a load on now, but the walk back to the hotel was long, and he stopped for a short one in a chrome-heavy bar at the top of Queen Street. At the bar Constantine met a Kiwi named Graham and his girlfriend, Lovey, and the three of them got stinking drunk trading shots of ouzo and Baileys Irish Cream. Constantine ended the night dancing on the bar to Curtis Mayfield's "Give Me Your Love," a song he had selected from the jukebox. He did not remember the walk home.

He woke the next morning with a top-ten hangover, realizing suddenly with a painful smile that he was fiercely drunk and in the bowels of a temperance motel. His back hurt from the paperback that was still stuck in the pocket of his jeans. Constantine vomited, took a bath, then grabbed his backpack and fell into a cab for the Auckland airport.

He caught his flight to Thailand and rode a taxi into the heart of Bangkok. Upon exiting the cab, he realized that it was very late at night, and that he was an American and without prospect in a country of Asian faces. The streets were narrow and unevenly paved, and rats moved freely around the closed stands of vendors.

Constantine stopped the driver of a three-wheeled tuk-tuk, who told him of Soi Cowboy, the party district whose bars were largely populated by expatriate Vietnam vets. The driver took him there and dropped him in front of one such establishment, Inside, Constantine made friends over a half-dozen Mekong beers with a bushy-side-burned American named Masterson, a burnout for sure but less of one than the others in the bar.

After a couple of shots to back up the Mekongs, Masterson took Constantine to Patpong, the area noted for its commercial prostitution. Constantine was a bit surprised at the organization of it all—the tuk-tuk driver, undoubtedly with his hand in the till as well, dropped them at the "most very clean place"—and at his first sight of women onstage wearing cardboard numbers strung around their necks. Two more beers and a joint of something sweet, and Constantine had chosen a woman who stood with a dispassionate smile on the plywood stage.

He came in her in the back of Masterson's place, a two-room affair down another dark alley. Afterward, she pulled a crumpled piece of yellow paper from her jeans and read a poem, in English, to Constantine. Her ability to speak the language puzzled him, as she had repeated the words "No English" to him several times before they stripped off their clothes. It puzzled him, too, that she slept in his arms the entire night, until he reasoned that his room was probably nicer than anything she had to go back to. He settled with her in the morning. Later, he casually mentioned to Masterson the whore's "No English" mantra. Masterson laughed and said, "But it don't mean 'no *speak* English,' mate. It means 'I no suck your dick.'"

Constantine left Bangkok quickly, hearing of the beautiful south and huts on the beach. After an overnight train ride and the ferry to

Ko Pha-Ngen, he rented such a hut, at less than two American dollars a day, a serviceable dirt-floored living arrangement that housed a corner slab of cement with a hole drilled in the cement for excrement. The beach and green water were some of the finest he had seen, and there was a nearby eatery called the Happy Restaurant that served "special" mushroom omelettes, which kept him right for half of every day. But he soon tired of the fierce mosquitoes and the repetitive conversations of backpackers — where to eat cheap, where to sleep cheap — and after a few weeks on the Gulf of Thailand he headed north.

In the course of his travels he found a guide and trekked up into the hills close to the Burma border. Small tribes practiced slash-and-burn farming there, and each tribe had an opium professor, opium being the most prized of crops. In one village he visited the hut of the tribe's opium professor late at night, and lay on his side on a straw mat as the professor prepared his pipe. The hut had been built up on stilts, and Constantine could hear the sound of pigs running beneath him as the mixture was carefully heated to its boiling point. Constantine did three bowls, and stared without thought at the candles in the hut until he fell to sleep.

His months in the hills were uneventful, and later he could not remember exactly what he had done to pass the time. He bathed irregularly and ate very little. In the ancient walled city of Chiang Mai he smoked some heroin offered to him by his guide, then sat in a folding chair on a riverbank, under a black sky. He sat with his guide the entire night, both of them uninterested in conversation, as the muddy river flowed by.

Eventually Constantine made his way south once again. His intention was to leave Asia and visit Europe. He spent nearly the balance of his cash on a cheap flight out of Bangkok, and took it all the way to Brussels. In Brussels, very late one night, he caught a train headed for Paris.

Constantine chose an empty compartment, but soon the compartment was filled with three backpackers — two young British women and a thin Jamaican man—and a well-dressed Parisian woman in her early twenties, a transplanted Italian named Francesca. The Brits and the Jamaican stared at Constantine with a curious, grinning contempt, but Francesca broke the discomfort with some spirited conversation, buoyed by her delight at Constantine's command of French. Constantine confessed to her that he was now quite broke, and Francesca gave him an address where he might find some work. Soon the Brits and the Jamaican were asleep, and then Francesca's head dropped to Constantine's shoulder, and later her face fell full in his lap. Constantine closed his eyes, eventually nodding off with an unwanted but unshakable erection.

Constantine left the train at the station in Paris, giving Francesca a guilty kiss before he waved her off. The station was busy with well-dressed Parisians and backpackers, and the air was thick and aromatic with the smoke of Gauloise cigarettes. He hitchhiked south and was picked up by an amiable young man who was playing a cassette of Bob Dylan's "Pat Garrett and Billy the Kid" loudly through his rear-mounted speakers.

The tip from Francesca led him to Tours, a university town on the Loire, on the northeast edge of central France. The address she had given him turned out to be the local orphanage, and the mention of her name brought an instant smile to the chief of staff. Apparently Francesca was some sort of angelic philanthropist, making Constantine's lecherous thoughts from the train seem somehow even more unclean. He was hired immediately as an interpreter, with a small salary to go with his room and board.

Constantine settled in to the slow, easy life of the town. He rode an old bicycle for basic transportation, and to run errands to the local pharmacy. Mostly his job consisted of acting as an interpreter in the crucial first meeting between French child and English-speaking parent. He suspected that there was something a bit illegal in these transactions, and that there was much money being passed below the table. But he remained emotionally detached from the children and the dynamics of the adoption process, preferring to pursue perfection in the art of being alone. In general he stayed away from trouble, though he did steal a Citroën one night, returning it to the unsuspecting owner's parking spot before dawn.

One year after he had arrived in Tours, Constantine packed his JanSport and rode the train to Amsterdam with the intention of having a short holiday. Once there, he took a room at the Hotel My Home, a boardinghouse near the station run by a couple of humorless but kind old men. On the first night of his stay Constantine had a few genevas with beer chasers at the pub below the hotel, the Café Simone. He was surprised to see middle-aged men smoking marijuana at the bar. Other than that the place was like any local, complete with the requisite red-faced, cap-wearing drunk at the end of the bar doing his atonal rendition of Del Shannon's "Runaway." He took to Amsterdam immediately and did not return to France. A week later he took a job as a barback in a lesbian club named Homolulu's, and a week after that he met a blonde named Petra Boone, who became his girlfriend until he left Amsterdam, quite suddenly and for no explainable reason except to travel, six months later.

He drifted south by rail into Italy, and later took the ferry from Brindisi to Patras, in Greece. A bus dropped him in Athens, where Constantine checked immediately into the local hostel. Athens was no place to experiment on accommodations if one didn't know the language. It reminded Constantine of New York City with heightened emotions.

The desk clerk at the hostel was a Greek girl named Voula, a tightly curled brunette with mahogany eyes and a small, wet mouth. The manner in which she used her hands to navigate through her broken English attracted Constantine, along with her low-stanced, hippy shape. They were friends immediately and lovers three days later, when Constantine moved into her room, the best and most private in the house.

Beyond his desk duties at the hostel, which paid his room and board, Constantine did not work during his stay in Greece. He spent his days drinking Nescafé in the *cafeneions* and his nights in the tavernas eating rich, garlicky food washed down with Amstel and the occasional retsina. Late at night he and Voula would lie in beach chairs on the roof of the hostel, smoking cigarettes and laughing over the sounds of crazed, honking cabdrivers in the street below. He was beginning to like Greece, revising his original opinion of its people from incivility to a kind of unrestrained passion.

One day, after a rainfall, Constantine sat in the National Park Garden near Syntagma Square. He noticed a small boy crying and pointing at his tricycle, which was stuck in the middle of a large puddle on an asphalt track that surrounded a small pond. Constantine walked into the water and retrieved the bike, carrying it to the boy. The boy was wearing elastic-banded trousers and red suspenders over a striped green shirt. He said "thank you" in Greek, and receiving no response, put his arms out to hug Constantine. Constantine picked him up and held the boy to his chest, immediately feeling something that scared him, a connection to the child that brought on an odd but acutely heavy sense of loss. He realized then that the road he had taken had not been natural or right but rather the long, aimless act of a man who had no center. He realized the import of the stability that had eluded him, and that realization frightened him. Constantine put the child down and returned to the hostel, where he loaded his pack and walked, without a good-bye to Voula, out into the street.

He drank that night, wandering from one taverna and discotheque to the next, catching an early-morning cab to the airport, where he boarded a flight to New York City. Landing in JFK, the first American voice he heard was from a uniformed man who was loading luggage onto a moving belt. The voice sounded foreign to his ears.

Two weeks later he had taken a job in Annapolis, and then he had run from that, and now he was sitting next to a puckish old man in a hopped-up Mopar, cruising the interstates of Maryland. He drummed his fingers on the dash, thinking that after seventeen years the sum of his accomplishments had been one big broken circle with a gaping dead end. But Constantine had been wrong about a lot of things, and he would be wrong about this too. Everything always added up to something, and the real trip was about to begin.

CHAPTER 4

THE CAPITAL Beltway was a jumble of sooted automobiles tailgating at a steady sixty by rush hour's ass end. The sun hung gauzy through the filmy grayness of the cloudless sky, and the air smelled of tar and exhaust. There had been a Beltway when Constantine left town in 1975, and in fact it had been in place for ten years before that. But what it had become since then—a twisted ring of stinking metal, circling the city—was madness in the mind of Constantine.

"Seventeen years, huh?" Polk said.

"That's right."

"Still got family here?"

Constantine shook his head, answered without thinking. "No."

Sometime later they took the exit ramp at Georgia Avenue and headed south. Polk drove into downtown Silver Spring, stopping at a red light where Route 29 crossed Georgia. Constantine looked at the tall, clean, partially unoccupied office buildings, and at the Silver Theatre, a deco house now boarded up and locked. His mother had taken him there to see *Goldfinger* when he was eight years old, and from it he remembered only an oriental man with a deadly iron hat, and his embarrassment at his mother's loud, gin-fueled comments throughout the show. Later, in a conciliatory gesture, she had bought him a yellow-and-green parakeet at the wooden-floored Woolworth's up the street. Constantine had let the bird go free that same night.

"Where we going, Polk?" Constantine said as the car lurched forward on the green.

"Charlotte lives in a rent-controlled job on Connecticut," he said. "I'll head west at Missouri, take Military from there."

"Any motels along this way?" Constantine said, thinking that Military would take them along the perimeter of the old neighborhood.

"Sure, there's one at the District line."

Constantine said, "Drop me there."

Polk waved his hand. "I told you, Connie, you're with me. Charlotte's got an extra room and an extra bed." He smiled and winked once again. "Maybe an extra friend."

"This is what I want, Polk. Do me a favor and don't argue it. Drop me at the line and pick me up in the morning. Okay?"

Polk nodded. He drove under a railroad bridge and up an incline, and a little past that they crossed the line into D.C. He pulled the car to the curb in front of a motel sign advertising adult movies in each room, letting it idle as he reached into his windbreaker for a thin roll of bills. Polk unwound the rubber band that held the bills tight and began to count off some paper. Constantine put his hand over Polk's.

"I've got money, Polk. It's okay."

"You sure?"

"I'm sure. Thanks."

"I'll pick you up at nine, all right, Connie? You'll be here, won't you?"

"Yeah." Constantine opened the passenger door, reached into the backseat, retrieved his pack, and slung the strap over one shoulder. He bent down and put his head through the open window. "So long, Polk."

"So long, Connie. See you in the morning."

Polk put the Dodge in gear and drove off down the street. Constantine turned and walked through the glass doors, into the orange lobby of the motel.

CONSTANTINE BOUGHT cigarettes and checked into his small room two stories above and facing Georgia Avenue. A streetlight rose outside the frame of his window, though darkness had not yet fallen and the light had not yet been switched. Constantine had a shower and changed into a fresh pair of jeans and a clean denim shirt that had been pressed from the steam of the shower. He left the hotel and walked down the street.

At a Korean carryout named the Good Times Lunch Constantine ate a dinner of deep-fried cod and green beans, and washed it down with a can of beer. He had another beer sitting at the counter, listening to rap from the store's small radio, watching the traffic lighten through the window, as dusk came and then the dark. Constantine left the carryout, bought a fifth of Popov vodka at a liquor store two doors down, and walked back to the motel.

He poured a drink of vodka over ice in his room, and had it sitting on the edge of his bed. The drink backed by the two beers pushed him toward sleep, but he poured himself another and after that he did not think of sleep.

Constantine pulled a phone directory from the closet and looked up Katherine. He figured she would have kept her maiden name. He found her name and number in the Maryland book, along with her husband's. He pushed the numbers into the touchpad of the grid on the bedside phone. After three rings, she picked up.

"Hello?" It was her. More formal, no longer a child, but it was her.

"Katherine?"

"Yes?"

"It's Constantine."

She didn't answer. For a few seconds Constantine listened to her breath, and the raucous sound of young children, and over that a man's voice raised in exasperation.

"Yes, it's me. It's Katherine." So the husband was in earshot and she didn't want him to know who was on the line. Constantine smiled.

"I'd like to see you tonight, Katherine."

"That's impossible."

"I'm only in town for the night." Constantine waited. "Anyway, I think you've already decided. Am I right?"

A long silence. "I'll see what I can do," she said. "Where?"

"The library," Constantine said, chuckling. It was where she had told her parents she was going at night, years ago, when she met him on the hill at Lafayette playground.

"Come on," she said, an edge to her voice.

Constantine swirled ice and vodka in the plastic motel cup as he gave her the address. "I'll be in the lounge next to the lobby. Okay?"

"Give me an hour," she said, hanging up the phone.

To freshen up, he thought, as he killed the rest of his drink.

THE MOTEL lounge was done in burnt orange a shade down from the orange of the lobby. The customers and the staff of the lounge were all neighborhood types and in their late thirties and early forties, and the music on the sound system reflected their collective past. The bartender had been playing the Commodores, BT Express, and Ohio Players on the house stereo for most of the night.

Constantine sat on the vinyl seat of a booth against the wall, against a smoked-glass window that gave to a view of the lobby. He sipped a rail vodka over ice and dragged on a Marlboro between sips. Katherine sat across from him, a Glenlivet and water in the long fingers of her impeccably manicured hands. It was their second round of drinks.

Katherine nodded at the pack of smokes parked on the table next to Constantine's drink. "Give me one of those, will you? If I'm going to smell like it and breathe it I might as well enjoy it."

Constantine looked her over. Her brown hair was shiny and straight and hung to her shoulders, her dark makeup tasteful, highlighting concisely her light brown eyes. As a teenager she had been on the heavy side, and when she had walked into the lobby that night, a cream silk shirt tucked into a black skirt, Constantine had noticed the loss in weight. A workout queen, he guessed. Tight, tan legs, and no stockings.

He shook a smoke out of the pack and pointed it toward Katherine. "Here you go."

"Thanks."

Constantine lighted her cigarette.

She blew smoke across the table and shook some hair behind one shoulder. "I sell medical supplies. That's what I do. Anyway, I told Robert I had to go out tonight, to meet a client."

"What you told your husband makes no difference to me," he said.

Katherine said, "All right." She looked around the bar and smiled, moving her head arrhythmically to the music. The man was playing Bohannon's only Top 40 hit, the one where the background singers spell the name out into an echo machine and repeat it over a pre-go-go beat. "You remember this one?"

"I remember it," Constantine said.

"You took me to Carter Barron one summer night, to see this guy. Bohannon and two other groups, under the stars."

"You're talking about Funkadelic, and the Delfonics. That was a show." Afterward they had taken a blanket, a candle, and a bottle of Spanish wine and walked into Rock Creek Park, the dew soaking through the blanket as they made love.

Katherine shifted in her seat. "In a few years, my oldest girl will be out on dates. It's a shame—she'll never do the stuff we did, never know those good times. The nights in D.C., the concerts at Fort Reno. I won't let her, you know? It's too dangerous now, with the guns. It's crazy."

"So I've heard."

"Yeah, you heard. You haven't been around."

"I've seen the world," he said.

Katherine smiled. "You took a helluva slow boat."

Constantine nodded and butted his cigarette in the ashtray. Katherine did the same and looked at him coyly as she blew the last of her smoke in his direction. He looked around the place, listening to the music, watching a sad-eyed man bobbing his head to it at the bar, and then he looked back at Katherine. Her eyes were still on him.

Constantine said, "Let's go upstairs."

Katherine pulled a twenty from her wallet and signaled the waitress.

CONSTANTINE BROKE the seal on the motel cup and tore away the paper. He pulled some cubes from the room bucket, dropped them into the two cups, and poured vodka over the ice. He walked across the room, turning off the lamp on the way. He handed Katherine her drink where she stood against the wall nearest the window. He tapped her plastic cup with his.

She nodded and drank deeply, closed her eyes. Constantine looked out the window and saw rain falling thickly through the glow of the streetlight.

Katherine opened her eyes and placed her drink on the formica-top dresser. She slipped her hand behind Constantine's neck and pulled his face down to hers. Her lips were cool from the ice and her tongue bit of scotch against his.

Constantine put his hands up into her skirt and slipped them behind her panties. He pushed his groin into hers and freed one hand to unsnap the fastener on the side of her skirt. The skirt fell to the ground, Katherine kicking it away sharply with the toe of her pump. Constantine unbuttoned her blouse, his fingers brushing the warmth of her smooth belly as they traveled down. He released the hook on the front of her brassiere, peeling it back and off her shoulders. In the light he saw her chest redden, as it had always reddened when he undressed her, and he smiled. Katherine kissed him again, pushing her tongue aggressively into his.

3 8   •   G E O R G E   P E L E C A N O S

He led her to the bed, where she lay back, her feet still on the floor. Constantine undressed quickly and lowered himself onto her, rubbing his phallus along the front of her panties. He squeezed one dark nipple into stone, rolling it between his thumb and forefinger as he kissed her open mouth. Then he turned her over, pulling her panties down below her knees and off her pumps.

Constantine took Katherine in the yellow light that spilled in from the streetlight outside the window.

KATHERINE SHOWERED while Constantine freshened his drink. He sat on the edge of the bed and sipped vodka, listening to the water run behind the door. After a while it stopped running and ten minutes later Katherine walked out into the room.

She was dressed and made up exactly as she had been when he had looked at her in the lobby through the smoked glass of the lounge. He watched her walk to the dresser and clasp her watch to her wrist. He watched her straighten herself in the dresser mirror.

She looked at his reflection in the mirror as she pulled the cuff of her shirt down over her watch. For the first time that night he could not see a trace of the girl in the woman's face.

"You didn't have to do that," Katherine said. "Why did you have to do that?"

Constantine butted his cigarette in the night-table ashtray. "It was the one thing we never did," he said.

She looked him over. "So that's what it's about for you. New experience. Nothing deeper than that."

Constantine shrugged unconsciously. Katherine's eyes glazed.

"You want to know something?" she said, their eyes still connected in the mirror. "What I told you earlier, about those good times we had—that was all bullshit, Constantine. The truth is, I've got a life now, and a career, and a beautiful family. When I look at my children, and I think I ever knew guys like you, it just makes me feel dirty."

Constantine said, "How do you think you're going to feel when you look at them tonight?"

Katherine took her eyes from the mirror and picked her handbag up off the dresser. She tucked it under her arm and walked with her head up to the door. She opened the door and walked out, closing it softly behind her.

Constantine listened to her footsteps in the hall, and when he heard the bell of the elevator he rose and stepped over to the window. A minute later Katherine walked through the lobby doors and out onto the sidewalk below.

He watched her step off the curb into the wet street. A car filled with kids passed in front of her and accelerated at a puddle. Katherine stepped back and avoided the splash. She wound her straight hair back behind one ear, walking with a forced bounce in her step as she crossed the street. She slipped once on a patch of slick asphalt, the heel of her pump sliding out from under her. But she caught herself, and quickly put the key to the lock of her imported sedan. Katherine lit the smooth ignition, pulled away from the curb, and drove north toward the suburbs.

Constantine turned his head, stared deeply into the darkness of the motel room. So that was over now too.

CHAPTER 5

CONSTANTINE SAT freshly showered under the cloth awning of the motel the next morning at nine o'clock, his backpack leaning up against the brick wall at his side. The rain had continued in spasms through the night and now came steadily and with the added push of wind. He smoked and listened to the hiss of the southbound tires on the wet street.

The yellow Super Bee approached just after nine and stopped at the curb, pointing north. Constantine put his JanSport over his shoulder and trotted through the rain, across the street to the car. He threw his pack in the backseat and climbed in next to Polk.

"Mornin'," Polk said.

"Morning."

Polk wore the blue windbreaker buttoned high, with a triangle of white T-shirt showing below the neck. He held a styrofoam cup of coffee in his hand, a small ring of plastic cut from the top. He took another full cup off the dash and handed it to Constantine.

"This'll start us off," he said.

Constantine tore a piece from the lid. He blew on the steam that twisted out of the hole before he sipped. He took his Marlboros out of the breast pocket of his denim shirt and tossed them onto the deck of the dash. It was a gesture to let Polk know that the cigarettes were theirs. The ride south was going to be long, and everything from then on would be cut straight down the middle.

They rode out toward the suburbs of Wheaton and caught the Beltway east. A half hour later they were on Route 4, and soon after that the crispness of country had returned to the air. Gradually the traffic died out, and then it seemed to be just the two of them and the occasional pickup passing from the opposite direction. Constantine noticed a stone marker at the head of the unnamed two-lane that they had taken the previous day. Polk turned onto the road and gave the Dodge some gas.

They drove past woods and took a wide curve, past more woods fenced with a split rail, and then a clearing. The big colonial sat back in the clearing. Polk slowed and steered the Super Bee between the squat brick pillars, stopping at the iron gate. He glanced at his watch and shifted on the bench.

Through the windshield Constantine could see the figure with the field glasses framed above the portico in the center window. The figure moved out of the frame, and the iron gate opened inward. Polk eased through the gate and drove toward the house.

A thickly barred cage containing a doghouse stood thirty yards to the left of the house. In front of the doghouse, behind the bars, a black Doberman lay calmly on its belly, its thick head up and tracking the movement of the Dodge. The bars on the cage matched the thickness of those on the front gate.

They stopped the car between a late-model Buick and the black Olds, where Polk cut the engine. Constantine retrieved the smokes off the dash and slipped them into his breast pocket. He turned to look at Polk.

"In and out, right, Polk?"

"That's right, Connie. A quick twenty grand, and then we walk." Polk glanced in the rearview, wet his fingers with his tongue, and ran the fingers through the bristles of his flattop. "You're going to see some shit in there, and hear a little bit too. It's smoke, that's all you gotta remember. They're nothing but hoods. So keep quiet and don't sweat it."

"All right."

Polk pulled back on the interior latch. "Let's go."

They got out of the car and took the three steps up to the front door, Polk grasping the railing for support. He pushed on an oval button set to the left of the door while Constantine studied the brick face of the house. Floodlights hung from the top corners, facing out toward the lawn.

The door opened. Gorman, skinny and gray, stood back in the frame. He nodded at Polk and jerked his head back and up. Constantine marked Gorman as a boozehound, but there was something else—drugs, maybe, and nothing designer—that was eating off the color in his complexion and in his eyes.

They walked behind him through a white marble foyer, past large open rooms done in green leather and dark wood. Two staircases bookended the foyer, leading like bowed legs to the upstairs landing. Gorman chose the left, and they fell in behind him. Constantine ran his hand along the shiny cherrywood banister as he ascended the marble stairs.

The landing ran square around the second floor, with double doors centered in each wall. Gorman walked them around to the wall situated at the front of the house. He knocked twice on the door, turned the brass knob, and stepped in. Polk and Constantine followed.

Two men sat in armchairs upholstered in green leather, in front of a cherrywood desk set next to the large bay window that gave a view out onto the lawn. One of the men was Valdez. The other, a lean man with muttonchop sideburns, wore an open-necked lime green shirt tucked into pleated tan slacks. Neither he nor Valdez looked up or acknowledged the entrance. The lean man was using a thin metal file to pick dirt from his thumbnail.

Behind the desk sat a trim older man with short, slicked gray hair. He wore a navy sport blazer over a green polo shirt. His tan face was tight and handsome.

The man fingered a mound of magnetic chips on a black plastic base as he glanced briefly at Constantine and smiled thinly at Polk. It was a smile Constantine had seen on priests and salesmen.

The man said, "Polk."

Polk nodded. "Grimes."

Grimes did not get up, and Polk stood with his hands loose in the pockets of his windbreaker. They stared at each other blankly, though in the eyes of Grimes, Constantine could see a light, a flicker of history between the two men.

Grimes looked at the lean man and said, "Jackson," then made a sharp, economical movement of his head. Jackson slipped the file into the pocket of his slacks. He rose without speaking and walked slowly to a bookcase that had a ledge, where he sat with one foot brushing the floor.

"You too, Valdez," Grimes said.

Valdez got out of his chair and swept a stony glance past Polk and Constantine as he stepped to the far wall. Gorman was there, his arms folded, and Valdez took his place beside him.

Polk walked to the chair directly in front of the desk and took a seat. He folded one leg over the other and crossed his hands in his lap. Constantine settled into the chair where Jackson had been.

Grimes moved the magnetic toy and field glasses from the center of his desk and tented his hands in their place. "You're back," he said.

"Yes," Polk said.

"How long's it been?"

"I don't know. A couple, three years."

"Get into anything interesting while you were out on the road?"

"Some things," Polk said, and cut it at that.

Jackson had retrieved his file and was digging deeply into the cuticle of his thumb. No one spoke for a minute or so, and then Constantine heard the Mexican sigh behind his back. Grimes cleared his throat to break the silence.

"Valdez tells me you stopped by yesterday and inquired about the twenty thousand," Grimes said. "I thought we had that settled the last time you were in town."

"You had your muscle throw me out," Polk said. "That didn't settle it."

"Well," Grimes said, "I'm sorry you feel that way. Because you and me go back. But we've been going around on this thing for years now, and I think you know me well enough—"

"And you know me."

Grimes bit down on the inside of his lip and lowered his voice. "Yes."

Polk smiled and made an easy wave with one hand. "So, the money, Grimes. Then you don't see me again."

Grimes put a finger in the air and said, "Excuse me, one minute." He turned his desk phone around, picked the receiver out of its cradle, and punched a three-digit extension into the grid. "Hi...bring me a coffee up to the office, will you? Thanks." He replaced the receiver and looked back at Polk.

Polk patted the inside of his knee. "Back to the money, Grimes."

"Right. Well, I'm going to be honest with you, Polk. This whole discussion—it's all irrelevant now."

"Why's that?"

Grimes showed some teeth. "I just don't have it, old buddy. I simply haven't got it."

Polk laughed loudly, a short, cynical eruption. "You haven't got it? That's rich, Grimes. That's really rich."

Grimes's grin widened. "Listen, I won't bullshit you. Of course I can get it. But the way I have my funds tied up, to maximize return, it would take a few days to get you the cash. So this is what I'm thinking: since you're going to be hanging around for a couple of days, why not cut you in on something...*extra* we've got going on. Something big."

Constantine felt a tic, a weakness in the knees, and a brief rush of power. His thumb dented the leather arm of the chair.

Polk leaned forward. "Like what?"

Grimes shifted his gaze to Constantine and back to Polk. "We haven't been introduced."

"His name's Constantine."

"That doesn't mean anything to me," Grimes said.

Polk said, "He's a driver."

Constantine heard a grumble and some movement behind him — the unfolding of arms. Jackson looked up from his surgery and dropped the file into the side pocket of his slacks.

"A driver?" Grimes said. "It happens that we could use a driver."

Polk said. "What's the game?"

Grimes moved the magnetic toy back in front of him on the desk and ran his fingers through the chips. "The briefing's two-thirty this afternoon. All the details will be handled then, by Weiner."

"Condense it for us, Grimes. You can do that."

"Of course I can. But if you turn it down, how can I let you and your friend walk?"

"Because you know me," Polk said, making a head movement toward Constantine. "And I'm vouching for him."

"I don't like it," Valdez said, behind their backs.

Polk and Grimes kept their eyes on each other, ignoring Valdez. It was as if the Mexican were not standing in the room.

Grimes played with the magnetic chips, making a mound of them before he pushed the toy away. "All right," he said. "In a nutshell: we're talking about a knockover, this Friday. Two liquor stores, on opposite ends of Northwest."

"What's the payoff?" Polk said.

"Total take? I put it at three hundred Gs."

"How many men?"

"Six, not counting Weiner."

"The split?"

"The usual," Grimes said. "A hundred to me, inclusive of my bankroll — guns, automobiles, anything else. Twenty to Weiner, for logistics. The rest to the six who pull the job. That's thirty each, for you and your friend." Grimes grinned. "And something else."

"Keep talking."

"The extra twenty. It's yours when you complete the job."

"Why so generous?"

"I need you, Polk. I've looked at this closely, and it's as near to a sure thing as you can get. But it's never all cake." Grimes pointed over the desk. "You're good. I want to hedge my bet."

Polk let it settle. "What if I pass, just take the original twenty?"

Grimes said, "That's not an option."

Polk chewed on that for a while. He said, "If I decide to come on board—and I haven't decided—there's one more thing."

"Go ahead."

"If something goes down—if I don't make it—Constantine here gets my share. My thirty, and his, *and* the extra twenty. Agreed?"

"Yes," Grimes said, against the tightness in the room.

There was a knock on the door, and an entrance. A woman carrying a cup and saucer walked through the room and stopped at the desk.

Constantine took her in: a thirtyish blonde, natural from the looks of her—pale, unblemished complexion and blue, blue eyes. She wore riding jeans and low-heeled calfskin boots, with a chambray shirt tucked into the jeans and a red scarf tucked into the neck of the shirt. The scarf hid most of the neck, but not the best of it, the long swannish curve that ended at the chiseled chin. There was a freshness in her like newly printed money. Constantine could smell it from his chair, as if a window had been opened in the room.

The woman placed the setup in front of Grimes and ran one slender finger along the edge of the blotter. "Is that all?" she said. "Because I'm about ready for my ride."

"Yes, sweetheart," Grimes said, looking suddenly small and boyish behind the desk. "I'm about done here." He moved his eyes to his guests. "You remember Mr. Polk, don't you, Delia?"

The woman named Delia gave Polk a polite but disinterested smile. "Of course. Nice to see you again."

Polk nodded, his eyes fixed on the woman.

Constantine spoke for the first time. "My name's Constantine," he said, no longer wishing to remain invisible.

He stood and walked to the desk, where he stretched out his hand. Delia shook it, held on a second longer than necessary, looking him over before she released her grip. Constantine thought he saw something familiar in her eyes, but the sensation passed. The only thing familiar, he decided, was his own desire.

Delia turned and walked from the room. Jackson chuckled under his breath, stroking his sparsely goateed chin as he eyeballed Constantine. The door shut behind the woman, and Constantine returned to his seat.

Grimes had a sip of coffee. He placed the cup back on the saucer, staring once meaningfully at Constantine before he spoke to Polk. "Well," he said. "What do you think?"

Constantine thought of the money. He pictured it in tightly banded stacks. In the picture, next to the stacks of money, stood the woman. He looked at Polk, and he nodded.

Polk said, "We'll come to the meeting this afternoon. See what this thing's all about. I'll give you my answer then."

Grimes took a pen from a leather cup and wrote some words down on a green pad. He tore the top sheet off the pad and held it out to Polk. Polk got out of the chair, limped to the desk, and took the paper from Grimes's hand.

"I'd like you to take care of this," Grimes said, "before the meeting. Okay?"

Polk read the note, said, "Right," folded the paper, and put it into his windbreaker. "Let's go, Connie."

Constantine joined Polk and the two of them walked from the room. When the door was shut, Valdez pushed off from the wall.

"Mr. Grimes—"

"Save it," Grimes said, his palm up. "Just save it. I know what I'm doing, understand? You and Gorman, take a walk. And be back for the meeting."

Valdez and Gorman split. Jackson watched them walk—

raggedy-ass motherfuckers, out of the old school—until the door closed behind them. He looked at Grimes.

"You want me gone too, Mr. Grimes?"

"No." Grimes pulled a white envelope heavy with hundreds from his top drawer and pushed the envelope to the edge of the desk. "Come on over here and have a seat, Jackson," he said. "I've got a little extra something I want done on this one."

Jackson crossed the room, picked up the envelope. "This have somethin' to do with the old man?"

"Yes," Grimes said. "I'll let you handle it, any way you see fit."

"So, just get it done, right?"

"That's right." Grimes nodded, lowered his eyes to the blotter on the desk. "I think you'll like it."

Jackson ran his fingers through the deck of green. He smiled and said, "I think so too."

CHAPTER 6

POLK AND Constantine took the marble stairs to the foyer, Polk holding the banister for support. Valdez and Gorman had come out behind them. Valdez stood on the landing, his eyes following Constantine, his mouth moving gutturally, his face contorted. Gorman stared over the balcony, his hands dug rigidly into his pockets.

At the bottom of the stairs, by the open doors that led into a library, Polk pulled Constantine aside. Delia sat in an armchair on the opposite end of the foyer, one leg crossed over the other. She looked anxiously at Polk, as if she wanted to speak. Polk caught it, but first turned to Constantine.

"What do you think?" Polk said, keeping his voice low.

"About the woman?"

He frowned and shook his head. "I know what you think about the woman. I'm talking about the job."

Constantine shrugged. "I'll listen to what they've got to say."

"All right." Polk watched Delia get out of the chair and cross the room. "Good."

Constantine studied Delia's walk, admired it as she came to a stop in front of them.

"Mr. Polk," she said, "if you're on the way out, I'd like you to drop me at the stable. If it's not an inconvenience."

Polk smiled. "I'd love to, sweetheart. But I think I'm going to stick around, catch up with the boys upstairs." He pulled the notepaper and car keys from his windbreaker and handed them both to Constantine. "You don't mind taking Delia down to the stables, do you, Connie? After that, take care of this errand. And meet me back here, two-thirty."

Constantine pocketed the note and palmed the keys. "I'll see you then."

He began to walk for the front door, and Delia followed. Valdez looked down from above and ran his tongue across thick lips. His eyes trailed them to the door.

Out in the yard, Constantine stepped quickly across the driveway toward Polk's car. Delia trotted a few steps to catch up.

"You in a hurry?" she said.

"I walk fast," he said, keeping his stride. Constantine noticed, walking next to her, that the woman was nearly his height.

"I've got to get something out of my car."

Constantine said, "I'll meet you at the Dodge."

He dropped into the driver's side of the bench, moved the seat back, and cooked the ignition. Through the windshield he watched Delia reach into the Mercedes and pull a gadget from the visor. She walked to the Super Bee and slid in on the passenger side.

"Nice car," she said dryly.

"You could take yours." He motioned toward the Mercedes. "It is yours, isn't it?"

"Yes. But I don't want to take it. When I finish my ride, I always walk back to the house, through the woods. It's my routine."

"Some routine. Like working, I guess, only different" Constantine swung the Dodge around and headed down the driveway toward the gate. He looked at the beeper-sized gadget in Delia's hand. "That open everything around here?"

Delia said, "I suppose it does," and she rolled down the window to take some air. The rain had stopped, and with the window open a damp green smell settled around them.

Delia pointed the gadget at the gate. It swung in and Constantine edged through, turning left onto the two-lane. He punched the gas and felt the surge of the 383.

She looked at him, across the seat. "You're some sort of driver, aren't you?"

"They think I am."

Delia looked out at the road as it disappeared beneath the hood. "You're here for this new project."

"You don't know the particulars, huh?"

"He spares me the details."

"But you know something about it, don't you? It bothers you enough to pretend you're outside of it all. But not enough to walk."

"What are you talking about?"

"I'm talkin' about Grimes's business. It keeps you in designer scarves, and it keeps you in horses."

"I'm not interested in what you think."

"You're interested," Constantine said. "I felt it in your touch."

Delia said, "Just drive."

The woods ended, the split rail continuing to border the field where the stable stood. Delia pointed to an open gate. Constantine slowed the Dodge, turning in and driving slowly down the gravel road that ran a path to the stable. He cut the engine.

"Thanks for the ride," she said, not looking at him now.

Constantine made a head movement toward the stable. "Can I see it?"

Delia pushed some blond off her face. "If you'd like." She started out of the car. Constantine stopped her with his hand. Her arm felt soft beneath the chambray of her shirt.

"Listen," he said. "I'm sorry. I didn't mean anything."

"You don't know me," she said, and moved out of the seat.

Constantine exited the Dodge and followed her through a gate, into a paddock, and then through the dutch-doored entrance to the stable.

Two stalls stood inside the stable, with the head of a horse visible over the gate of one stall. The opposite stall was open and unoccupied. The stable appeared neatly arranged, clean, with the pleasant smell of damp hay. Hooves clomped the dirt as they entered.

"Hello, Mister," Delia said musically, opening the stall gate out and to the left. She stood protectively against the gate as the horse moved halfway out into the stable.

The stallion stood still as Delia patted his neck and forequarters. He was black and full and muscled, with a blue-black mane and tail, and a diamond of white between his eyes, covering the area from his forehead down close to his muzzle. Constantine looked at the horse's deep, intelligent eyes, and then at Delia's, crinkled at the corners as she traced her fingers down his face as she might the face of a lover.

"A thoroughbred," Constantine said, knowing nothing of horses, though this was something anyone could see.

"Yes," Delia said. "The son of an Arabian stallion and an English mare."

"Beautiful," he said, looking at Delia.

Delia walked to the back of the stable, took a leather halter and rope off a nail, and returned. She held the horse by the mane with her right hand, brought the nose band up, pushed the loose end of the crown piece over the head, and buckled it. She patted the black stallion on his hindquarters and watched him walk slowly from the stable out into the paddock.

"What now?" Constantine said.

"Nothing too exciting. I clean his stall—shovel it out, and lime it—and then I ride. When I get back, I feed him."

Constantine looked into the empty stall, the dirt damp with urine. A wooden manger sat half filled with hay, a bucket of water by its side. His eyes moved above and to the left of the stall, in a corner of the stable. A video camera hung there, pointed down, an indicator light burning red below the lens, a green button below the light. Constantine looked into the lens, chuckled, then looked at Delia.

"We being watched?" he said.

"Not necessarily. It's always on. They're not always monitoring it." Delia put a strand of blond behind her ear. "I can call them, though. That's what the button's for, below the light."

"It's a lot of security for an animal. Grimes got a thing about the horse?"

"He's got a thing about protecting his investment."

"When you've got something that sweet, I guess…you don't want to lose it."

"That's right."

"It is sweet," Constantine said. "Isn't it? I'm thinking right now how sweet it must be—"

"Don't," Delia said sadly. "Don't think about it."

She made a move to go around him, but Constantine stepped in front of her, blocking her way. Her blue eyes bored into his with determination, but there was something else there, something like an opening; Constantine took it, holding her chin in his hand just as she tried to jerk it away. He put his mouth on hers. Her lips were warm and almost at once there was no resistance, and Constantine took his hand off her chin, feeling her mouth open as she relaxed against him. He put his hands on her shoulders and smelled the clean scent of her hair, and the smell aroused him as much as the smoothness of her tongue and the pressure and warmth of her groin against his.

They broke apart. Delia stepped back, ran the back of her hand across her mouth, slowly looked him up and down.

"Why did you do that?" she asked quietly.

"You wanted me to."

"Yes," she admitted. "I suppose I did."

"You can't be happy."

She studied his face. "You're not going to make trouble, are you?"

"I might," he said.

She came forward, closing her eyes this time before they kissed. He felt her around him, felt her tongue slide over his. She took his fingers and put them to her breast, her teeth pressing into his lips as he touched her. They walked to the far corner of the stable, where they undressed.

Delia dropped Constantine's denim shirt into the damp dirt. He watched the muscles of her back wash over her rib cage as she carefully spread the shirt. She sat on it and reached for his hand. He came to her as barn swallows fluttered in the rafters.

AFTERWARD, THEY did not speak. Constantine held her, her tears hot on his neck. The feeling of her in his arms frightened him, the same fear that had gripped him when he had held the boy in the park, in Greece. He could just move on—there would be other children to hold, and there would be other women—but he was tired.

Delia looked up at him and smiled, wiping the tears off her face. She put her head back down and buried her face into his shoulder. After a while the fear that he was feeling went away.

CHAPTER 7

A CATALOG of power fashion packed the lunch-hour sidewalk at Connecticut Avenue and K, the downtown hub of the city's lobbyists, and blue-chip law and brokerage firms. Armani suits and Louis Vuitton handbags paraded by, sharing the concrete with the homeless and the vendors and the bums, the scent of Opium colliding with the stench of urine.

At one particularly busy avenue storefront, Washington's working women—secretaries, attorneys, and hookers—buzzed in and out of glass doors. Those exiting the shop carried white plastic bags emblazoned with a luxuriant blue logo depicting one delicate foot resting on a pillow. Mean Feet, D.C.'s premier shoe boutique, had begun to heat up.

Inside, Randolph worked the floor.

"What size, girlfriend?" Randolph said, to the woman in the red skirt. She was standing by the display rack holding a spectator, a black number with a blue vamp, in her hand.

"That depends on what you're doing tonight," she said coyly.

"Tonight?" Randolph said, buying time, looking away like he was thinking it over, really looking at the rest of the customers on the floor, making sure none of the other boys took one of his women.

Antoine, that skinny boy from Georgia, was edging over to one of his best regulars, a perfect seven and a half, a regular with a full-time paycheck and a government job. And Jorge, the Latin with the thin mustache and all the hair, was sniffing after something in a tight leather skirt, always lookin' to get next to that Man in the Boat.

"Yes, tonight."

Randolph looked down impatiently at the woman's foot. "You an eight and a half, right?"

"That's right."

"How's next Tuesday sound?"

"Tuesday's good," said the woman in the red skirt.

Randolph said, "I'll be right back."

On the way to the stockroom Randolph stopped at a large woman wearing a colorful dress and a headband to match. She was sitting on the end of the padded bench, and she was holding a sale shoe, some burlap-lookin' bullshit, some old-ass espadrille-lookin' shit, in her callused hand.

"You ready now?" Randolph said.

"Nine," said the woman.

"Be right back." Randolph paused before entering the stockroom. He turned and shouted across the sales floor, over the seventies funk—Rick James, "Bustin' Out of L 7"—that was booming out the store speakers, toward his regular, who was now holding a shoe and talking to Antoine. "What size, baby?"

The woman said, "Antoine's helping me today, Randolph."

Randolph bugged his eyes and shook his head. "Uh-*uh!* What you want to talk to that itty-bitty"—Randolph paused, grabbed the top of his thigh, shook what he grabbed—"you want a man with some *heft,* don't you, baby?"

The regular looked at Antoine, blinked apologetically, and turned back to Randolph. "Seven and a half," she said.

Randolph jetted into the stockroom, kicking boxes out of the way. He felt Antoine follow him back.

"What you want to go and disrespect me like that for?" Antoine shouted, as he entered the clutter of stock and stretching tools and empty cartons.

Randolph turned, gave Antoine his godfather stare. "You know better than to talk to my ladies, Spiderman."

"Don't call me no Spiderman, man."

Randolph softened his voice—he didn't need to throw gasoline on this shit, not during the rush. "Go on, man. There's plenty of money out there for everyone. Plenty of money and plenty of honey. Right, Antoine?"

Antoine smiled his country smile, said, "That's a bet. Sure is plenty of honey." He turned his arachnid's torso and loped back out the door, all arms and legs.

Randolph headed for the back of the stockroom, thinking that the boy Antoine could be good—*if* he concentrated more on picking up customers and less on his pride. Now the other one, Jorge, he'd wash out. All he thought about was the nappy, day and night. Randolph knew one thing: the day was for taking those shoes to the hole; the night was for the freaks.

Randolph climbed the wooden shelving to get red skirt's nine— she'd said eight and a half, but she sure was a nine—and he pulled it from the top. He jumped to the floor, feeling the impact, even on the thin green carpet, thinking that at forty-two maybe it was time to slow down. But he had forgotten that by the time he was looking for his regular's seven and a half. The name of the shoe was Panis, which he remembered 'cause it rhymed with Janis, the name of the redbone he'd been with the night before. The Panis—a slingback in black, he was sure that was the color she had held in her hand—was at the top of its stack, too, and he leapt up for that, got it on the second try.

On the way back out, Randolph took the biggest burlap shoe he could find for the woman in the colorful dress. She had said nine, but those big-ass, spread-out, Haitian-ass feet had to be elevens. Eleven at least—if they had stocked a twelve in the back, he would've brought that, too.

Out of the stockroom, Randolph surveyed the floor. The crowd had begun to thin out, the only new face a man who had entered and was now sitting on the bench. The man wore blue jeans and Timberland boots, and his black hair hung long and clean. A three-day black beard, trimmed and grown high, covered his jaw. His brow was thick and his eyes were blue and deep. Randolph's first thought: Jesus, just like in the pictures. But what the fuck is he doin' in my shop?

Randolph dropped the burlap shoes in front of the Haitian without a word, and moved to the woman in the red skirt. He opened the lid of the box, unwrapped the tissue with ceremonious care, and dropped to one knee. He took the right shoe and put it on her foot, and he placed the shoe on the top of his thigh as he tied it. He patted her on the ankle and ran his finger along it after the pat, saying, "Okay, darling," as he stood and walked toward his regular seven and a half.

"How you been, baby?" Randolph said as he arrived at his regular, a fine light-skinned woman with a spray of freckles across the bridge of her nose. She smiled and moved her eyes shyly away from his. Had he ever taken her out? He couldn't remember, just then. Randolph pulled the right slingback from the box, put her foot on his knee, and guided the shoe onto her foot.

The Haitian woman walked her shoes up to the register, where the manager, a balding, heavyset young man, sat ringing up sales. Randolph yelled to the manager, "That's a twenty-nine"—Randolph's sales number—"on that one, Mr. Rick."

Randolph excused himself, content that the Panis was going to fit just fine, and walked around to the freak in the red skirt. "Those spectators gonna do it today, girlfriend?"

She scrunched up her face. "These shoes are too *hard,* Randolph."

Randolph countered: "Don't you like hard things?"

She laughed. "Not my shoes!"

He took the shoe off her foot, patted her ankle once again. "I'll stretch these out with some magic shit"—it was plain old alcohol, and he kept it in the back—"okay? And, oh yeah, don't forget about Tuesday night, hear?"

The woman in the red skirt smiled. "I won't forget. I'll lay those spectators away today, get them out on Tuesday."

Randolph grinned. The front door opened, and a man and three women walked in. The man wore a matching shirt and slacks combination and the women wore hot pants and halter tops and tight-assed skirts.

Randolph crossed the sales floor, stepping around Jorge, who was sitting on the bench next to his girlfriend-of-the-week, and walked up to the pimp, a guy by the name of Felix. Randolph shook Felix's hand, using a handshake that he used only on Felix, a handshake that he had otherwise stopped using with friends since 1975.

"All right, man," Felix said.

Randolph said, "All *right* "

"You gonna hook my ladies up today, hear what I'm sayin'? Some evening shoes, man."

"I got just the thing, man." Randolph could feel Antoine's envious stare burn into his back. He postured theatrically, spread his palm out in the direction of the ladies. "Sizes?"

Felix pointed down the line, starting with two pretty fine ones and ending with some West Virginia–lookin' girl. "Nine, seven and a half, and ten."

Ten said, "I be a nine, Felix." *I be,* shit. Randolph had to check his grin. West Virginia talked blacker than the black freaks.

Felix nodded as Randolph looked at her feet. Randolph said, "Have a seat, all o' y'all. I'll be right back."

He started for the stockroom, noticing the man with the long black hair staring at him from his seat. What did he want? If he was into pumps, then Randolph didn't mind; he made plenty over the years, selling high heels to men. But this one didn't look like a punk, didn't even look like the type to be buyin' shoes for his woman. No, this one wanted something with *him.*

But Randolph put it out of his mind. When Felix walked in, twice a year, he dropped five hundred, sometimes a grand. So this was a special day, maybe a three-thousand-dollar day—a triple dot. At ten percent, three hundred dollars for a day's work. Not bad for where he came from. Not bad at all.

In the stockroom, he tried to remember the sizes as he picked out the shoes. Nine, seven and a half, and…the West Virginia–lookin' ho, with those country-ass feet—she had said nine. But she meant ten.

LATER, WHEN the rush had ended, just as Felix and his girls had left the store, Randolph looked across the littered sales floor to the bench in the corner, where the man with the long black hair still sat. The Isley Brothers' "Groove with You" came sweetly from the store speakers—Antoine had taken the funk down a few notches for the post-rush chill—while Jorge stood in the stockroom, putting dead soldiers back up on the shelf. It had been a good day, and Randolph had made some money. Now he'd see what that man had on his mind.

He crossed the sales floor, stepped up to the man. The man had risen out of his seat, a near-friendly smile on his thoughtful face. He was taller than medium, like Randolph, though not as solid, more on the loose-limbed side.

Randolph stroked his black mustache, looking hard into the man's blue eyes. "All right, man. What you want?"

The man took a piece of paper from his pocket and handed it to Randolph. Randolph took it, read it, tossed it on the bench.

"Right now?" Randolph said.

"Yes," the man said.

Randolph shrugged sadly and headed for the front door, the man walking beside him. Before he reached the glass, Randolph shouted over his shoulder, to the manager. "I'm takin' the rest of the day off, Mr. Rick."

Mr. Rick, running a tape on his calculator, did not look up. "See you in the A.M.," he said.

Antoine shouted from the entrance to the stockroom in the back of the store, pointing down at the erratic pile of shoe boxes at his feet. "Where you goin', Shoedog? You ain't goin' nowhere till you put up these thirty-fours!"

"You put 'em up, Spiderman. I got something I got to do."

Antoine shook his head slowly as Randolph and the man walked out the door.

Out on the sidewalk, Randolph turned to the man. "You got wheels?"

"Right over there," the man said, pointing.

Randolph looked it over, said, "Uh-uh." He nodded to a late-model T-Bird parked on the street. "We'll take my short."

They walked to the T-Bird, Randolph tipping a bill to an old man who sat by the car, putting quarters in the meter on the half hour. Randolph gave the old man some parting instructions, along with a handful of change. The old man thanked him and walked slowly up the street.

Randolph went to the driver's side, put his key to the lock. He peered over the roof at the man with the long black hair, who was standing by the passenger door, waiting to be let in.

Randolph studied the man. "You're new," he said.

"That's right."

"You got a name?"

The man pushed his thick hair behind his ear, reached into the pocket of his denim shirt, and withdrew a cigarette. He paused before putting the filter between his lips, and squinted his blue eyes.

"Yes," he said. "I've got a name."

Randolph said, "What is it?"

And the man said, "Constantine."

CHAPTER 8

WEINER LOOKED down and studied the contents of the glass case. The ring he wanted sat near the back, wedged in the slotted felt of the display. He pointed in the general direction of the ring, waited for the liver-spotted hand of the clerk to light on the correct one.

"That's it," he said. "May I see it?"

"Of course," the woman said, spreading cracked lips to reveal a perfect row of artificially white teeth. She retrieved the ring and laid it on a square of blue felt that she had spread on the glass.

Weiner picked it up—a simple number, a tiny diamond set in 14-karat gold—and examined it as he fingered the track winnings that were rolled in the pocket of his trousers. Nita had said, innocently enough, that she had never owned a diamond anything. She had said it the day before last, when Weiner had finally asked her out for coffee. She had said it as she looked down into the black of the coffee.

Weiner put the ring back down on the felt, deciding now that Nita would have her diamond.

"I'll take it," Weiner said.

"It's lovely."

"Wrap it for me, will you?"

"Of course."

The clerk took the ring and glanced once at Weiner before she disappeared into the back room. Weiner took the roll from his trousers and unwound the rubber band, counting out the bills. He took what he needed for the ring and put it in his right pocket and rebanded what remained and put that in his left pocket. He looked into the mirror behind the counter.

He wasn't so old. At least he didn't look his age, not fifty-five. No way did he look fifty-five. He had put on a few pounds, but on him it looked good, and the goatee he had worn for thirty years had come back in style. He had seen it on the young people, first the African-Americans and later the whites, over the last few years. He looked good anyway, and now the goatee, it made him look younger. He figured he looked good because he had never married, since married cats always looked older, on account of all that stress. Some people said it was clean living, but clean living, in his case, had nothing to do with it. Anyway, he didn't know what kept him young, but he knew he wasn't too old for Nita.

That day in the coffee shop he had asked her to go to the Sonny Rollins show at One Step Down, the jazz joint in the West End. He had met her buying music at Olsson's at Dupont Circle, where she worked as a clerk when she wasn't studying for her undergrad degree at GW. He had been looking to pick up an old disc, "Mulligan Meets Monk," that had been reissued on CD. Olsson's didn't stock the CD, but she knew of it, and he had been impressed. Her looks—dark hair, black clothes, heavy on the eyeliner, heavy in the hips—had impressed him as well. She reminded him of the zaftig Beat chicks he had known in the old days, at Coffee and Confusion. The memory saddened him, but at the same time it made Weiner realize that all he wanted was to get next to it—to touch it—just once.

But Nita had hedged on the date, telling him to swing by Friday afternoon, her next shift, where they'd discuss it. He figured she needed to think it over—the age difference, and like that—and that was natural. But the ring might help things along. The ring might close the deal.

Three C notes seemed steep and a bit of a gamble, but that day Weiner felt lucky. He had cased both liquor stores in the morning, diagraming them and taking notes just after his visits. As usual, his memory had been dead on, his stay brief and uneventful.

Afterward he had driven out to Laurel for the one o'clock post, settled in his spot in the grandstand, and quickly surveyed the form. For the first race he laid a win bet at the five-dollar window on the four horse, Arturo. Arturo was to be ridden by Prado, the hot and hotheaded Peruvian. Weiner gave equal weight to the jockeys as he did to the horses, and Prado had been his man since Desormeaux had hightailed it for Del Mar. Arturo went off at eight to two and won the six-furlong contest; Prado had pushed him to a roll at the rail.

In the second race Weiner played the seven-two combination and hit the exacta for six hundred twenty-six dollars and twenty cents, his biggest payday in months. He would have stuck around for another race—his friend Kligman pleaded with Weiner to "parlay it," the favorite strategy of track losers—but he had to make the two-thirty meeting. He felt relieved, really, driving to the jewelry store at Laurel Mall, that the money he had won still rested, for a change, in his pocket. He'd pick up the ring, drive out to Grimes's house, and lay out the whole deal.

As for the twenty grand that Grimes would give him to strategize the job, that would pay off old debts. And of course there was his debt to Grimes, for keeping the shylock's muscle from crippling him that one time, two years back. He owed Grimes for that one still, and he supposed he would always owe him. Everyone owed Grimes something.

The thought of it made him feel hollow, but only for a minute, when the clerk returned from the back room with the ring and placed it, beautifully wrapped, in his hand. He gave her the three hundred and asked for a receipt. Walking out the door, Weiner could only imagine the look on Nita's face when she would unwrap the paper, and open the box. Maybe then she'd let him get next to it. Maybe then, he decided, she'd let him touch it.

VALDEZ STARED out the window of his room, stroking the long whiskers of his black mustache. His room was small, with a perpetually unmade bed and an unvarnished nightstand and bureau, and a color television on an unvarnished stand set in the corner. His .45 sat on the nightstand, under a naked-bulb lamp, next to the bed.

Valdez didn't mind the room. After a while he really didn't notice the size of it or the furnishings. When he used the room, it was only to watch television or to sleep. It had been generous of Mr. Grimes to let him live there, in the back of the house, though at night he could often hear Gorman coughing into his shitty handkerchief in the next room, forcing up and then hawking phlegm. That would annoy him, the way a bug might annoy him, but Valdez would just turn up the sound on the television, and that would be that.

Anyway, the room in this house in the country seemed a million miles from where he had been. First Mexico, then Los Angeles as a kid, then back down to Mexico, the border towns where everything—reefer, coke, pills, and women—could be bought, and everything of value needed protection. Valdez used muscle and a major set of balls there to earn his rep—he killed his first man at eighteen, one bullet to the head—until he became as valuable as that which he had been hired to protect. In Miami, in the early eighties, it had spun out of control; the ones he went up against had crazy, speed-stoked eyes. The retribution kills piled up and got bloodier— near the end, Valdez macheted a man in a dirt-floored warehouse, hacked at his shoulders and neck while the man cried out for his "mamacita"—until finally he gave up on it and drifted north, where an old contact put him on to Mr. Grimes. His decision to move on had nothing to do with fear. Valdez didn't know fear, not like most men know fear. But he figured that the odds would catch up with him soon. And Valdez had no particular wish to die.

Compared to his days as an enforcer, working for Mr. Grimes had been a blessing, a fat slice of angel food cake. Every year or so there would be a job, something to keep Mr. Grimes interested, though from where Valdez sat Mr. Grimes didn't need the risk, what with all the pretty things he already owned, the horses and the blonde and the cars. But everyone had a kick, and the kick for Mr. Grimes was moving the men around the playing field, and the reasons for that did not interest Valdez. Unlike the others who had to stay, the ones who owed Mr. Grimes, Valdez stayed because he liked the life. In that way, he supposed, he owed Mr. Grimes too.

Today, at two-thirty, Valdez would put on his black jacket and go to the meeting, and he would listen and not ask too many questions, because in the end you just shut your mouth and did the job and got out. The new one, the one with the long black hair, he bothered Valdez a little, maybe because he couldn't read what was in the man's eyes. And the old man—Valdez watched him now through the window, limping along the edge of the woods, smoking a cigarette—he would have to be dealt with this time. But what bothered him most today was the timing of the meeting—it would run over and cut into his show, "A Lifetime of Love." He'd missed it yesterday, and now he was going to miss it again today. And he'd been waiting all month for Taurus, the international spy, to nail the brunette.

Valdez sighed, stroked his mustache. He didn't know why he got so worked up over it. Christ, the way they worked it on that show, Taurus and the brunette, they'd be in bed together for the whole goddamn month.

POLK DRAGGED hard on his cigarette, felt the burn as the paper touched the cork of the filter. He dropped the butt and crushed it in the grass beneath his right shoe. He exhaled the last of it, then spit into the woods. He looked at his left foot as he limped along the tree line, and cursed softly. This time of year the air was always cool and damp, and with the dampness came the pain.

He had been a gimp for forty years, since Korea, so he had been this way for most of his adult life. He no longer thought about it, except on days like this, when the dull ache traveled up his leg, reminded him with the nagging insistence of a cold touch on his shoulder. Of course, it could have ended there, on a frozen reservoir in Korea. It could have ended, if not for Grimes.

But that had been two young men, and now the men had grown old and into something else. He didn't owe Grimes a thing, not after what Grimes had done. Not after Grimes had done the very worst thing that a man could do.

Polk thought of Delia—she had become a truly fine-looking woman—and of Constantine, and of the look that had passed between them in the office of Grimes. Standing under the branches of a pine, thinking of Constantine, Polk had a brief but cutting rush of guilt. It wasn't that Polk had a particular fondness for him. In the end, Constantine was no better or worse than any man, and in his drives and desires he was certainly as predictable. But he supposed that it came down to priorities. And he believed that it was still possible, perhaps for the last time, to fix what he had done, and not done, so many years ago. So he would keep pushing Constantine, and he would not think about the bad things that could happen to the young man with the long black hair.

Polk pulled some needles from the branch that hung over his head. He rubbed the needles on his fingers, then put the fingers under his nose. He smelled the bite of green pine against the blackness of nicotine. He turned, and limped back toward the house.

THE WAY Gorman saw it, the time of day didn't matter much when a man wanted to get high. The meeting would be coming up soon, and he'd go to it, and he'd listen. A standard knockover, that's what it was, you go in with a hard look and a drawn gun, maybe rap the barrel to someone's head, let them feel the weight, and then you book. He'd done it enough to know the routine, and there wasn't one good reason why he couldn't listen to Weiner run it down without a little buzz in his head. No good reason at all. Gorman sat on the edge of his unmade bed and squeezed a line of clear glue out of the orange-and-white tube, moving the tube around in a circular motion to spread the glue into the opening of the brown paper bag. He quickly put the bag, bunched at the opening, to his face, letting the bag seal his mouth and nose. He closed his eyes and took long, deep breaths.

When Gorman felt the rush in his head, a pleasurable pounding that seemed to levitate his skull, he took the bag away from his face and let himself drift back, until his head rested on the bed's pillows. He opened his eyes, watched the room glide, closed his eyes again, and dropped the paper bag to the floor.

He smiled. A poor man, living like a rich man in a country estate. A long way from the west side of Viers Mill Road in Wheaton, where he had grown up in a cramped GI-bill house, in a neighborhood of tradesmen. The old man, gaunt and chronically unemployed, had tried to raise him and his two brothers, but soon after the old lady died the boys went wild, and the old man gave up, crawling into a bottle of St. George's scotch until his death. His older brother died too, soon after that. He had been fucking off on a construction site after dark, cooked on Schlitz and paint fumes, and trying to impress some heifer. He got his head tore off by a crane.

Gorman joined a gang in the early sixties, a loosely knit group of greasers brought together by their distrust of foreigners and spades. They played only Motown at their parties, low-lit basement affairs where the girls wore sleeveless Banlons and heavy black eyeliner. Gorman and his boys wore baggy work pants called "Macs" from Montgomery Ward, Banlon pullovers, black high-top Chucks, and three-button black leathers. They hung out at the Cue Club in Glenmont—it was in that pool hall's bathroom where Gorman first huffed glue—and the bowling alley at Wheaton Triangle, where they shook down junior high school kids for spare change. They always hung together.

Gorman wondered, what happened to those boys? Some of them, he heard, bought it in Vietnam. Others became tradesmen like their fathers, mechanics mostly in the gas stations that ran along Georgia Avenue from Rockville down into the District. A couple of them did time, first for theft and later for dealing grass and dust. Suckers, all of them.

Gorman had dropped out of Wheaton High his junior year, headed south to Daytona, where he heard about the parties and the girls and cars on the beach. He spent the next ten years dodging the draft and working a succession of odd jobs, warehousing and clerking auto and appliance parts. On the side he dealt reefer and dust and crystal meth, the cocaine of bikers and the working class. Gorman dug crank himself, but not in the same way that he dug the glue.

In the late seventies he killed a man for money in the alley behind a bar, pushed a switchblade knife between the man's shoulder blades as the man climbed into the saddle of his bike. It had been easy, and he did it a couple of times after that, always for money, and always from behind. Gorman had always been skinny, never a fighter, though he was good with a gun and a knife.

Some years later Gorman met Valdez as Valdez headed north, passing through Daytona, shacking up with mutual friends. Valdez told him about a man named Mr. Grimes, just outside of D.C., who was looking for hired help. Gorman left with Valdez, as now he felt tired and too old for the Florida scene. He had stayed and worked for Grimes ever since, and it had been just fine.

There in that room in the back of the house, Gorman had everything he needed. At forty-seven, he had lost interest in most things, including women. Women had never dug him in the first place, he knew that, and anyway it was easier to think about a broad and jerk his dick over the toilet bowl than it was to talk to one. Life was just that simple.

All he needed, Gorman figured, as these thoughts spun dreamily inside his head, was a place to sleep, a little spending money, and the glue. The glue would get him through all of it, the hassles and the orders and the jobs. The glue would take him away. The glue was good.

*   *   *

JACKSON PULLED the car over to the curb on Wisconsin Avenue and cut the engine. He looked through the windshield, took in the block: upper Northwest, a row of specialty, white-interest retailers— camping gear, Persian rugs, gourmet baked goods, women's books—and ethnic restaurants, pizza parlors, and beer halls servicing the students of American U. In the middle of it, all glass and fluorescent banners, stood a liquor store a quarter length of the block. The double glass doors swung in and out with regularity, even on this weekday, alkies and society folk and students alike cradling their brown paper bags like babies as they carried the goods to their cars.

Jackson pushed his shades up on the bridge of his nose, straightened the Hoyas cap on his head, and glanced once more at the sign over the doors: Uptown Liquors. So this was the motherfucker he was going to hit on Friday.

He pocketed the ignition key and got out of the car, walked across the sidewalk to the doors, pushed on the doors, and stepped inside. The first thing he thought, the way the aisles lined up, the big selection, the bright tags, the cashier stand with the conveyer belt to move the juice along: this was a supermarket for booze.

Jackson stepped around the maze of wine displays in the center of the store, barrels filled with bottles capped by neon tags. The liquor racks ran behind the wine displays, and past the liquor a wall of glass-fronted coolers stocked with beer. He headed for the brown liquors in the center aisle, passed bourbon and scotch, and settled in on the brandies. He pretended to study the brandy bottles, looking over the top of his shades to the sales counter against the wall.

Three men stood behind the counter, speaking loudly to the customers and each other, ringing sales on two old-fashioned registers. Shelved behind them: miniatures and pints, expensive champagnes, cordials, and liquor in seasonal, decorative decanters. An old women in a red sweater stood at the front cashier station, ready to ring, but the store action centered on the counter.

The way it worked, the customers came in, stepped up to the counter, ordered from one of the loud men, and the men—Jews, Jackson guessed, two old and one young—would bullshit about the quality or the price, maybe suggest something else, and then the men would scream the order toward the entrance to the back room, at the end of the counter. After that a black man would carry the order out to the counter, dolly it out if it was more than one case of beer, and when the customer had paid the tab the black man would take it out to the customer's car. The customers came to Uptown Liquors for that ritual. Jackson could see that they came here for the show.

The two older men, with their double-knit pants pulled high over their soft bellies, they would be no problem. The younger one, with his Rolex and diamond pinky ring, he had nothing, a cocky strut and a big mouth, but nothing underneath. The brother, the one the others called Isaac—"A case of long-neck Buds up front, Isaac, we need it now, the gentleman's in a hurry!"—he'd be the one to watch.

Jackson studied Isaac—the steady eyes, the solid walk—and decided he'd seen enough. Jackson did not step up to the register, where the lenses of two wall-mounted video cameras remained focused. He turned away from the brandies and walked down the aisle, negotiated the wine displays, and exited the store.

Jackson fed the meter and sat in his car for the next half hour. Sometime around one o'clock Isaac walked out the front door of Uptown Liquors and into the small garage. A minute later Isaac drove his Monte Carlo out of the garage and headed downtown. Jackson pulled away from the curb and followed.

Jackson sat low and relaxed in the driver's seat, stayed two cars back. This liquor store thing, it looked easier now than he had first imagined. If this boy Isaac fell in line, then the whole deal would be down. Maybe nobody, except of course the old man, would get hurt. Jackson would be a hero, might even get off the hook with Grimes, even things out after Grimes had bailed him out on his card game

debt. Not to mention the thirty grand. The thirty grand was nothin'
but sweet.

Jackson tailed Isaac east, across town to 13th Street, south on 13th
to Fairmont. Isaac drove to the middle of the residential block and
parked. Jackson stopped at the top of the street and pulled over. Fairmont Street consisted of row houses sectioned off into apartments,
glass and litter, young men wearing beepers, and children playing
ball on the blacktop. It was exactly the kind of dead-end bullshit
Jackson had come back to after Vietnam, before he got hip to the B
& E and then the fencing business. Those had been the best days, the
seventies, when it *had* all been business—before the cocaine and
the cards.

Jackson was through with gambling now and he had kicked the
freeze, and maybe with this job he'd take his thirty and be through
with Grimes. He watched Isaac cross the cracked concrete sidewalk,
walking toward his place—the raggedy-ass motherfucker had a job,
and he still had to go home and eat his lunch—and he thought, yeah,
if this brother comes around, and this job goes down clean, I'm out
of the life. Out of it, in a large way.

CONSTANTINE LOOKED across the buckets, over at Randolph. The man
sat low, pressed jeans and a pressed cotton shirt, one arm straight out
on the wheel, the other at his side, his free hand stroking his black
mustache. They had not spoken since Randolph had driven them east
on Pennsylvania Avenue, straight out of the city on Route 4.

"That skinny guy," Constantine said, cutting the chill. "He called
you Shoedog."

"Just a name," Randolph said.

"He told you to pick up your 'thirty-fours.'"

"Yeah. 'Thirty-four,' as in 'three-four, out the door.' Those the
shoes left over from the bitches who didn't buy. The bitches who
walked out the door. I let 'em pile on up. It gets the other boys
all...emotionally distracted, and shit. Makes 'em forget what
they're doin'."

Constantine checked out the T-Bird's cockpit. The Detroit R & D men had turned an American original into a Jap lookalike, an imitation rice rocket. "You like the car?" Constantine asked.

"It's all right," Randolph said, his eyes ahead.

Constantine offered, "I never been much of a Ford man."

"For city cruisin', it'll do." Randolph shifted in his bucket. "You know somethin' about cars?"

"A little."

"What else you know? You know why Grimes called me out?"

"Yeah, I know."

"How about fillin' me in." Randolph turned smoothly onto the unmarked two-lane.

Constantine looked out the window at the wild dogwoods dotting the woods. "Two liquor stores. Day after tomorrow."

"You in?"

"Yes," Constantine said, thinking of the woman. "I'm in."

"As what?" Randolph asked.

"A driver."

Randolph shook his head thoughtfully. "Man, you greener than a motherfucker." He added, "Grimes does like 'em green, though."

"What about you?" Constantine said.

"What about me."

"What do *you* do?"

Randolph ran his hand along the top of the dash. "I'm a driver, too, man."

Constantine looked at Randolph's pressed clothes, the man's style. "I don't get it. I mean I watched you back there, in the store. You're already hooked up, man. You don't need it."

Randolph laughed sharply. "You ought to know better than that, Constantine. What's Grimes got on you, anyway?"

"Nothing," Constantine said, still thinking of Delia.

"Grimes got something on everybody."

"What's he got on you, Randolph?"

Randolph slowed the car, stopped it between the pillars of the black iron gate. He turned, stared into Constantine's eyes. "Look, man, you seem all right. But you don't know me all that well to be askin' those kinds of questions. Okay?"

Constantine nodded, looked away. The gate opened in and Randolph drove through, up the drive to the parking area in front of the house. A few more cars now stood in the group.

Randolph parked next to the Caddy. The two of them climbed out of the T-Bird and walked up the steps to the house. Constantine turned the knob without a knock and walked into the marble foyer. Randolph walked behind him.

Gorman stood on the landing above, leaning over the railing, his face drawn and gray. "You're late," he said, directing it down to Randolph.

Randolph ignored Gorman, looked back at Constantine. "Motherfucker's a glue head. You know that?"

Constantine hit the stairs and said, "I figured it was something."

CHAPTER 9

THE MEETING had been set up in a room adjacent to Grimes's office at the top of the stairs. When Polk saw Randolph enter, he rose from his chair, crossed the room, and held Randolph by the arm, looking in his eyes as they talked. Constantine could see that the two of them had worked together before.

The room had two rows of metal folding chairs facing an easel and desk. A coffee urn and setups had been placed to the side. Weiner sat on the edge of the desk at the head of the room, one foot on the floor.

Valdez sat in a chair in the second row, staring ahead, sipping his coffee. Gorman entered, grabbed an ashtray off the coffee table, and had a seat next to Valdez. Jackson sat in the second row as well, away from Valdez and Gorman. He picked at his thumbnail with his metal file.

Constantine poured black coffee and took it, along with an ashtray, to a seat in the first row of chairs, where Polk and Randolph had settled. Constantine dropped the ashtray, along with his smokes and matches, on the seat next to Polk, and sat to the right of that. Polk shook a smoke out of the deck, struck a match to his, leaned across the seat, and lighted Constantine's.

"Thanks for picking up Randolph," Polk said, smoke dribbling from his mouth. He winked. "Get along all right with the girl?"

Constantine brushed that away. "I left your car downtown, Polk, out on the street."

"Don't sweat it." Polk made a short head movement to his right, in the direction of Randolph. "His man will feed the meter, make sure it doesn't get towed. We'll pick it up later."

The door opened and then closed behind the men. Grimes entered, took a seat in a large chair—the only one with arms and upholstery—at the back of the room. No one turned around. Weiner moved off the desk and stood next to the easel. Constantine heard a match strike and afterward the pleasant aroma of fine cigar drifted toward the front of the room.

Weiner checked his wristwatch, cleared his throat. "All right, gentlemen," he said. "Let's get started."

Constantine pigeonholed Weiner: an old, bookish hipster—the hipster tag came from the goatee and the cocked beret Weiner sported on his bald head—with three rings on one hand. A small-time gambler, no casino action, a backroom poker player or maybe a pony romancer. Constantine could picture the guy at the track, standing under the odds board, head down, specs low-riding his nose, his hand gripping a stubby pencil, drawing circles on the racing form.

Weiner picked a wooden pointer off the coffee table, draped it shotgun style across one arm. "Two liquor stores," he said, "this Friday, on opposite ends of town. Two three-men teams. Each team has two inside men and a driver. The first hit goes down at eleven-fifteen, the second at eleven-thirty."

"Talk about the teams," Valdez said.

"I'll get to that," said Weiner. He tapped the end of the pointer to the diagram on the easel. "The first hit is Uptown Liquors, on the east side of Wisconsin Avenue, just north of Brandywine, past where Forty-first splits off. It's your basic market-style setup, except for the counter"—Weiner pointed—"right here. Two cameras point down at the counter. Alarm buttons underneath. Next to the counter, the stockroom."

"Describe the staff," Polk said.

"Three Jewish gentlemen," Weiner said. "They stay behind the counter. An old lady works part-time. And there's an African-American gentleman, a stockman, does the heavy work."

"Guns?" Valdez grunted.

Weiner shook his head. "I don't think so. Nothing out front, anyway. They've never been touched, not in that neighborhood. If there's heat in there, it's coming from the back—the stockman's the one to watch."

Jackson nodded, thought of Isaac. As usual, the hymie had it nailed.

Valdez said, "What kind of take?"

"I put it at a hundred grand, in three separate spots from what I could make out, all under the counter, with a little in the registers. They keep the Thursday deposit out, combine it with Friday's. They need cash up there for money orders, their own payroll. And to line their own pockets. Friday's the day they skim their nontaxable income. Which I figure, from what the gentlemen are driving, is four times the amount they declare."

"So we just stroll in," Gorman said. "Right? Is that what you're saying, Weiner? I mean, it's that easy. And we wear stockings on our faces, on account of the cameras, and we raise our voices a little, and we walk with a hundred grand. And all we got to worry about is some old spade—I mean, *African-American gentleman*—who works in the back room."

Randolph turned in his seat, spoke slowly to Valdez. "You tell the little bitch to watch his mouth, hear?"

Valdez grinned, gave Randolph the once-over.

Gorman said, "Maybe after this, you and me take it outside."

"Maybe," Randolph said. "Soon as you pull your head out of that glue bag."

Polk laughed while Constantine butted his cigarette. Grimes

dragged on his cigar, watching the bunch from the back of the room. Jackson kept his eyes clear and ahead, thinking of Randolph, the driver: he was down but just too sensitive. This here was only business.

Weiner said, "If the Uptown job's too simple for you, Gorman, then you're in luck. You're not on that team. You're on the second hit, at eleven-thirty." He turned the page back on the easel to reveal another diagram. "EZ Time Liquors, on the northeast corner of Fourteenth and R."

Randolph said, "Talk about it."

Weiner shifted his weight "As you can see, this is a small place, about eight thousand square feet. Liquors, beers, a small selection of fortified wines. And convenience store items, inner-city style— condoms, dream books, disposable lighters, a numbers machine— that sort of thing." Weiner pointed to a small square in the right area of the store. "Here's the counter where the staff stand. Two Irish gentlemen, father and son, and another Irishman, older, an uncle I'd guess. Hard guys, all of them."

"Guns," said Valdez.

"All over the place," Weiner said. "No plexiglass between the customers and the staff. The Irishmen wear vests under their shirts. I figure each one of them's got access to a gun behind that counter. Also, I've been in the place on two separate days, and on both occasions I saw the same newspaper spread out—same date, same edition—under the left register. I figure there's a sawed-off underneath the paper."

"So they're heeled," Polk said. "What's the take?"

Weiner smiled, made a victory sign with his fingers. "Two hundred grand."

Polk thought it over. "That's why the hits are staggered, fifteen minutes apart. You make some noise uptown, where they don't hear that kind of noise too often, and you draw all the units up that way, and then you make the jackpot hit down on Fourteenth and R. Am I right?"

"Precisely," Weiner said.

Constantine put fire to another smoke, heard Gorman do the same. Everyone stared at the diagram then, all of them considering the alternate weight of money and death.

Constantine exhaled, blew a jet of smoke across the room. "Why not just rob a bank?" he said.

Gorman snorted a laugh while Valdez shifted his wide ass. Jackson moved his eyes to the right but did not move his head.

"What's that?" Weiner said. He had not expected the young man with the long hair and blue eyes to speak.

"Why not rob a bank?" Constantine repeated. "I mean, you're going in there against more guns than you've got, and these guys are protecting their own turf, so why not hit a place that's got one uniformed gun, a security guy, a guy who's got nothing at stake?"

"It's a good question," Grimes said from the back of the room. "Answer it."

"All right," Weiner said. "Simply put, we *are* going to rob a bank. For the people of the inner city, the liquor store *is* the bank. Most African-Americans, Hispanics down there, they aren't able to open checking or savings accounts—they have no credit, or they can't afford the charges, or they don't trust the primarily white banking institutions. So the liquor store is where they cash their checks, get money orders to pay their bills. On the morning of the second Friday of each month—which is this Friday—EZ Time Liquors brings in a hundred and fifty grand via Brinks just to fill those orders. Combine that with the fifty they've got stashed, and you're looking at a possible two hundred, if you hit it just before the noon rush. It's payday in the ghetto, and the liquor store's the bank. Only this time, gentlemen, the payday is ours."

Gorman put his hands together, clapped three times. It was just like Weiner to make a political speech in the middle of a business meeting. So the spades in the ghetto couldn't get no credit, couldn't get no jobs, didn't trust whitey's banks, blah, blah, blah. Fuck 'em all, anyway.

Valdez stroked the whiskers of his mustache and said, "Now the teams, Weiner."

"Right." Weiner used his pointer. "On the Uptown job: Jackson, Polk, and Randolph. On EZ Time: Valdez, Gorman, and Constantine."

Valdez stood out of his chair, pointed his finger at Constantine's back. "That green sonofabitch is not gonna be my driver, understand?"

Grimes spoke calmly. "Sit down, Valdez. I picked the teams. You can drop out or you can do it the way I say. Those are your options."

Valdez sat, lowered his head, shook it slowly from side to side.

"The rest of it's standard," Weiner said. "I'd like you gentlemen to drop in on your respective targets between now and Friday, get a feel for the place. We meet here at ten A.M. on Friday morning, pass out guns and ammunition for those not already carrying."

"I won't need a gun," Constantine said.

"Everyone carries," Weiner said. "Equal responsibilities, equal risks, equal rewards." Weiner turned to Randolph. "You and Constantine pick out your vehicles, tomorrow morning, nine A.M."

"Rego?" Randolph said.

"Right. He'll explain the procedure on the drop." Weiner cradled the pointer. "Any other questions?"

The room went silent except for the long, heavy exhales of cigarette smokers and the creak of hinged metal chairs. Grimes stood, said, "That's all, then. Good luck, all of you. Constantine—see me in my office, right after this." Grimes turned and exited the room.

When the door slammed shut behind him, the men relaxed. Valdez stood once again and kicked his chair back with his heel. Constantine did not look back, knowing that the gesture was meant for him.

Polk put his hand on Constantine's arm. "I'm sorry, partner. I thought the two of us could ride together on this one."

"I'll be all right," Constantine said, thumb-flicking some ash off his cigarette, noticing the unsteadiness in his hand.

"I'll meet you downstairs," Polk said.

"Right."

Constantine sat in the chair and finished his cigarette, waiting for the others to leave the room. Weiner left last, putting his notebooks and pencils into a battered briefcase, patting Constantine's shoulder on the way to the door. Eventually, Constantine was alone. He heard their voices out in the hallway—Valdez and Gorman's anger, Jackson's simple laughter—and then their heavy footsteps on the marble stairs.

Constantine ground the butt of his cigarette into the ashtray, rubbed his face around with his hand. The gray smoke of the meeting hovered in the center of the room, turning slowly in the light. Constantine got out of his seat and moved through the cloud.

CHAPTER 10

GRIMES PUT his hand to his temple and smoothed back his steel gray hair. He had a seat behind his desk, then randomly rearranged the accessories that sat on the blotter of the desk. He placed his cigar in the lip of his crystal ashtray. His hand came to rest on the mound of magnetic chips piled on the black plastic base. He fingered the chips, listened to the footsteps of the men descending the marble staircase outside his office door.

These meetings exhilarated him but tired him as well. Gorman and Valdez always asked the wrong questions. And Jackson, his own stupidity magnified by his groundless self-confidence, asked no questions at all. But Jackson did as he was told, absolutely, and the value of that was great.

The cleanest of them was Randolph, and with him Grimes never worried; Randolph had always done his job, and done it precisely and without incident. He knew Randolph's worth, and the importance of keeping him in the fold.

Polk, too, had always been a professional. There was no reason to believe he would not acquit himself well on this one. Still, this would be Polk's last job. Polk was becoming irrational, careless, dangerously close to spoiling it. He would have to go. Friendship meant little now, its worth receding with time, fading behind the primary concern of self-preservation. Grimes believed in nothing if not protecting the things he valued most.

And there was Constantine. The young man with the long black hair asked the right questions, and kept his mouth shut when there was nothing pertinent to say. Grimes believed he would deliver when things heated up. Constantine's strengths, though—his lack of emotion, the absence of a moral center—also made him a dangerous man. If Constantine had a weakness, it was the weakness that plagued most men. He had seen it in Constantine's eyes when Delia had entered the room. But Grimes wouldn't use it. He would find something else in Constantine, some kind of opening. And then Grimes would break him, like he had broken the others.

Grimes looked at the brown spots on the back of his hand as his fingers moved through the magnetic chips. He had noticed the spots only recently, and then he had noticed the cracks and deep wrinkles around his knuckles, and the thinness of his fingers at their joints. He pictured the brightness in Delia's eyes when Constantine had touched her hand. He tried to remember the time when Delia had looked at him in that same way.

Grimes heard footsteps approach his door, heard a knock on the door, saw the brass knob begin to turn. He straightened in his chair, softened the tightness that had crept into his face.

CONSTANTINE KNOCKED on Grimes's door, entered.

Grimes sat behind his desk, wearing a canary yellow polo shirt under a blue blazer, his gray hair swept back. He motioned for Constantine to sit in the chair in front of the desk. Constantine walked across the room, had a seat in the chair, and crossed one leg over the other. He waited as Grimes relighted his cigar.

Grimes let some smoke pass from his mouth. "Would you like one, Constantine?"

"I don't smoke them."

Grimes looked lovingly at his cigar. "This one's got a Dominican filler, with a Connecticut Valley wrapper. Assembled in Jamaica. I go for the pyramid tip, myself, though that's a matter of preference over taste, the way it feels on your lips." He drew on it, looked back at Constantine. "It's a shame. You really should be interested in good things. As you get older, your more basic passions decrease. Naturally, your desire for material pleasure gets greater."

"Possessions only complicate things," Constantine said. "I can't fit a sixty-thousand-dollar car into my backpack."

"Or a woman," Grimes said.

"No."

"But you could fit a nice cigar into your pack, couldn't you?"

"What's your point?"

"Only this. Within the scope of his ambition—even his limited ambition—a man should always strive to have the best. And by extension, to do his best." Grimes parted his thin lips into something resembling a smile. "I think you've got that quality in you, Constantine. I think you just don't know it."

"My ambition is to keep moving," Constantine said.

"You might think so," Grimes said. "But I saw something in you yesterday, when I first mentioned the job. You were interested in the money—any man would be—but it was more than that. You were hopped on the job itself."

"Maybe."

"It's why I put you on the downtown hit. You're into the challenge of it. I think you're going to do fine."

"Valdez and Gorman don't think so."

"They're plumbers. I don't worry about what they think. Neither should you."

Constantine rubbed his thumb on the green leather arm of the chair. "So what's in this for you? You obviously don't need the money."

"That's right." Grimes tapped ash into a crystal tray on the corner of his desk. "I don't have to be doing this at all, Constantine. I think, in your own way, you could get along without it too. So I think you can understand it when I say that, from time to time, I *need* this sort of thing."

"Need what, exactly?" Constantine said. "Not the rush. You're not in the middle of it. You watch it go down, from behind that desk."

"I've seen all the action I'll ever want to see. And I killed plenty of men in the war, if you think that means something. No, this is something else."

Something else, maybe, but nothing mysterious. Grimes was frightened of his mortality, his fading virility, his diminishing worth. The affliction of time. Constantine thought of Randolph, how he'd been summoned, like his draft number had come up, and Polk, who couldn't walk away. The only thing Grimes had left was the grip he kept on his men, the ability to bring them back every year, through blackmail, for one more job. Constantine didn't like Grimes, and he didn't trust him. But now he knew him, and knowing him diminished his power. Grimes, all polish and hunt country gloss—just another pathetic old man.

"Anything else?" Constantine said. "Polk's waiting for me downstairs."

Grimes dragged on his cigar, rolled the lit end around in the ashtray. He glanced at his watch, then back at Constantine. "One more thing. Come over here to the window, will you? I'd like you to see something."

Grimes got out of his chair and stepped behind it. Constantine rose, walked behind the desk, and stood next to Grimes in the square of sunlight that fell into the room. They looked out the window.

At the tree line, a hundred yards from the house, Delia stepped out of the woods. She walked with her head down, a stick in her hand, her hips moving languidly, her blond hair loose, the breeze keeping it off her face. Constantine felt his stomach drop; from the window, he thought that he could smell the freshness of her hair.

"Every day," Grimes said smoothly, "I watch her walk out of

those woods, same time. It's a small thing, really. But to watch her, to know she's mine—"

"I understand," Constantine said.

"Of course you do." Grimes kept his gaze on Delia. "You were taken with her yourself, earlier today. Everyone is. The others, when I'm around, they act like she's invisible. Then, behind my back, they laugh, talk about her, talk about what they'd do to her. They're cowards." Grimes's face, deeply wrinkled, turned grim in the light. "I admired your courage today, when you stood out of your seat to touch her hand. I admired it, and at the same time I hated it. Do you know what I mean?"

"I think so."

"Good." Grimes turned to face Constantine. "Because if you ever act on it, I'll kill you. I'll kill you and I'll bury you, out in those woods. Understand?"

"My friend's waiting for me downstairs," Constantine said.

Grimes said, "Then go."

Constantine turned and walked for the door. Before he reached it, he heard the voice of Grimes. "You should be more clean, Constantine. There's dirt all over the back of your shirt."

Constantine thought of Delia lying on the shirt, quivering wet, naked in the mud of the stable. He felt a touch of the Beat as his hand turned the knob of the door.

CHAPTER 11

POLK, **RANDOLPH**, and Weiner waited in the driveway for Constantine to come from the house. Jackson had walked out behind them, gotten in his car. He pulled the car alongside the men and rolled down the window.

"Pick a good one tomorrow, hear?" he said to Randolph, and Randolph knew he meant the car. Jackson winked at Randolph, but Randolph did not acknowledge the wink. Randolph considered Jackson a loser, worse than a bum. There were those who could work, and those who couldn't; those who could and who chose the hustle were worse than those on the bum.

As Jackson drove toward the gate, Delia walked from the woods, past the men. The men tracked her walk, admired it, Polk more deeply than the rest. She did not look at them as she passed them and entered the house.

Five minutes later Constantine opened the front door and stepped out. He crossed the driveway to where the men had grouped themselves around Randolph's T-Bird.

"What's going on?" Constantine said.

Randolph said, "Waitin' on you."

"Well," Constantine said, "here I am. What now?"

"We usually go out after the meeting, have a few," Polk said. "Like a tradition. You up for that, Connie?"

"I guess I am," Constantine said. "I need to check back into my motel, take a shower, change my clothes."

Randolph said, "We'll pick up Polk's heap, swing back out."

"You guys can meet me in the motel lounge," Constantine said.

Weiner said, "Where would that be?"

"On the west side of Georgia, just over the District line. Place doesn't have a name, just says 'Motel.'"

"I know the place," Weiner said, then looked at his wristwatch. "I'll see you gentlemen around eight."

Randolph said, "Right"

Weiner marched to his car, a midsized, cookie-cutter GM product—from where he stood, Constantine could not make out if it was a Buick or an Olds—and drove off. Randolph, Polk, and Constantine climbed into the T-Bird, Polk squirreling himself into the backseat. Randolph turned the ignition key and headed down the driveway to the open gate.

"What'd Grimes want with you?" Polk said.

"Pat on the back," Constantine said.

Polk said, "Thought it might have something to do with the woman."

Constantine said, "It didn't."

"She is fine, though," Randolph said.

"Yes," Constantine said.

"Too fine," Randolph said, "for a poor motherfucker like you."

"I guess you're right," Constantine said.

Polk tapped Constantine on the shoulder. "Hey, Connie, how about passing me back a smoke?"

Constantine took the pack from his shirt pocket and tossed it over his shoulder to Polk in the backseat. Polk took a cigarette, wedged it between his lips, passed the pack back up to Constantine.

"I thought for sure," Polk said, "that Grimes was going to talk to you about the woman."

"Come to think of it," Constantine said, "he did mention something."

CONSTANTINE ASKED for and checked into his old room after Randolph dropped him at the motel. He napped in the room, falling asleep immediately, the venetian blinds sealing out most of the light. He awoke a short time later in the dark.

After his shower Constantine had the last of his vodka while he cleaned up his beard and dressed in fresh clothing. Before he left, he checked himself once in the mirror, then switched off the light.

Coming out of the elevator, Constantine could hear the Ohio Players' "Sweet Sticky Thing" playing from the lounge. He entered, scoped the bar. In a far corner, he saw Polk and Randolph sitting with a woman at a roundtop. Constantine crossed the room, passed juicers huddled over their drinks at the bar, and stopped at the table.

"Connie!" Polk said, standing at once, shaking Constantine's hand. Polk had put on a textured dress shirt, a Puerto Rican–looking number, over his white T-shirt. His windbreaker was spread over the back of the chair.

"Polk. Randolph." Constantine smiled politely, extended his hand to the middle-aged woman in the chair. "My name's Constantine."

"Charlotte," the woman said, closing and then opening her eyes slowly in drama-class fashion. She had deep purple eye shadow and penciled-in brows, sharply pointed at the tips. A shock of white-blond hair had been bleached into the front of her black bouffant. Straightaway, Constantine thought of Lily Munster.

"Good to meet you."

"And you, honey." Charlotte gave him a nicotine-tinted smile. "Polk told me you were a looker. He was right."

"Thanks."

"Sit down, lover," Randolph said, "and have a drink."

Constantine sat, pushed the netted orange candle away from him, to the center of the table. A bandy-legged waitress came by, jutted her chin upward at Constantine. The motion revealed a scar beneath her chin.

"Vodka rocks," Constantine said.

"What flavor?" the waitress said, impatiently jiggling change in her black apron.

"Just vodka."

The waitress gave the rest of the table an eye-sweep. "Anybody else?"

"Two more of these, sweetheart," Polk said, twiddling his fingers between his and Charlotte's glasses.

"You?" the waitress said to Randolph.

"I'm good," Randolph said, cupping his hand over his glass of soda water. The waitress gave Randolph an unclean look, wiped quickly at the area in front of Constantine. She brushed ashes off the table, half of them going into her hand, the other half drifting into Constantine's lap. The waitress turned to walk away, and Randolph watched her feet.

Randolph said, "Eight and a half."

"What's that?" said Constantine.

"The lady wears an eight and a half. An A width, though. Tougher than a motherfucker to fit." Randolph eyed Constantine's denim shirt. "Speakin' of threads, man, that outfit there—what the fuck is that, your uniform?"

Constantine flashed on his high school military academy and service days, chuckled to himself. "I guess so," he said. "Too many choices, too many complications. You know what I'm saying?"

"I know you're a little off," Randolph said. A softness came into his eyes. "But you're down, I guess."

Constantine glanced at Polk and Charlotte, huddled across the table, laughing. Eddie Kendricks's "Keep on Truckin'" had begun to blare through the bar speakers. Randolph sipped at his soda.

"You don't drink," Constantine said.

"I drink," Randolph said. "But I keep it in check. Drinkin's ruined most every man I know. When I get into the store every morning,

I got to be on my game, one hundred percent. Can't let those other boys get the jump on me, man."

"But you do something," Constantine said, looking into the pinkish white of Randolph's eyes.

RANDOLPH GRINNED. "I do like my herb, now and again."

"You holdin'?"

"Sure am. Shit I got'll make your dick hard. You wanna get high?"

"That would be good," Constantine said.

The two of them excused themselves and headed for the bathroom in the back of the lounge. Constantine went in first, motoring quickly to one of two urinals. Randolph had a look around the blue-tiled bathroom, then leaned back against the wall, next to a casement window. He pulled a manila coin envelope and some papers from his maroon sport jacket.

Constantine urinated while Randolph shook a line of pot into two papers he had glued together. He twisted a tight one, passed it through his lips, then ran a flame beneath the number to dry it, give it a seal. Constantine washed his hands in the sink as Randolph flicked his lighter and burned one end of the joint.

Randolph hit the weed, closed his eyes, held it in. He cranked open the window, looked through the crack, saw a barely lit alley, and blew the smoke out into the night. Randolph passed the joint to Constantine. Constantine blew the ash off the end, took a hit. He paused, felt the smooth warmth in his lungs, exhaled.

"Nice taste," Constantine said.

Randolph formed an "okay" sign with his thumb and forefinger. "Sens."

"What if someone comes in?"

"The bartender ran with this lady I used to know," Randolph said. "Homeboy's cool."

Constantine passed the joint back to Randolph just as the bathroom door swung open.

"Gentlemen!" Weiner said, marching in. His floral print shirt had been buttoned to the neck, the tails tucked into his brown Sansabelt slacks. A beret, the same shade of brown as the slacks, sat cocked on his head.

Randolph re-produced the joint that he had cupped when the door had opened. He put it to his mouth, hit it once more, and passed it to Weiner. Weiner smelled the sweet wisp coming off the burning end, smiled, hit it, and talked as the smoke passed through his lips.

"Nice tea," Weiner said.

"Sens," said Randolph.

"What about Polk?" Constantine said. "He comin' in too?"

"Not his bag," Weiner said. "He knows what's going on, though. Said you guys were in here doing one of two things—fucking each other or smoking grass." Weiner grinned as he handed the number to Constantine. "It made Charlotte blush. And it takes something to make her blush."

Constantine drew on the joint, then turned it around in his hand. He felt himself smile stupidly. "Hey, Randolph. Come on over here, man, let's get serious."

Constantine blew the ash off, put the lit end in his mouth, felt it singe his tongue. Randolph stepped up, cupped his hands around his mouth, and took the shotgun from Constantine.

"If you don't mind," Weiner said, "I'll have some of that." Constantine turned, blowing a great jet of smoke into Weiner's face.

The bathroom was filled now with the heavy smoke of marijuana. Constantine took another pull, handed the joint to Randolph.

The door opened. A middle-aged man wearing a loosely knotted tie stepped inside. He stopped walking, had a look at the three men, and went to the head to urinate. When he was done, he zipped up his fly and faced Randolph.

"How 'bout a hit off that stick?" he said.

"Why not?" Randolph said. "Everyone else in this motherfucker's had some."

The man hit it, kept hitting it until Randolph plucked the joint from his mouth. The four men stood in the bathroom and laughed.

Constantine lighted a cigarette, savored the good taste of the tobacco in his lungs. He patted Randolph on the shoulder and said, "Let's get out of here, man."

The four of them were still laughing as they walked out into the lounge.

The stranger waved them off and returned to his seat at the bar. The Isley Brothers' "What It Comes Down To" played now in the lounge. Constantine heard himself singing it as they walked to the table. The ground felt soft beneath his feet; the room and the people in it glowed faintly in the barroom light.

Constantine sat, noticing that Polk had ordered him another drink. He killed the rest of the watered-down vodka and quickly had a sip of the new, toasting Polk with the glass. Polk, his arm around Charlotte, winked back. Constantine dragged on his cigarette, blew a smoke ring in the direction of Randolph.

Randolph said, "Heard you singin' that song."

Constantine smiled. "The Isleys, man. 'Three Plus Three.' Ernie *wailed* on that one."

" 'Who's That Lady,' 'Summer Breeze'—shit, Constantine, he wailed on that whole motherfucker. Boy *played* some guitar."

"I wore the grooves out on the disc. I had the original—"

"On T-Neck," Randolph said, giving Constantine skin.

"Nineteen seventy-three," Constantine said. "I had just got my license, bought this Dodge—a sixty-six Coronet Five Hundred. Yellow, with black buckets, a swivel tach." He closed his eyes, had a taste of his drink. "I had this girlfriend then, girl by the name of Katherine. I used to drive her in that car through Rock Creek Park, on Saturday afternoons. The Mighty Burner was the deejay on WOL, remember?"

"You know I do," Randolph said. "I had just moved up here, from North Carolina."

"When I'd ride with Katherine in that car, I practically used to pray the Burner would play that song."

Randolph said, "Yeah, well, you older than a motherfucker now. So you might as well forget all about your first nut, hear?"

Constantine thought of Katherine, what he had done the night before. He thought of Delia, in the barn. He took a drag, stubbed out his smoke in the ashtray.

"I guess you're right," he said.

Weiner had been looking around the bar, moving his head to the music. He signaled the waitress, ordered a Brandy Alexander. Randolph asked for a cognac. The rest of them held.

"How about you, Weiner?" Randolph said mockingly. "This tune remind you of anything?"

Weiner pursed his lips, shook his head broadly. "If it's after Phil Ochs, I can't identify it. The Beatles ended it for me, gentlemen."

"Who the fuck is Phil Ochs?" Randolph said.

Weiner waved his hand. "Never mind. Suffice it to say that there was a scene in this town that you two can't even imagine—Constantine, you in particular were kicking the slats out of your crib in the era I'm talking about."

The waitress returned with the drinks, served them clumsily. Constantine ordered another vodka.

The waitress said, "Why didn't you order your drink when I was here before?"

"Because I didn't," Constantine said.

The waitress rolled her eyes and slouch-walked away.

"Anyway," Weiner said, raising his Brandy Alexander. "Ladies and gentlemen? To success." The five of them tapped glasses in the middle of the table. Polk and Charlotte returned to their private conversation.

"Like I was saying," Weiner said. "There was this scene in D.C. A real Beat scene, an underground. I used to go to this one club, Coffee and Confusion was the name of it, over on Tenth and K."

"That was your bar?" Randolph said.

"Oh, there were other joints. The Java Jungle, the Ontario Place—but Coffee and Confusion, that was it for me. Guys playing guitars, bongos, wearing shades inside the club. A real scene. And the chicks there"—Weiner's eyes, already glazed, deepened at the memory—"my God, you should have seen them. Long, straight hair, parted in the middle. Heavy makeup, black around the eyes. Their breasts, their young breasts—the whole package, I've got to tell you, was terrifically sexy. Totally and terrifically sexy."

"Sounds like a winner," Randolph said.

Weiner smiled wryly. "Well, of course, you're patronizing me. But you've got to agree, Randolph, everyone has their time. And everyone knows that their time was the best. Do you agree?"

Randolph thought of the Zanzibar, in the seventies. "Yes," he said.

The waitress returned, served Constantine. He nodded to her, hit the drink. "After this round," he said to Randolph, "let's get out of here."

"I'm down with it."

Polk broke away from Charlotte. "We'll head downtown," he said. "Charlotte's got a friend, wants to hook up with us. That okay by you guys?"

Constantine nodded. Randolph watched the feet of a woman who walked past their table.

"Hey, Weiner," Randolph said, nudging him with his elbow, nodding toward the woman's feet. "What you figure her shoe size is?"

"I have no idea," Weiner said.

"I'll bet you ten bucks she's a nine."

"You make your living selling shoes." Weiner shook his head. "That's a sucker's bet."

"Anyway," Randolph said, "she would have told you she's an eight and a half. But believe me—the freak *is* a nine."

AFTER A while they got their tab and left eight on thirty-three for the waitress with the bandy legs and the scarred chin. Despite her attitude, Constantine had argued for the heavy tip. He had known many waitresses in his life, and he liked even the bad ones.

Out on Georgia Avenue, the five of them walked to Polk's Super Bee. Polk limped alongside Charlotte, Randolph at their side. Constantine stayed with Weiner, smiling fondly at the little man's march. Something had loosened in Constantine; he could not tell now if it was the marijuana or the alcohol that had unscrewed his head. But he'd forgotten about the things that were behind him. He'd forgotten, just then, about the thing that he'd agreed to do.

CHAPTER 12

POLK DROVE the Dodge downtown, Charlotte at his side, her thigh touching his. Randolph and Constantine flanked Weiner in the backseat. A cool April mist cut the air, came through the open windows.

Constantine let the mist and wind bite his face as he stared out the window at the neon life of Georgia Avenue. Small bars, Caribbean nightspots, athletic-shoe stores, funeral parlors, independent insurers, Korean beer markets, and liquor stores blurred by. On every block there seemed to be an easel set on the sidewalk, advertising beepers and answering services. Constantine noticed the cursive, neon sign for Posin's, the Hebrew grocery store where his mother had taken him weekly as a child to shop for meat. It was the only business on Georgia that Constantine could recognize.

Constantine said, "What's with the beepers?"

"Man, you *have* been away," Randolph said. "The beepers are for all these young entrepreneurs and shit."

A young man in a hooded jacket and baggy jeans stood on the corner of Georgia and Buchanan, watching the Dodge and its occupants pass. He formed his hand into the shape of a pistol, pulled the trigger on Constantine. Constantine looked away.

"The thing I noticed," Constantine said, "since I been back in

D.C. The young people—none of them smile. It's like they don't know how to smile." He rubbed at his beard. "What the hell's going on here?"

"Simple, man," Randolph said. "It's the end of the motherfuckin' world."

Weiner squirmed between the two men. "Polk, put on some music, will you?"

Polk clicked the radio on to an easy-listening station. A string version of "When Doves Cry" came through the trebly dash speaker.

Randolph groaned. "Come on, man, turn this Geritol bullshit off."

Polk notched the volume down. "Hey, Connie, how about passing me up a smoke."

Constantine put the pack on Polk's shoulder. Charlotte turned, took the pack, smiled at Constantine. She put a cigarette to her lips, pushed in the dashboard lighter, and handed the pack back over the seat. Constantine slipped the deck into the pocket of his denim shirt.

"Where we headed?" Constantine asked.

"Place in southeast," Polk said. "A joint where cops hang out, believe it or not. Charlotte's friend wants to meet us there."

"That's that joint on Eighth and G," Randolph said. "Right?"

"Yeah," Polk said, taking the lit cigarette from Charlotte's hand, wedging it between his teeth. "Place called The Spot."

THE SPOT was a windowless, cinder-block establishment set on a dark corner of the city, east of the Hill. Its transom, a dirty piece of rectangular glass framed above the door, functioned as the only source of natural light. As the group walked to the front door, Constantine noticed the rag-swathed feet of a man protruding from a nearby alley.

The six of them stepped inside, stood on a two-step landing. To the left, a mahogany bar ran along the wall, lit by hanging conical lamps. A handful of men, some alone and some in groups, sat on barstools, their drinks and ashtrays set in front of them. One of the men who sat alone, a bearish man with short, dirty blond hair, talked quietly to the bartender. A bulge in the shape of a gun butt protruded from the back of the man's tweed jacket. Three other men sat grouped at the end of the bar under a large Redskins poster, arguing loudly over the results of a fifteen-year-old playoff game. Bluesy slide guitar played loudly through the house stereo, but none of the patrons seemed to notice.

Polk and Charlotte stepped down into the bar area, went straight to the tender to say hello. Constantine looked to the room at his right, an unpopulated green room with scattered tables and dart boards.

"Let's sit in there," Constantine said, pointing to the empty room. "There's cops in the bar."

"Cops and liquored-up rednecks," Randolph added.

"That's okay by me," Weiner said, "but hold on just one minute." Weiner pointed to the bartender, a dark-haired man with a blue bar rag hanging off the side of his jeans. "The bartender— now keep in mind that I've never been here, and I'm assuming that neither have you—he looks to me to be a person of Mediterranean descent. If I were to bet on it, I'd say Italian. In fact, a twenty says the man *is* an Italian." Weiner paused for effect. "What would you gentlemen say?"

Constantine felt himself check the bartender out, though he was not a betting man. He shrugged. "If you say Italian, Weiner, then he is."

"I'll take that bet," Randolph said. The man could have been Italian. But from where they stood, the man *could* have been damn near anything. It seemed like a good bet.

"Come on," Constantine said. "Let's sit down."

The men pushed two four-tops together and took seats. Polk entered the room with his arm around Charlotte, the two of them laughing.

"I ordered us a round," Polk said loudly, limping to the table. "Connie, how about one of them smokes?"

Constantine tossed the deck of Marlboros to the center of the table.

"Hey, Polk," Randolph said. "You know the man behind the bar?"

"Yeah," Polk said, lighting a cigarette off the table's candle. "I've seen him around."

"He's an Italian," Weiner said, nervously touching his beret. "Am I right?"

Polk shook his head, let smoke stream from his nose. "He's a Greek."

Randolph said, "I'll take that twenty, Weiner."

"God-*damn* it, though," Weiner said, reaching for his wallet. "I was close."

A short young Latino walked into the room carrying a round of drinks balanced on a bar tray. He sorted them out, served them, and left with a careless bow and a gold-toothed smile. The party lifted their drinks to Weiner's toast. Charlotte and Polk returned to their private conversation.

"Well, anyway," Weiner said, holding the bill out in his hand, "I can afford the twenty tonight. I hit at the track today. I hit pretty good."

Randolph took the twenty, folded it neatly, and slipped it into the inside pocket of his sport jacket. "So I guess that means you're buyin', too."

Weiner shook his head. "Actually, I spent half of my winnings already."

"Spent it on what?" Randolph said.

"A gift for my lady friend," Weiner said, his eyes reflecting wet from the flame of the candle. "Well, not exactly my lady friend yet. A young lady I met in the record store." Weiner hit his drink.

Randolph nudged Constantine. "I do believe our man here's in love."

Constantine pulled on his vodka, ignoring Randolph. He said to Weiner, "What's she like?"

Weiner smiled. "Like the girls I used to know, the ones I told you about. The ones who used to hang at Coffee and Confusion.

She's real hip, this one. Not beautiful, exactly, I know that. But she has it." He looked into his drink, spoke quietly. "It's been a long time since I've known someone this…clean. I'll give you odds, she barely has a smell to her. I swear to God, if I could just touch that pussy, just touch it one time"—Weiner put his palms together, as if in prayer—"I'd die a happy man."

The bar's front door swung in, and a small bell sounded above it. A woman with a pale complexion entered, looked around, and bounded down the two steps into the room. She wore a short black cocktail dress with a plunging neckline; her stockings were black, and her black hair had been teased and brought forward like the curl of a wave, frozen in the last quiet seconds before it hits the shore. She moved forward quickly, winking once at Charlotte, her purplish lips twisted into a warm, crooked grin, her arms out-stretched.

Randolph looked first at the woman's eyes, then he checked out her shape. His appraisal stopped at the black pumps on the woman's feet: seven, maybe seven and a half.

The woman fell into Polk's arms as he stood to greet her.

"Hello, Polky!" she said.

"Hey, Phil," he said, kissing her roughly on the edge of her mouth. "How the hell's it goin', sweetheart?"

"It's goin'," she said, punctuating her two-pack-a-day laugh with a slap on her hip. "I looked in the mirror this morning and saw that it was going fast. So someone better take advantage of it, real quick." She smiled, her dark eyes lighting on Randolph.

"The name's Randolph," he said, extending his hand. Constantine noted the velvet in Randolph's voice, the same velvet from the sales floor, earlier in the day.

"Phil," she said. "Short for Phyllis."

Randolph ran a long finger along his black mustache. "Don't look like you're short on a *damn* thing," he said.

Phyllis said to Polk, "I like your friends."

"That's Constantine," Polk said. "The man in the cap is Weiner."

Constantine and Weiner nodded at Phyllis. She tilted her head pleasantly and returned her gaze to Randolph.

"Come on, honey," Charlotte said, rising to her feet and grabbing Phyllis by the arm. "You're way behind. Let's go into the bar, have a coupla shooters. We'll come back in, join the party."

"I'm ready," Phyllis said, thrusting out both fists and doing a brief cha-cha, two steps forward, two steps back. She pointed at Randolph and smiled. "Don't go anywhere, boys."

Polk got up, followed Charlotte and Phyllis back into the bar. Weiner stood and said, "I think I'll join them." Constantine and Randolph watched him walk away.

"Looks like you got a date tonight," Constantine said, "if you want it."

"I might," Randolph said.

"You like them like that?"

Randolph shrugged. "I just like 'em."

The busboy came back into the room with a round of drinks balanced on his tray. He put a double vodka rocks in front of Constantine and a cognac with a side of ice water in front of Randolph.

"Hey, amigo," Randolph said. "We didn't order these."

"You fren," the busboy said, grinning.

Randolph shrugged, sipped his cognac as the busboy walked away. "I'm way past my limit," he said. "You could stand to slow down too."

"I'm drunk," Constantine admitted. "But I don't want to slow down." Constantine lighted a cigarette off the table's candle. "If you slow down, you get hit. Can't hit a moving target."

"Yeah, you the king of the drifters," Randolph said softly, looking Constantine up and down. "And if you had a brain in your head, you'd drift the fuck on out of this town—tonight."

"*You're* in this thing. Polk's in it." Constantine blew smoke at the table. "I'm in it too."

"We *have* to be in it," Randolph said. "You don't. Not yet."

Constantine drank deeply of his vodka, swallowed, felt the cool sting of the alcohol in his chest. "Earlier today—you said Grimes had something on everybody."

"That's right" Randolph said. "Valdez and Gorman are losers. They stay around 'cause they got nowhere else to go. Jackson, he's a loser too. Owes Grimes on a card debt. Weiner, he's locked in on an old gambling beef as well."

"And with Polk it's the money."

Randolph shook his head. "I don't think so. I used to think, you know, it was that thing with his foot."

"What do you mean?"

"Polk and Grimes," Randolph said. "They were in the same outfit, C Company, in Korea. Got into some serious shit during the Korean offensive, east of the Chosin Reservoir. It was colder than a motherfucker there—Siberian cold. Subzero. The company got stopped at a blown bridge, at the base of Hill Twelve Twenty-One, on the way to Hudong. That's when the Koreans attacked. C Company, Chosin—all that shit is legendary, man, the old-timers were talkin' about how fierce that shit was when *I* was in the service. Well, Grimes and Polk made it over that hill, made it to the other side, and kept right on going, crossed that frozen reservoir to a place called Hagaru. By then Polk had the frostbite bad. The way I heard, Grimes carried him most of the way across the ice." Randolph swallowed water, put the glass back down on the table. "They air-lifted Polk, took off damn near half his foot. But if Grimes hadn't looked after him…"

"That doesn't sound like the Grimes I know."

"Friendship and loyalty. It means something, when you're young." Randolph sat back in his chair. "But Polk paid his debt a long time ago—he's been in on these jobs, going back near twenty years. It doesn't explain why he's still here today."

Constantine swirled the ice around in his glass. "What about you?" he said.

Randolph looked into Constantine's eyes, then looked away. "When I first came up here, in the early seventies, I got a job as a stockboy, at this shoe store on Connecticut Avenue. My cousin was a salesman there at the time, and he hooked me up. Over the years, you know, I got to be a salesman myself, and a damn good one. My cousin, though, he just got further into that street bullshit, till finally he was into the heroin thing and out of a job. At the time the company was really doin' it—we had ten stores, and we were moving some inventory. The owner, he wasn't declarin' most of the cash money that was coming in, and the way he turned it was to do cash deals with the New York vendors, for a discount on his purchases. He did this every second Thursday of the month. My cousin knew about it—he knew when the owner brought in the cash, and where he stashed it the night before."

"Your cousin knocked the place over," Constantine said.

Randolph nodded. "Grimes bankrolled the job. My cousin's dealer—he owed Grimes a favor—hooked the two of them up."

"What happened?"

"It was a night job. They came in through the skylight, at the office above the Connecticut Avenue store. They got away with it, too. The owner couldn't even report the theft—all that cash." Randolph closed his eyes, tilted his tumbler back, and sipped cognac. "Anyway, I knew about it, and I didn't do a damn thing to stop it. The man was my cousin, understand? The thing is, he died two months later, anyway. Overdose."

"Grimes is blackmailing you."

Randolph lowered his voice. "I come from a little tobacco farm, Constantine, outside of Wilson, North Carolina. If you could see the place I'm talkin' about, compare it to what I've got now, my life now, at that shoe store..."

"I understand," Constantine said. He butted his cigarette, smiled at Randolph. "That skinny kid, at the store—"

"Antoine."

"Yeah. He called you 'Shoedog.' You gonna tell me now what that's all about?"

"You might not understand, man. It's about having some kind of direction in your life."

"Try me."

Randolph leaned over the table. "You ever see a dog, man, when he's walkin' across a bridge? Well, that dog, he doesn't look left and he doesn't look right. He keeps his head down, lookin' at his paws makin' a straight line, all the way. And the only thing he's thinking about, the whole time, is gettin' to the other side of that bridge."

"So?"

"So this. You saw me today, on that floor. While those other boys were thinkin' how to get the jump on me, or thinkin' about the pussy, all I was concentrating on was doin' my job. From twelve to two, that's what the fuck I do. I put my head down, just like a dog, and I cross that bridge. And every single day, I'm the only one in that joint who gets to the other side." Randolph sat back, pointed at Constantine. "I'm a shoedog, man. Might be time for you to be some kinda shoedog too."

Constantine finished the rest of his vodka, put the glass down on the table. "Maybe so, Randolph," he said. "But I never found that one thing—"

"Not yet."

"No. Not yet."

A few minutes later, the party moved back into the room. They grouped themselves around the table, stood over Randolph and Constantine.

"Let's go," Polk said energetically, his arm around Charlotte. "We'll get a nightcap over at Market Inn."

"Great piano bar," Phyllis said, smiling at Randolph. "You boys up for it?"

"I could listen to some standards," Randolph said.

"Come on, Connie," Polk said.

Constantine shook his head. "I don't think so. I'm comfortable here. I'm gonna hang out, have another drink."

Weiner had a seat and said, "I'm with Constantine."

Randolph stood up, moved smoothly to Phyllis, slipped his arm around her back, his hand resting on her waist. "Suit yourself, Constantine. I'll pick you up in the morning, at your place. Eight A.M. We goin' shopping, remember?"

"I'll see you then," Constantine said, nodding at Phyllis, then looking back to Randolph. "Have a good night, man."

Randolph raised his brow. "Bet."

"We took care of the tab," Polk said. "See you fellas later."

Constantine took his cigarettes off the table and tossed the pack to Polk.

The two couples walked toward the door. Charlotte broke away, came back, leaned over the table, and put her mouth close to Constantine's ear. "Polk's got plans for you," she said. "He's really impressed. For the record, so am I." She kissed him on his cheek.

"Thanks, Charlotte," Constantine said. "Take care of him."

"Honey?" she said, standing straight and capping the movement with a broad wink. "I always do."

She turned and moved quickly to the door. As she walked out, Constantine could hear their laughter over the blues shouter coming through the bar's speakers. The door closed, and the laughter died.

Weiner looked over at Constantine. "Hope you don't mind me staying with you. I would of been a fifth wheel in that group."

"I don't mind," Constantine said.

Weiner looked around the room, touched his beret. "You want another drink?"

"Yeah," Constantine said. "One more."

CHAPTER 13

CONSTANTINE AND Weiner killed another round, then got up to leave. Constantine paid the tab and pinned a damp ten under his rocks glass for the busboy. The busboy chin-nodded Constantine as he walked with Weiner from the room.

On the landing, Constantine stepped aside as the big cop walked toward the head. The cop gave him a jittery, unfocused look on the pass. Constantine did not look him in the eye.

Constantine dropped quarters into the cigarette machine that stood on the landing, took his Marlboros from the long slot that ran along the bottom of the machine. He grabbed a blue book of D.C. Vending matches off the top of the machine and stuffed them into his jeans, pushing on the front door. He caught the toe of his shoe on the sidewalk as he walked out, stumbled, and stopped clumsily next to Weiner, who was standing on the edge of the street.

"You all right?" Weiner said.

"Yeah," Constantine said, realizing then that he was irreparably drunk. "Where we goin'?"

"Across town for a quick stop," Weiner said, motioning for a cab that was approaching from two blocks away.

"I don't need any more to drink."

"Neither do I," Weiner said, as the cab stopped at the curb. "Come on."

A soft-spoken young Arab drove them into Northwest. Constantine stared out the window, tried to focus on the buildings. At a stoplight, he saw a shadow of a man walk into the blackness of a storefront, his head down, his hands buried in the pockets of his jacket. Constantine looked at his watch, tried to focus on it in the darkness of the backseat. He could see only that the hour hand tilted to the right of midnight.

At Weiner's direction, the cab stopped on a corner of 9th Street. Weiner paid the man—Constantine did not know how the man had arrived at a figure, as there was no meter in the cab—and the two of them got out.

Constantine could see some club action on F Street, the lettered block that ran to 9th. A group of kids stood halfway down the block, most of them smoking, leaning against the gated front of a shoe store. They wore flannel shirts, all of them; it looked to Constantine as if the boots they wore on their feet were the same style as those he had worn in the marines. One of them yelled something at him, and the rest of them laughed. Constantine wished he were with them— he wanted to laugh too. Weiner tugged on Constantine's shirt, and Constantine followed Weiner down the block.

They crossed to the east side of 9th, walked a half block down, to a group of businesses lit by yellow blinking globes. Constantine recognized these businesses as porno shops. Somewhere in this area Constantine and his friends had come one night as teenagers to check out the strip clubs, the tail end of an already dead downtown burlesque scene. His first experience had been at the Gold Rush, then at the Silver Slipper, where he had eagerly sat at the table nearest the stage as an aging transvestite lisped the introduction—"Welcome to the fabulous...fabulous...Silver Slipper"— and where he had been promptly thrown out after refusing to buy the minimum amount of watered-down drinks. Later that evening he had paid for some head in a place called Benny's Rebel Room, twenty-five dollars for a sensationless squirt. He supposed that these places, like most of the places he had known as a youth, were gone.

Weiner entered a door under a white sign that read FUN PALACE. Constantine followed. Inside, the fluorescent light and cigarette smoke burned his eyes. Two dour Salvadorans stood behind the counter, casually examining their new customers. Constantine walked behind Weiner past the product aisles, through a corridor lined on both sides with books and magazines, to an area where men stood silently, waiting to enter curtained booths alternately marked RED SYSTEM and BLUE SYSTEM.

Weiner took a spot behind a man wearing a red, black, and green knit cap on his head, and folded his hands below his waist. Constantine stood at the back of another two-man line, next to Weiner.

"What's the system?" Constantine said to Weiner.

"I don't know," Weiner said. "You got quarters?"

"Yeah," Constantine said, reaching into his pocket. "I think I got some quarters."

Weiner's number came up first. Constantine watched him throw back the curtain on a blue-system booth and slip inside. A little while later a dead-eyed man walked out of a red-system booth, and Constantine took his place.

In the booth, Constantine dropped two quarters into the slot next to a television set in the wall. Dried, tear-like lines of jism ran down the screen of the television.

The quarters dropped and a picture came on the set: group action on a waterbed set to wah-wah pedaled, cheesy background music, three women and a man, the usual cluster-fuck. One of the women, a terribly skinny coke whore, moved aggressively, her mouth self-consciously frozen in an O. Watching the acne on her back, Constantine felt a brief wave of nausea. He could smell the alcohol coming through his own pores, and the stench of cigarette smoke on his clothes and in his hair. The film loop ended as quickly as it had begun, and Constantine walked unsteadily from the booth.

He bumped into a man who was pushing by to get in the booth. Neither he nor the man acknowledged the contact. Constantine moved to the product wall, saw some blunt rubber instruments called "butt plugs," scanned the wall further, saw some sealed replicas of penises redundantly labeled COCKS, and further still, COCKS, *WITH BALLS!* Finally he studied a group of suspended rubber penises that had been arranged by size, culminating in a three-foot member capped on both ends by fist-sized heads. Constantine wondered passively, what could anyone do with that? A case of one's eyes, he decided, exceeding one's stomach. He plucked a latex vagina off the wall and held it absently in his hand.

"Constantine," Weiner said, behind his back, "come over here."

Constantine replaced the vagina on a metal hanger and moved over to the magazine section, where Weiner held a cellophane-wrapped publication in his hand.

Weiner handed Constantine the magazine. "See anything funny about this?"

Constantine looked at the title of the mag: *A Man and a Woman.* His first thought was that the magazine was oddly named, as only one person stood posing on the cover. But his eyes traveled down, past the wig and lipstick and the perky brown breasts, down to the crotch, where he suddenly understood. This was a man—*and* a woman.

"Who do you suppose," Constantine said, "gets off on this?"

"Other he-shes, I guess," Weiner said, with a shrug. "How was your flick?"

"A daisy chain," Constantine said, "on a bed."

Weiner said, "Same as mine. I thought for a minute, you know, that the red system had different movies from the blue."

"Can we go now?"

Weiner touched his beret. "Sure, let's go."

Weiner stopped at the front counter before leaving the shop. He called one of the clerks over with a curl of his finger. The clerk got off his stool and walked tiredly to the counter.

"Quandes el difference," Weiner asked, "donde el systemo rojo y el systemo azur?"

The clerk looked back at his coworker, shook his head slowly, leaned over the counter, and stared at Weiner. It was a while before Weiner realized that the man was not going to speak.

"Thank you," Weiner said to the clerks. "You gentlemen have a nice evening."

CONSTANTINE DRIFTED in and out of consciousness as the cab drove north on Georgia Avenue, the damp air from the open window blowing pleasantly against his face. He awoke several times to Weiner's voice, to the sudden stop and forward lurch of the cab, and on each occasion he tried to remember where he was, what things he had done that night. The concentration became too difficult, and after a brief, hazy glance out the window, Constantine let his eyes close once again and fell into the easy arms of sleep.

Weiner woke Constantine in front of the motel near the District line. "Come on," Weiner said, "I'll walk with you inside."

Constantine rubbed his face, felt the idle of the cab. The driver's head was tilted in shadowy profile, listening to the backseat conversation.

"I'm not ready to go inside," Constantine said.

"Okay. Well, I've paid for the cab."

"Thanks, buddy. Thanks for the night."

"Take care, kid," Weiner said, patting Constantine's arm. "I'll see you Friday morning."

Constantine watched Weiner exit the cab, march across the street to his GM sedan. He sat in silence until Weiner pulled away from the curb.

Finally the driver looked in the rearview, caught Constantine's eye. "Where would you like to go?" he said, with the careful enunciation common to Middle Easterners.

Constantine looked out the window. "Take Thirteenth Street to Missouri. Catch Military and head west."

The cabby nodded, swung the car out on Georgia, cut a U, and gave the Chrysler gas.

CONSTANTINE HAD the driver stop the cab at 27th and Military, across from an entrance to Rock Creek Park. He gave the man ten dollars, told him not to wait. The driver took off down the empty street. Constantine stood under a streetlight, strained his eyes to focus on his wristwatch. He could see that it was sometime after three.

Constantine crossed to the west side of 27th, started down the sidewalk. He buttoned his shirt to the collar against the chill as he walked past St. John's, his Catholic military academy high school.

Constantine had no feeling for the school at all, not like the boozehounds he met in all the bars around the world, guys who talked incessantly about "those days" as if those were the only days that still carried significance in their bitter, empty lives. Constantine had not wanted to attend St. John's—his father had insisted—so his years there had been spent working toward a kind of deliberate separateness from the school and its students. He supposed now that he had achieved what he set out to do.

At a curve in the road, 27th became Utah. Just past that, Constantine turned left and walked down McKinley. The structure of the neighborhood, its impression of low-key wealth, had not altered. Elegant, porched colonials sat rowed on the block, complemented by sensitive Volvos and Ford Taurus wagons parked on the street in front of them. Only the trees had changed, their height and fullness exuding an old-world, botanical charm on the homes that stood beneath them.

Constantine quickly crossed Nebraska Avenue, continued west on McKinley. He walked to 33rd, made a right. He had done nearly a mile on foot now, and though he knew that he was loaded, he felt oddly invigorated. The feeling accelerated as he brushed past hyacinths and shrubbery, taking the steps up to the playing field of his old elementary school, Lafayette.

He went around the concrete walk that encircled the baseball field, passed a concrete pedestal water fountain that had been jammed on. Constantine slowed at the backstop, curled his fingers through the fence. He looked out at the fog moving slowly in the night, across the wet diamond. Behind him, the water of the fountain arced over and cleared the pedestal, drumming faintly in the mud.

Constantine remembered the year—1973—and his team, a ragtag group of D.C. Rec boys. They took the city championship that summer, against Anacostia, under the lights at Turkey Thicket. Constantine played second base, went two for three that night, a cheap single and a line double to left. The double had knocked in a pair of runs. Closing his eyes, he could still see the faces of his teammates in the infield: a stoic Irish boy at first, a genial, rifle-armed Indian at short, a fireplug Irish Catholic at third base. The pitcher was a tall, lanky kid whose black eyeglasses, held together at the bridge by white surgical tape, slid down his thin nose at the completion of each pitch. The kid threw serious heat—the opposing teams reverently called him "The Greek from Rock Creek"—but Constantine could not remember his name. Standing there, he could not remember the names of any of them.

Constantine pushed away from the backstop and walked toward the school, remodeled now since his youth. He saw the brick wall where he had played stickball as a child, walked past the basketball court where as a teenager he had smoked reefer and shot hoops daily, walked past the hill where he had drunk Tango and Boone's Farm, where he had made love to Katherine on summer nights. He could smell those nights—the bite of wet, freshly cut grass, the taste of nicotine and fortified wine on Katherine's breath, the faint, briny tang of her young vagina—even now. These memories were clear, though he did not feel as if he owned them; he had the feeling that these were memories told to him by someone else.

He walked over a grassy hill, slipped in the dew, slid a few feet to the bottom of the hill. Getting to his feet, he brushed wet grass and mud off his jeans as he crossed Broad Branch Road. Constantine walked straight down Oliver, made a left into the alley that ran to the street after the first house.

He walked along a privacy fence, turned right at the back of the house. The privacy fence told him that the Bradfords had passed away—they would never have erected a fence, and they would never have left their beloved house for anything less than death. At the next house, Constantine stopped, stood in the alley under a light, rested his forearms on a chain-link fence.

He looked into the yard. The shrubbery, the border around the walkway, the double-locked wood shed—all of it fastidiously and impersonally maintained. The pear tree was still standing, pruned back, flowering now with small white blossoms. At nine years of age, one August evening in 1966, Constantine had reached for a pear in that tree, reached absently and with anger as his parents had argued violently in the house, their voices carrying into the backyard. The pear had been filled with bees, and the bees stung his palm and forearm just as he put his hand around it, and he knew instantly from the horrible sound and then the unbelievable pain that he had made a terrible mistake. He had run screaming down the alley, frantically rolling in a puddle at the end of it. Afterward, Mrs. Bradford had held him and treated him, and he went home very late that night. By then his mother was so far into the bag that she could not recognize the swelling in the hand and arm of her own son. His father, of course, had gone to bed.

Constantine looked into the second-story window of the Dutch Colonial. The blue light of a television flickered in the room. In silhouette he could see a thin head rising over a high-backed chair, and from the head, sparks of sparse, white, disheveled hair. He wondered what his father thought, sitting there, old and alone in the middle of the night, staring at the empty, insane images moving across the television screen.

Did the old man think of his wife? Probably not. Constantine himself rarely thought of her, and when he did it was with effort, a futile attempt to reconstruct her face, her radiance, before the gin and ugliness, before the slow sickness came and drained the blood and youth right from her. Oddly, he found it difficult to bring her image up in his mind, though he remembered the cloth of her brilliant blue housecoat as she sat at the side of his bed, rubbing his back. Sometimes, too, in the dawn hours that bordered between consciousness and sleep, he could hear her voice, saying his name. He'd awaken suddenly, and the sound of her voice would still be in his head, and he would not return to sleep.

Constantine took his cigarettes and matches from his shirt pocket and put fire to a smoke. He stood there, his arms on the fence, staring up at the silhouette of his father in the window of the house that he'd grown up in, and he lowered his head and laughed. The sound of his laughter carried in the night. A light came on in a house down the alley, and with it the deep bark of a large-breed dog.

So if the old man came out of the house, what would he do? Would the father recognize the son after seventeen years? He would, Constantine decided. He would look at the long hair, the twisted, drunken face, the muddy clothes, and simply turn around and walk slowly back into the house. There was no reason to think, after all, that anything between them had changed. But standing there, Constantine felt himself hoping, against his cynicism, that his father would leave his chair just then, descend the pine staircase, pass through the small, dim kitchen, and walk out the back door, into the yard, to see and wrap his arms around his son.

The old man did not walk from the house, and after a while the light went out down the alley and the dog no longer barked.

Constantine ground his cigarette down into the concrete and walked out of the alley to Broad Branch Road, following that all the way to Military. He crossed to the other side of the street and put his thumb out at the first group of cars. At the tail end of the group an old Lincoln came to a stop near Oregon Avenue. Constantine went to the passenger door, opened it, and got inside.

CHAPTER 14

RANDOLPH SAT low in the driver's seat of the T-Bird, side-glanced Constantine. He looked at the man, slumped down, his eyes covered by dark shades, his long, uncombed hair blowing in the wind of the open passenger window. Randolph issued a low chuckle as he drove toward Virginia, over the 14th Street bridge.

"You look like some dog *shit* today, boy," he said.

"But I feel like a million bucks," Constantine said, stretching left and pushing in the dash lighter. "How'd the rest of your night turn out?"

"Nice lady," Randolph said.

"A little old," Constantine said, "even for you."

"Old ladies," Randolph said. "They love you right."

Constantine touched the hot end of the dash lighter to a Marlboro. He pulled on it, felt the heat in his lungs, watched his exhale shimmer and disappear in the flash of the morning sun.

"This guy we're going to see—"

"Rego," Randolph said.

"You know him?"

"I've used him."

"He all right?"

"Grease monkey. Talks nickel-dime bullshit all day long." Randolph looked over the rail at the brown water of the Potomac River, back at Constantine. "But he's down."

They took the GW Parkway into Alexandria, drove through a poor residential district and then over railroad tracks into an industrial part of town marked by low cinder-block structures and two-story warehouses. Constantine did not recognize any of it. As a boy growing up in D.C., anything over the river had been irrelevant.

Randolph cut into the last group of warehouses in the complex, stopped in front of an open garage where coveralled mechanics lethargically circled foreign and domestic hood-raised cars parked in the bay. Randolph got out of the T-Bird, made a head motion to Constantine, and Constantine followed.

They walked around the side of the warehouse to the asphalt alley in the rear. Randolph pushed on a buzzer set next to an entrance to the left of a pull-down garage door. Constantine urinated in the alley while Randolph conversed with a voice coming through the speaker mounted below the buzzer. The door swung out as Constantine pulled up on the zipper of his fly.

A small man with a thick head of curly blond hair stood in the doorway. He appraised Constantine, smiled at Randolph as he ran his hands clean over the chest of his gray coveralls.

"Rego," Randolph said.

"Randolph," Rego said, shaking Randolph's hand. "Come on in."

Randolph and Constantine walked through the door, stepped into an immaculate, fluorescently lit bay that held four cars: a Ford, a Chevy, and two Chryslers. All had been painted flat black, stripped of their feathers—no stripes, no monster scoops, no spoilers, no oversized tires or mag wheels—but Constantine could see straight on, knew from the make and model years, that these cars had been manufactured for speed, and for the street.

"You two want some coffee?" Rego said, out the side of his mouth.

"I gotta get to work," Randolph said, looking at the cars. "What do we got?"

Rego drew a cigarette and matches. Constantine watched with amusement as Rego, in the windless bay, cupped his greasy-nailed hand around the match, a gearhead affectation. Rego exhaled slowly, dramatically. The guy was handsome, almost a Redford type, with blue eyes and deep laugh lines ending at the cut of a square jaw. But the blue eyes were a bit wide-set, the jaw a little slack.

"You got your Ford Torino here," Rego said, pointing his cigarette at the farthest car on the left. "Cobra model, four twenty-nine Ram Air, with a four-barrel—"

"Skip the Ford," Randolph said, looking past Rego. "That the way you look at it, Constantine?"

Constantine nodded.

Rego said, "What about the Chevy?"

"Fuck a Chevy," Constantine said. His head hurt awfully bad.

"I guess you two know what you want," Rego said.

"We're lookin' for somethin' serious," Randolph said.

"I got these Chryslers," Rego said. "They're serious as a heart attack."

Randolph said, "Talk about it."

Rego nodded in a scholarly manner as he dragged on his cigarette. He walked over to a long, clean-lined Plymouth parked third in the row, and touched his hand gingerly to the hood, as if the hood were hot.

"This Fury should do it," Rego said. "Nineteen-seventy. Four-forty V-8, automatic, completely hopped up on the rebuild."

"Six barrel?"

Rego closed his eyes with reverence, nodded slowly. "Three two-barrel Holley carbs."

Randolph walked to the driver's side, opened the door, climbed in. He sat behind the wheel, ran his hand along it, gripped it and ungripped it as he studied the dash.

"What about that one?" Constantine said, pointing his chin down the line at a black sedan that looked benign as a taxicab. "Fast?"

"Faster than shit through a goose," Rego said. "Road Runner, four-forty. Six-pack, same year as the Fury. Four-speed Hurst."

"It moves, huh?"

"It really screams," Rego said, widening his eyes broadly, as if a stranger had just grabbed his dick. "I'm serious as cancer."

Constantine got in the bucket of the Plymouth, looked at the tach mounted on the steering column, put his hand on the shifter, depressed the clutch, moved through the gears. He pushed on the car horn, heard the "beep-beep" of the Road Runner cartoon character, shook his head, and chuckled. He glanced through the passenger window, caught the eye of Randolph, still sitting in the driver's seat of the Fury. Both of them got out of their cars and went to Rego, who was crushing his cigarette under the toe of his work boot.

"About that horn," Constantine said.

"Purists," Rego said, shrugging his shoulders. "If it don't have the horn, it ain't a Runner."

"Keep it," Constantine said, considering it for only a second. "It's all right with me."

"The two Chrysler products, then."

Randolph said, "Right."

"You pick 'em up tomorrow," Rego said, handing Randolph a folded slip of paper from the pocket of his coveralls. "Here. The drop location is the same."

"Plates?" Randolph said, putting the paper in his pocket.

Rego winked. "Fresh in the A.M., right out of satellite parking at National. They won't even make the hot sheet by the time you roll. Guaranteed."

"All right, man," Randolph said. "You all straight?"

"Weiner fixed me," Rego said.

"Then that'll do it," Randolph said, shaking Rego's hand. Randolph exited and Constantine followed. The door closed behind them as they hit the alley.

Randolph and Constantine walked along the side of the warehouse to the parking area, got into the T-Bird. Randolph turned the key on the smooth engine, backed out of his space, put the car in drive, and pulled out of the lot.

"You sure you all right with that car?" Randolph said, looking at the road.

"It's fine," Constantine said.

"And you don't mind that simple-ass horn."

"No, I don't mind."

"You serious, man?"

"Yeah, I'm serious." Constantine pulled hair off his face, pushed it behind his ear, and grinned at his friend driving the car. "Serious as a hangnail, Randolph."

VALDEZ AND Gorman sat in the black Caddy in front of Constantine's motel at the District line, Gorman's thin arm out the driver's side window, a cigarette dangling in his fingers. Jackson sat alone in his own car, behind them. Constantine noticed them as Randolph pulled to a stop on the east side of Georgia Avenue.

Randolph cut the engine. "Here's where we split up," he said to Constantine.

"You goin' with Jackson?"

"Yeah."

Constantine nodded past Randolph, to Valdez and Gorman in the Caddy parked across the street. "What am I supposed to do with those lovers?"

"Go with 'em, have a look at the joint." Randolph prodded his finger gently into Constantine's arm. "And keep your mouth shut. Don't let Valdez fire you up into talkin' about nothin', hear?"

"What are you sayin', man?"

"I'm talkin' about the woman, Constantine. I didn't mention it 'cause it wasn't none of my goddamn business. Any fool can see ...listen, man, you got a death wish, that's your thing." Randolph cut it, shook his head. He scooted up in the seat, pulled his wallet, pulled a card from the wallet, flipped the card over, and wrote something on its back. "Here, man"—Constantine took the card—"you need me, you can reach me at work, or on the number on the back. You might want to talk, 'specially tonight. Hear?"

Constantine slid the card into his breast pocket. He got out of the car and closed the door, bent over and leaned his elbows on the frame of the open window.

"Thanks," Constantine said.

"Ain't no thing," said Randolph.

Constantine pushed away, waited for a break in the traffic. He jogged across Georgia to the black Caddy, got into the backseat. Valdez and Gorman were both wearing shades, staring straight ahead. Valdez took the toothpick that was lodged in the corner of his plump mouth and dropped it out the window. He looked in the rearview at Constantine.

"You're late," Gorman said.

Constantine looked away. "I was picking out the car."

"You pick out a good one?" Valdez said.

"It'll do."

"Maybe you want to drive right now," Valdez said, shooting an ugly grin toward Gorman. "Seeing as how you're the driver."

"And maybe," Constantine said, "you'd like to kiss my white ass."

Gorman laughed sharply, punched Valdez in the shoulder. Valdez squirmed in the seat, looked back up in the rearview.

"I don't know why Grimes put you on this thing," Valdez said, "but I hope we all make it through. 'Cause after it's over, brother, you can believe one thing: I'm gonna fuck you up."

Constantine stared back in the mirror. "Can we just go?"

Gorman dragged his cigarette down to the filter, flicked it out onto Georgia Avenue, and turned the key in the ignition.

"Come on, Valdez," he said. "We sit here all day, you gonna miss your fuckin' show."

CHAPTER 15

Randolph drove north on Wisconsin Avenue, looked across the seat at Jackson. The man had been talking shit the whole trip, since he and Randolph had argued in front of the motel over who would drive. Randolph had ended it when he told Jackson to get his seventies-lookin' ass inside the car. Now Jackson had brought out his pick—a black plastic comb with a black plastic fist clenched on the end of it—and he was raking the comb up the front of his modified Afro. Randolph hadn't seen a pick like that in years.

Jackson whipped his head to the right, rolled his window down, and yelled something out to a large-breasted, long-legged woman walking up the street in a short leather skirt. The woman kept walking, her alternating-piston ass moving with beautiful efficiency, her eyes straight ahead. Randolph gave the T-Bird gas and sped past.

"Hey, slow down, man!" Jackson said.

"She ain't look like she want to talk to you, man," Randolph said.

"I'll make the bitch talk"—Jackson smiled, ran his fingers across his crotch—"right into the goddamn microphone." Jackson turned his head once again to get a final look, lowered his voice to a mumble. "She looked like Pam Grier, too."

Randolph parked a few doors down from Uptown Liquors. The

time was a little after eleven, and already there was some early alky action, in and around the shop. Jackson strained his eyes to see through the plate glass of the store: in the back, near the end of the counter, stood Isaac, gathering and breaking down cartons. Jackson knew that Isaac would have to take the cartons out, to the green dumpster in the garage beside the store.

Randolph checked his watch. "We meetin' Polk here?"

"Uh-uh," Jackson said. "He's still shacked up with the nappy, that old freak of his. Said he'd swing by later in the day, check the place out."

"Then let's get on it, man. I got to get my ass down to the shoe store, for the noon rush."

"You go on," Jackson said. "I done took the tour yesterday." Through the glass, Jackson watched Isaac head into the back room, the cartons under his arm.

Randolph opened the door, put one foot out on the asphalt. "All right, then. I'll be right back."

Jackson put his hand around Randolph's arm. "Take your time. I know you just the driver, but Grimes wants you to know the place real good. Get yourself an education, hear?"

Randolph pulled his arm away, shifted his shoulders beneath his jacket as he climbed out of the T-Bird. He walked down the sidewalk to the double glass doors of Uptown Liquors, went inside. When the door closed behind him, Jackson bolted from the car, jogged past the store, and entered the darkness of the small garage.

He took off his shades, folded them, hung one stem in the pocket of his shirt. Adjusting his eyes, he moved quickly toward the green dumpster. To the side of it, a door opened, and Isaac stepped out into the garage. Jackson stopped walking, watched Isaac put the broken-down sheets of cardboard into the dumpster. Isaac looked bigger, harder up close.

"What's goin' on, brother?" Jackson said.

"Nothin' to it," Isaac said, looking at Jackson for only a fraction of a second, the look disinterested, as if Jackson were a salesman who had come to his door.

Jackson said, "Got a minute?"

Isaac closed the lid of the dumpster. This time he did not bother to look at Jackson. "You take it easy, man," he said, and he turned to walk back through the door.

Jackson reached into his pocket, pulled the hundreds that were bound with the heavy rubber band, used his forefinger and thumb to fan the stack. The sound of it cut the stillness of the dark garage.

Isaac stopped walking. He knew the sound, had heard it every night at closing time, when old man Rosenfeld and young Rosenfeld counted out the money. He had gotten used to hearing the sound. But now the sound was aimed at him.

Isaac turned, squinted his eyes at the hustler with the mutton-chop sideburns and the tight green pants. "What you want, man?" he said.

Jackson slapped the stack of hundreds against his palm. "Tomorrow morning," he said, "quarter past eleven—me and a couple of boys gon' knock this motherfucker over."

Isaac shifted his weight. They stared at each other, listened to the hiss of cars passing by on Wisconsin. Isaac cocked one eyebrow. "What you tellin' me for?"

Jackson smiled. "Maybe I'm takin' a chance. But I been watchin' you, man. I figure I'm takin' a bigger chance walkin' into that shop tomorrow mornin', havin' to face you down. So I've told you." Jackson's smile faded. "And now I've crossed that line."

Isaac's eyes went to the money, then back up at Jackson. "You ain't done talkin'."

"Isaac," Jackson said. "That your name, right?"

"That's right."

"Sounds like a slave name."

"Talk about the money."

"I am," Jackson said. "See, I been in that shop, heard the way that Jewboy with the Rolex and the chains talks to you. The old man too.

'Isaac, fetch this, Isaac, fetch that.' Thought it might be time for *you* to get you some, brother."

Isaac looked away from the man's eyes, spoke in a low and steady voice. "What've I got to do?"

It was done now, easy. Jackson had not figured Isaac to turn so quick, but it proved what he already knew: a man would do anything, when it came down to it, for the green. *Especially* a raggedy-ass motherfucker like this.

Jackson fanned the stack, stepped up close to Isaac. "There's ten grand here, Isaac. I'll be comin' in tomorrow with an old white man, a little dude. When I get all the money, I want you to step out of the back."

"And?"

"I want you to doom the white man. Kill him, understand what I'm sayin'?"

Isaac stared at Jackson without emotion. He reached out, took the money.

"You need a gun?" Jackson said.

Isaac shook his head.

"After you kill the white man," Jackson said, "I'm gonna put a round over your head. Way over, for show. You drop down behind the counter, and that's when I get out. You be a hero, I take the money, and everything's clean. We down, Isaac?"

Isaac nodded. Jackson patted the man's arm, noticed the torn flannel of Isaac's shirt.

"Eleven-fifteen?" Isaac said.

Jackson said, "Right."

Isaac did not shake Jackson's hand. He folded the stack of hundreds and shoved them down into the pocket of his blue work pants. Then he turned and went back through the door, into the stockroom.

Jackson walked slowly out of the garage, putting on his shades as he moved into the light. He got to the T-Bird, sat in the shotgun seat just as Randolph emerged from the front door of Uptown Liquors.

Jackson relaxed, took a deep hit of the cool April air.

From inside, Isaac watched a tall man in a maroon sport jacket leave the store and meet the hustler at the car. There was something familiar about the tall man—something familiar and good. It bothered him, not knowing what it was. But then he heard the sound of the old man's voice.

"Isaac," Rosenfeld said, gesturing toward a man in a tweed jacket, standing at the counter. "The gentleman needs a case of Guinness, please."

Isaac nodded, and headed for the back room.

CHAPTER 16

GORMAN LAUGHED loudly. "Look at that fuckin' guy," he said.

Gorman pointed into a brightly painted concrete park at the corner of 14th and Girard, at a man standing, talking, and gesturing on a redwood pedestal. The man wore a fluorescent Gianni Versace jogging outfit, with thick gold chains hung out across the top. Young men dressed in hooded sweatshirts and low-rider jeans stood around the pedestal, listening to the man with the expressive hands.

"See that outfit?" Gorman said.

"Yeah?" Valdez said.

"Black man's tuxedo," Gorman said.

"Blind leadin' the blind," Valdez said, with a grunt.

Gorman said, "Fuckin' boofers."

The street opened up and seemed to brighten at U, at the bottom of a steep hill. It had taken twenty-five years, but the signs of regeneration—new businesses, new bars, theaters, and offices—grew through the ruin, like buds blooming impossibly from the concrete. When Constantine had left town, 14th Street had still been bloodied from the riots of '68, long rows of charred storefronts, all plywood and black iron. Constantine could still remember the tension when the city burned, how the smoke hovered over the downtown skyline, the way his parents had sat quietly with jittery eyes and folded hands at the dinner table that night.

"Pull over," Valdez said, as the car drove by the projects named Frontiers, at S Street.

Gorman slowed, guided the Caddy into a spot in front of a block of shabby row house storefronts on the west side of 14th, and cut the engine. Across the street stood a place called For the Love of Children, its faded wooden sign hung over the pocked door. Next to that was a partially demolished structure, a banner slung loosely across its falling brick facade, announcing the coming of City Center. The mayor's signature, in black, was scrawled boldly beneath the announcement.

"Liquor store's just around the corner," Valdez said, "on R. City's gonna tear that down, too."

"Looks like we're hittin' it just in time," Gorman said.

"They're making room for a new shopping center," Valdez said. "These people got nothin' but plenty of time to shop."

"Be new for maybe a week," Gorman said. "Then they'll do to the shopping center what they done to the projects. The spades keep tearin' them down, and the city keeps rebuildin' 'em. 'Your tax dollars at work'—like the sign says." He added, "I do like that mayor, though." He looked in the rearview, winked at Constantine in the backseat. "How about you, driver? You like to get a piece of our fine mayor?"

Constantine did not look at Gorman and he did not answer.

"He likes 'em more on the blond side," Valdez said. "Don't you, Constantine?"

"Let's get this done," Constantine said.

Gorman lighted a cigarette off a match, tossed the match out the window. Valdez pointed down the row of storefronts, to a beer market on the end.

"See that door, to the left of the market?" he said.

Constantine could see that the door stood in place, but it was not hung on its hinges.

"I see it," Gorman said. "So what?"

"Come on," said Valdez.

The three of them got out of the Cadillac, walked down the sidewalk, passed a pawnbroker, a restaurant supply house, and then the Iglesia Pentecostal Onda Hispana, a storefront church with blue lace curtains hung in its windows. A man in a torn jacket walked up to them, asked Gorman for the time. Gorman said, "Fuck off." Just past the neighborhood beer market they stopped at the door that Valdez had pointed to. Valdez pulled the door back enough to accommodate his wide frame, held it steady for Gorman. Gorman followed Valdez through the door, and Constantine followed Gorman.

They stood at the bottom of a steep flight of stairs, in a garbage-strewn foyer. The air smelled of vermin and human waste. At the top of the stairs darkness played against gray light, and in the grayness Constantine could see a faint veil of smoke. Valdez made a head motion and started up the stairs.

The three of them went up to the second floor landing, nails, wood, and squares of plaster crunching beneath their feet. Valdez pulled his gun when they reached the landing, looked left down the dark hallway. A rat scurried to the end of it, bumped a door, flipped in the air, ran, and found a patch of darkness.

Valdez looked up the next flight of stairs, to the third floor. "All right!" he yelled. "Come on down, I'm talkin' about now!"

They heard footsteps above, then saw, through the slats of the banister, ragged pants legs descend the stairs. Four men—young to middle-aged, emaciated, flat-eyed men—shuffled slowly past them on the landing. Valdez held his gun at his side, growled at the men to "move it." None of them looked at him, or at Gorman or Constantine. They continued slowly, down the stairs, through the door without hinges, out onto the street.

"Pipeheads," Valdez muttered.

"What now?" Gorman said.

Valdez said, "Up."

The third floor was brighter, illuminated from the skylights spaced evenly in the detailed ceiling. The doors in the hall—there were three of them—had all been opened. Constantine followed Valdez and Gorman through the doorway of the room that fronted the building.

The sour rot of human excrement and the smell of cooked cocaine hit Constantine as he entered the room. The room had no furniture; a moldy mattress sat next to an overturned milk crate in the corner. On the raw wood floor, burnt matches had been tossed and scattered. Above the mattress, sun-faded magazine portraits of Martin Luther King, Jr., John Kennedy, and Jesus Christ were scotch-taped to the wall. Black, watery waste had been splashed and heaped on a newspaper spread open on the floor, and smeared on the room's four walls. Constantine lighted a cigarette, pulled nicotine into his lungs, gagged up his morning coffee.

Valdez stood by the bay window that gave a view to 14th Street, called for Constantine to join him. Gorman walked to the corner of the room, unzipped his fly, and urinated on the mattress. The urine made a dull sound as it hit the springs.

"When in Rome," Gorman said, turning to grin at Valdez. Valdez shook his head as he gazed through the large window. The sunlight blew through the window like a torch, illuminating the porcine features of the Mexican.

Constantine exhaled a jet of tobacco smoke that swirled and then hung in the light "What are we doing here?" he said.

"From here," Valdez said, "it makes more sense." He pointed below and to the right, the low-rise structures at the intersection of 14th and R laid out like a grid. "There's EZ Time. We're going to come in from Thirteenth, down R. You park across from the mission, just away from the liquor store. R's one-way, heading west. The next two streets to the south, Corcoran and then Q, they're one-way going east. You got that?"

"Sure," Constantine said.

"I'm not kidding," Valdez said, his voice dull and quiet.

Constantine said, "I'm listening."

Gorman walked across the room, his thick-soled oxfords clomping noisily on the wood floor. He stood next to Valdez, buried his small hands in the pockets of his suit.

Valdez tried again. "There's a coupla major alleys behind this building, wide enough for two cars. The street vendors keep their carts in a garage back there. One connects R to S, and the other crosses Johnson and continues on to Fifteenth. Fifteenth Street is one-way, heading uptown."

Valdez looked at the silent Constantine, cleared his throat and sinuses, brought the whole mess together in his mouth. He turned his head back away from the window and hawked a wad of mucus across the room. Valdez wiped his mouth on the sleeve of his jacket.

"You need to know this shit," Valdez said, "in case the shit falls apart. One time, on one of these jobs—"

"I'll get myself a map," Constantine said.

"A map," Gorman said, chuckling, rocking back on his heels. "This guy's cute, you know it?"

Valdez stroked the whiskers of his black mustache. He stared out the window to the street below, waited for Constantine to finish his smoke.

Constantine ground the cigarette beneath his shoe, looked over at Valdez.

"That do it?" he said.

Valdez said, "Let's just go."

ON THE ride uptown, none of them spoke. Constantine sat back, closed his eyes, let the cool air from the open window brush his face. They dropped him sometime after noon in front of the motel on Georgia Avenue.

Constantine said, "I'll see you guys tomorrow," as he climbed from the backseat of the Cadillac. He quickly crossed the street, did not look back or wait for a reply.

Valdez watched Constantine walk through the orange lobby, punch the button for the elevator. The man stood there, waiting, his long black hair falling lazily to his shoulders, his hands hung loosely at his side, cool as a cowboy.

Gorman said, "Shit, Valdez, look at that!"

Valdez turned his attention to the street, to the black Mercedes coupe parked a few spots ahead.

"You see that?" Gorman said.

"I see it."

"It's hers, isn't it?"

Valdez said, "It's hers."

"What's she doin' here, Valdez?"

Valdez stared at the coupe. "She's fuckin' him, you moron."

Gorman giggled, said through the giggle, "You gonna tell Grimes?"

"I haven't decided," Valdez said. He checked his watch. "Come on, let's get back to the house."

Gorman engaged the transmission, pulled out onto Georgia, headed north.

Both of them kept their mouths shut for the next five minutes. Near the Beltway, Gorman suddenly whistled through his teeth, laughed, and shook his head.

"You gotta admit," he said, "the guy's got balls."

"Yeah," Valdez said, "he's got balls."

"Might surprise us," Gorman said. "Make a good driver."

"I was thinkin' the same thing." Valdez shifted in his seat. "So maybe I'll wait till after the job," he said, "to talk to Mr. Grimes."

CHAPTER 17

CONSTANTINE TURNED the key, opened the door. He stood in the doorway, looked at the woman on the bed.

"Hello, Delia," he said.

She pointed her chin in his direction. "Constantine."

Constantine stepped into the room, closed the door behind him. He tossed his room key onto the formica top of the varnished dresser.

"How'd you get in?" he said.

"I made friends with the concierge."

"The concierge?" Constantine said, and laughed.

"Yes," Delia said. "You know, the guy behind the desk."

"He likes to read, that guy."

"Uh-huh. He was reading something called *Skank* when I walked into the lobby."

Delia smiled. Constantine knew it was a smile because the corners of her mouth turned up when she did it. On her even a smile looked a little bit sad.

"So you made friends with the genius down in the lobby."

"With money," she said, "it's easy to make friends."

"I guess so."

Delia uncrossed her legs, stood up, smoothed out her skirt against her legs as she walked toward Constantine. Constantine traced the muscles on Delia's back through the silk of her shirt as they embraced. He kissed her on the lips.

After a while, she pulled away, shook her blond hair away from her face with a toss of her head. Constantine touched his finger to the vein in Delia's neck, felt the drum of her pulse.

"Not in this place," she said. "Okay?"

"Okay," said Constantine.

He went to the bathroom, urinated, brushed his teeth, and washed his face. He combed his hair, pushed it behind his ears, and walked back out into the room. Delia stood by the window, looking down onto the street. In the light that came in through the window, Constantine could see the crystalline blue of her eyes from across the room.

"I'm hungry," he said. "You hungry?"

"Yes," she said, "I'm hungry."

"Come on," Constantine said. "Let's grab somethin' to eat."

CONSTANTINE AND Delia ate lunch in a small Italian restaurant on Sligo Avenue, a few blocks north of the District line in downtown Silver Spring. The place had been thoughtlessly decorated, one square dining room with clown-face prints hung carelessly on salmon-colored walls. But the food was both reasonable and good, and the tables had turned over twice during their visit. Their waiter, a deeply lined guy with the manners of a two-day drunk, had been properly surly throughout the meal. Constantine gave the place high marks.

Constantine finished the rest of his anchovies and peppers, took the heel of the loaf from the bread basket, sopped the heel in the olive oil that remained pooled in the dish. He ate that and poured house red from the carafe into his glass. He topped off Delia's glass and set the carafe back on the table. Delia swallowed the last of her white pizza, wiped her mouth on the checkered cloth napkin that had been folded in her lap. Constantine watched the cloth move across her lips as he sipped the red.

During lunch he had told her much of what he had done in the last seventeen years. His story sounded romantic, even to him, as if the telling of it had altered the reality. Delia was a good listener, and she was beautiful, and it was easy to have lunch with her, sit across from her and talk.

"In all of that," Delia said, when Constantine was finished, "you never mentioned your family."

Constantine took the Marlboros from his pocket, shook the pack in Delia's direction. She refused, and he lighted one for himself.

"My folks are dead," Constantine said, the words coming easily. "You?"

Delia looked into her plate, back at Constantine. "My mother died a few years back. I don't know if my father's alive. I don't know anything about him. He left when I was an infant."

Constantine thought of Grimes, the substitute for the father she had not known. With the money added to the quotient, that explained the relationship. He kept his mouth shut, smiled thoughtfully at Delia.

"Ready to go?" he said.

"Sure," she said. "Let's go."

Delia signaled the waiter. He came, took her credit card, muttered something under his breath about credit cards, and walked away. Constantine dragged on his cigarette, watched the little waiter run the card through the machine, standing there in his tight pants and crooked bow tie, still mumbling hatefully under his breath. The guy looked like the dark side of Vegas, one scotch away from a ruptured aorta.

"Where we headed?" Constantine said.

"My mother's place," Delia said. "I still keep it, you know... in case I want to get away."

Constantine nodded as he stubbed out his smoke, killed the rest of his wine. The waiter returned, dropped the voucher on the table.

Delia signed it, added ten percent for the tip, and the two of them got up to leave.

Constantine pinned a five under his wineglass before heading for the door.

THEY PICKED up a bottle of dago red from an Indian market on Fenton Street, then drove a mile to a group of garden condos at 16th Street and East-West Highway. The buildings had been whitewashed, their shutters painted a forest green.

Delia parked the Mercedes next to a brown dumpster in the lot. On the way to the apartment Constantine watched two Vietnamese boys chase each other across the lawn. The chaser, a skinny boy no older than eight, screamed, "I get you, muthafucka!" to his friend. They disappeared over a rise behind the building, their laughter fading in the air.

Constantine and Delia entered a bleak stairwell, took the stairs down to a door marked 11. Delia used her key, pushed on the door, and Constantine followed her inside. She switched on a light.

The apartment was sparsely furnished, Early American on faded hardwood floors, ropy throw rags. Currier and Ives prints centered on white walls. They walked through the living room, passed a dinette set on the way to the kitchen. Delia switched the kitchen light on by pulling on a string that hung from the ceiling fixture. Constantine could see the silhouette of bugs lying in the globe of the fixture.

"I'll be in there," Delia said, pointing across the narrow hall to the only remaining room. "Why don't you open the wine?"

Constantine found glasses and a corkscrew. He corked the wine and walked into the darkness of the room across the hall.

The Venetian blinds had been lowered and drawn in the room. Delia stood in her bra and panties by a tall dresser, removing her earrings as she stared into the mirror. Constantine stopped behind her, traced a group of freckles sprayed across her shoulders. He poured two glasses of wine, placed the bottle on the dresser, and handed one of the glasses to Delia.

"This your mother's room?" he said.

"Yes."

"You don't mind?"

"No, it's all right." Delia put the wine glass to her lips, wrinkled her nose, smiled. "It smells like ginger," she said.

"That Indian place," Constantine said.

Through the window, in the stillness of the room, they could hear the laughter and taunts of children, playing on the grass behind the building. They spoke in English, their accents Asian and Hispanic. "Your mother!" said one, and then "Your father!" from another, and after that more laughter.

"It would be good to be a child," Delia said. They were naked on the bed now, lying side by side, the cotton bedspread and sheets drawn back.

"I don't know," Constantine said. "Nature corrects itself, I think. There's something good about every time." He kissed her on the lips, then touched his tongue to the cup of her armpit. He tasted her perspiration and perfume.

"Children don't have this," he said.

Delia's blond hair fell around the pillow, her arms back and underneath it. She stared at the brushstrokes patterned in the ceiling, swallowed, half-closed her eyes. Constantine kissed her belly, the inside of her thighs. He blew softly on the light brown hair of her pudendum, and took in her scent. He spread her lips with his thumb and forefinger, ran his tongue along the silk of her pink flesh, blew his breath inside of her.

"Constantine," Delia said.

She came quietly. Afterward they sat facing each other on the bed. Delia put her legs over his thighs, held him in her warm hand. She lowered herself onto him, moved him inside her, kept him there. He kissed the long curve of her slender neck, smelled her hair, held her. He rested his head against her breast.

*   *   *

CONSTANTINE POURED wine into his glass. He walked to the window, stood naked beside it, peering through the spaces in the drawn blind. Dusk threw vague slashes of light across his hips and chest.

Delia rose from the bed, moved across the room, stood behind Constantine. She put her arms around his shoulders. He felt the wetness of her groin against his skin.

"What about tomorrow?" Delia said. "Are you going to be here after tomorrow?"

"I don't know," said Constantine.

"I'd like to go away," she said.

"Where would you go?"

Delia shifted her weight, ran her fingers lightly through the hairs at the top of Constantine's chest. "It doesn't matter," she said. "I'd raise horses somewhere, I guess."

Constantine sipped wine, stared at the lines of gray in the blinds. "You're doing that now. You're doing it in style."

"I want to get away from *him,* Constantine."

Her hand fell to his hips, then touched between his legs. She wrapped her fingers around him. Her fingers brushed the end of him, where the remains of their lovemaking still came and dripped to the hardwood floor.

"You made a mistake," Constantine said. "You never should have—"

"It just happened," she said. "I wasn't looking for anything. He came into my life, just after my mother died. I don't even remember how we met."

"It's not going to be easy."

"I know it, Constantine."

She moved around to face him, then dropped to her knees. He felt the cool sweat on her hair as it touched his thighs. He felt her breath on him, her lips around him, her tongue. Constantine braced his hand against the trim of the window, and closed his eyes.

*　　*　　*

THEY FELL to sleep on the bed, woke to darkness. Delia found a candle, pushed it into the wine bottle, lighted it, and set it on the dresser. They showered together, then dressed together in the bedroom.

Delia stood in front of the mirror and brushed her hair. Constantine stood next to her, took his wristwatch off the dresser. Among the woman's articles on the dresser, he saw a St. Christopher's medal, a cloth patch embroidered with the numbers 1221, and a scuffed baseball. He fastened the clasp on his wristwatch.

"Did a man live here, too?" Constantine said.

"No," said Delia. "I found those, in the bottom of the dresser, after she died. My mother had friends, after my father left. But only friends."

"A woman can get along all right without a man, I guess."

"She lived a long life. But she was never happy." Delia's eyes were wet in the light of the candle. She blew out the flame, touched Constantine's hand in the dark. "Come on," she said. "Let's go."

DELIA DROVE Constantine to the motel on Georgia Avenue, stopped the Mercedes out front. She kept the headlights on and let the engine run. Constantine leaned across the seat, kissed her on the edge of her mouth.

"Thanks."

Delia wrote the number of her private line on a card, handed it to Constantine. She touched his cheek.

"This isn't over," she said.

Constantine did not answer. He got out of the car, shut the door, moved across the sidewalk to the doors of the motel, heard the Mercedes pull away from the curb. He bought a pack of smokes from the machine in the lobby, went to the elevator and pushed on the up arrow.

Constantine waited for the elevator, listened to a Johnny Guitar Watson tune coming from the lounge. He smiled a little, shook his head, turned, and headed for the lounge.

At the entrance, he passed a middle-aged man holding the wall for support. The man nodded at Constantine, tried to focus his eyes.

Constantine smiled. "A real mother for ya," he said.

The man pushed his hat back on his head and said, "Ain't that cold?"

Constantine entered the lounge and took a seat at the bar.

CHAPTER 18

ISAAC SAT on the edge of the bed, polishing his .45 in the yellow light of the lamp that sat on the nightstand. Next to the lamp, a General Electric clock radio, the dial set on WHUR, played softly in the room: Norman Conners, "You Are My Starship." Isaac loved that one. He rubbed the oilskin down the barrel of the Colt, and sang along.

He had cleaned and oiled the gun while Nettie, his wife of twenty-three years, cooked dinner one floor down. Isaac could smell the garlic of the pork roast, the biscuits, the onions frying with the potatoes, all of it coming up the stairs, warming the house. It felt right, sitting there, the aroma of the dinner in the room, Nettie working in the kitchen, the sounds of her pans clattering below, the fit of the .45 in his hand.

It had been a while since he killed a man. Twenty-two years, back in Vietnam. The way he felt then, he would have done anything to get back to his young wife and baby girl. He would have killed them all.

Besides, it had been work, and when a man was paid to do something, he did it. He had gotten back to the world, and he had gotten a straight-up job, and the baby girl had grown up fine, a junior now at UDC. He had stayed married to Nettie, too, not always an easy woman to live with, but a fine woman just the same. Good God, the woman could cook.

The job at the liquor store, that had always done him right. His paycheck read two fifty-five, but young Rosenfeld added two hundred in green to the envelope every single time, and it was the saving of that cash over the years that had bought his daughter's education, some other things as well. Yeah, the Rosenfelds had always done him right.

And there was the other thing. Isaac's father had been a stone drunk, a street-corner fixture in the LeDroit Park neighborhood where he had grown up. Old man Rosenfeld had taken Isaac's father in, taken him off the street, and given him a full-time job at the old liquor store on 5th and T. Isaac's old man straightened up then, and though the damage had been done—a rotten liver and a chest full of cancer—he lived out his last years with some dignity.

So when Isaac got back from the war, he took his father's place at the new liquor store on Wisconsin and Brandywine. In the garage next to the store he taught young Rosenfeld not to drop his left when throwing a right, and he showed him how to get down in a three-point stance. He watched him grow up, and he watched the father grow old. He listened to their trash-talking bullshit every day, how they played each other and the customers, and sometimes he winced at it, but always he kept his mouth shut. He owed the family for what they'd done, for his father and for him. He did his job.

Now the hustler had given him ten grand to kill a man, and he'd do that too. He'd make a modest dollar on the sale of the house, and he'd hook that up with the ten, and move with Nettie off Fairmont, to someplace safer, Oxon Hill maybe, or Landover, or Capitol Heights. Nettie could grow tomatoes, some spices in the yard. He'd buy her a few things, a new dress, and some shoes—good God, the woman loved shoes—and a few things for himself.

He thought of the man in the maroon sport coat, the man the hustler had met outside the liquor store, at the car. It bothered him a little bit, 'cause he *knew* the man. He forgot about it, though, as Nettie's voice called from down the stairs.

"Dinner, Isaac."

"I'll be right down, baby!" he yelled.

Isaac palmed a full clip into the butt of the .45, safetyed it, placed it in the top drawer of the nightstand. He switched off the radio, then the light, and walked out of the room.

GORMAN CUT the Caddy's engine, got out of the car, and walked across the lot. He checked the lot for undercover boys, guys sitting in their Fords wearing mustaches and shades and Peterbilt caps. He couldn't see a one. Most likely, they were parked across 261, bayside, in the lot of the Rod and Reel. They alternated stakeouts between the Rod and Jethro's, the crab house and bar that sat back on Fisherman's Creek, the marina area on the canal that dumped into the bay. Jethro's was where Gorman was headed.

Gorman felt comfortable in Chesapeake Beach. The drive was only thirty minutes from the Grimes estate, and he liked the water, and the air smelled salty and clean. And not too many spades. Always plenty of bikers, though, which meant that Gorman knew he could take the short drive down to Chesapeake, anytime, and cop. There was always reefer, and if he wanted green, he could get it, the good shit too, not Mexican sprayed with Raid. But tonight Gorman wasn't interested in smoke. Tonight Gorman was looking to score some crank.

He walked into the open-air lounge at the side of Jethro's, had a seat at the bar to the left of a group of young steamfitters he had seen before. The steamfitters, a loud row of beards, were all sloppy drunk. They watched a pro basketball game on the television set mounted over the call rack, and every time a shooter would miss, one of them would say, "That was close," and another would add, "Close only counts in horseshoes and grenades," and all of them would laugh.

Gorman nursed a draft and pretended to watch the game, though Gorman did not follow sports much, and he especially did not follow basketball, basketball being a game for bootheads. After a few sips of his beer, Gorman nodded across the horseshoe bar to a long-haired man in a leather jacket, and then Gorman went to the head in the back of the restaurant to take a piss.

Gorman drained in the urinal, then washed his hands in the sink. As he dried his hands on a brown paper towel, the long-haired man in the leather jacket walked into the bathroom.

"Spunk," Gorman said. "Thanks for comin'."

"You called, man. I'm here."

Gorman tossed the crumpled towel in the wastebasket, drew a fifty from his wallet, handed it to Spunk. Spunk leaned his back against the bathroom door, took a snowseal from the pocket of his leather, and put it in Gorman's palm.

Spunk's hair looked wet. He shook it away from his face. "You want to take a look?"

"Uh-uh. It's got weight." Gorman put the drug in his pocket. "You never fucked me before, Spunk."

"I wouldn't fuck you, man."

"I know it."

Spunk went to a dispenser mounted above and to the left of the sink. He put quarters in the slot, cranked a wheel, and reached into a slot at the bottom of the dispenser. He pointed the matchbook-sized packet at Gorman.

"Linger-On," Spunk said, turning the packet so he could read off the label. "Apply contents to area of organ covered by foreskin and massage until ointment disappears. Wait five minutes before ma . . . marital relations."

"Quicker to jerk off," Gorman said.

"Yeah." Spunk shrugged, gave Gorman a chew-stained smile. "The old lady likes it, though."

Gorman said, "Take it easy, Spunk," and left the head.

Gorman returned to the bar, drank his beer standing, left fifty cents on two-fifty for the barmaid, and walked back out to the Caddy in the lot.

He lowered the window, started the engine, and turned on the radio: "Ain't No Mountain High Enough"—at least they were good for somethin', man, god*damn*it they could sing. Gorman eye-swept the parking lot, unfolded the snowseal in his lap. He okayed the weight—no, Spunk knew better than to fuck him—and checked out the texture. Solid, specked with blue throughout.

Gorman used a double-edged razor to cut a line on a flat glass paperweight he kept in the car. He bent his head, did the line, felt his eyes water immediately. He wanted a smoke right away, but he waited. Gorman's blood began to rush a little faster. He drummed his thumbs on the steering wheel, bobbed his head to the music, cut out another line of crystal meth. Afterward, he lighted a cigarette, drew on it deeply. Some blood dripped from his nose, stopped on the cleft of his upper lip. He wiped it off, and smiled. This was real good shit.

Gorman pulled out of the lot, headed for 260. He kept the window down, turned the Motown up. Gorman wanted another hit, but he figured he could ride the high all the way to the house. Then he'd kick back, huff a little glue in his room, relax. Besides, the crank was for tomorrow. He'd save it, do it then.

VALDEZ HELD a juice glass in his thick hand, swirled scotch. One drink, just like always, the night before a job. Then early to bed.

A portable black-and-white played at a low volume in the room. Valdez sat in his boxer shorts on the bed, sipped scotch, watched the program on the screen. This was the one where the young guy runs an advertising agency, and the agency gets taken over by a bigger company, and the bigger company sends in some broad, a broad with brains and a big set of tits, to run it. So the guy, now he's got to answer to this broad, and he doesn't like it. But he likes those tits. So, for the whole season on this show, the two of them trade insults, and he checks out her ass every time she turns around, and she does the same to him, and nothing ever happens. Valdez figured, he could tell from the way the guy smiled, that the actor playing the role took it up the ass in real life. But they should have let him nail the broad on the show. It was a pretty good show, funny and all that shit, but him nailing the broad would have made the show a whole lot better.

Valdez tried to think about the last time he had been with a woman. He tried hard to remember. He thought of the time, a couple years back, when he and Gorman had gone down to Thomas Circle and bought a whore, a white broad wearing white hot pants with coffee stains on the crotch. She had sucked him off in the stairwell of an apartment house a little ways north of the Circle, on 14th. It had cost him twenty-five bucks, and Gorman had waited in the car. He guessed that had been the last time.

Valdez got off the bed, walked in front of the mirror that hung over his dresser. He fingered the gold crucifix that hung between the saddlebags of his chest, his eyes traveling down to his great brown belly. Under all of that he knew he was as hard as any man. He knew, too, that he was an ugly man, and that the ugliness added to the weight made it hard for any woman to want him. Men feared and respected him, though, and that was something.

From his bedroom, Valdez could hear the muffled, raised voices of the woman and Mr. Grimes upstairs. He walked back to the television set, turned up the volume. The beam of headlights—that would be Gorman, back from his run—passed through the room.

Valdez finished his scotch, placed the juice glass on the dresser. He touched the barrels of his two .45s, touched the extra clips laid neatly at the guns' sides. He turned off the television, turned off the lamp on the nightstand, lay on his back on top of the covers. Valdez folded his hands across his chest, listened to the muted emotions of the voices above, listened to the heavy wheeze of his own breath. He closed his eyes.

WEINER LAID an LP on the platter—the Jazz Messengers, on the Columbia label, three-hundred-and-sixty-degree sound—and turned up the volume on his Marantz tube amp. Man, this one really cooked.

He fixed himself a Brandy Alexander at the counter of his kitchenette, took it out to the living room, and had a seat on his brown corduroy sofa. Weiner put his feet up on the glass table that fronted the sofa, rested his glass in his lap. He closed his eyes, listened to the jump of "Infra-Rae," Hank Mobley's tenor sax blowing wild against Art Blakey's drums.

Weiner had taken in a five-thirty show at the West End, had one drink after that at the bar of Madeo's, a restaurant next door to the theater, then walked the three blocks to his Foggy Bottom apartment. He had changed into paisley pajamas, a velour robe, and brown leather slippers.

Tomorrow morning he'd meet the men at the Grimes place, answer any questions, collect his fee from Grimes, and finish his end of the deal. Then, while the men did the job, he'd go meet Nita.

Weiner looked at his wrinkled hand wrapped loosely around the glass. It really didn't bother him—a man his age, he'd have some gray hairs, a few wrinkles. The important thing was, he'd look good tomorrow, dress with a little flair. Nita liked his confidence, his wit—he knew that, could tell from the way her eyes danced when he told a joke—and she liked the way he wore his beret, a little off center, like he looked at the world different from everybody else. And the ring, man, that would turn her head all the way around. Sure, three Cs was steep for a ring like that, but he knew—he could just *imagine*—that Nita was worth every last penny.

Weiner got up, went to the window, looked out at the street below. A young man strutted down the sidewalk, his arm around his girlfriend. He kissed her ear, smelled her hair, and she leaned into him and laughed. Weiner watched them cross the street, turn a corner, pass through the light of a streetlight, and disappear.

He stood there staring at the light, the spot where the lovers had been, and his thoughts went back thirty years, to a terrifically sexy girl he had known, a young waitress at Coffee and Confusion. He could still see her, leaning over the tables, serving drinks, her long black hair falling around her face. He wondered where that girl was now.

Weiner closed his eyes, put his head back, and killed his drink.

"WHAT YOU thinkin' about, baby?"

Randolph said, "Nothin'."

"You thinkin' about somethin'."

Randolph rolled onto his elbow. He put his hand to the woman's breast. His fingers traced her nipple in the darkness. He lowered his head, kissed her there.

"Wasn't I good to you?" he said.

"Mmm-huh."

"I ain't thinkin' about nothin' but you, baby."

The woman said, "Come here."

CONSTANTINE LISTENED to the Isleys' "Live It Up" on the house stereo, had a taste of his drink. More ice water than vodka now, but that was all right. He'd have one more, call it a night.

He had sat alone at the bar for the last half hour, listening to the seventies funk favored by the tender. Solo drinkers took up the remaining stools, spaced evenly apart. The booths and deuces were largely unoccupied; a few adulterous couples talked quietly in the dim light.

Constantine heard a familiar voice call his name, turned his head left toward the entrance to the lounge. Through the smoke of the barroom he saw Polk, limping toward him.

Polk unsnapped his windbreaker as he took a seat next to Constantine. Constantine shook his hand.

"Polk."

"Thought I'd find you here." Polk strained a smile. "How's it goin', Connie?"

"It's okay."

"Got a cigarette?"

"Sure."

Constantine picked his Marlboros off the bar, shook one out of the deck in Polk's direction. Polk took it, flipped the filter between his teeth. Constantine stuck one in his mouth, lighted Polk's, put fire to his own. He dragged deeply, tossed the spent match into the ashtray that sat to the right of his drink.

"You ready for another?" Polk said.

"Yeah," Constantine said. "One more."

Polk signaled the bartender. "An Absolut and tonic here, and a vodka rocks for my friend." Polk turned to Constantine. "You take a special kind?"

"Just vodka," said Constantine, and the bartender went away to fix the drinks.

"You ought to try the good stuff," Polk said.

"It's all alike."

"Just the same, you ought to try it sometime. It's okay to have nice things."

"You sound like Grimes."

"Well," Polk said, "just look at him. Whatever you think of the man, he's got it all. Doesn't he?"

The bartender served the drinks. Polk tapped Constantine's glass with his, had a healthy pull off his cocktail. Polk put the glass back on the bar.

"I talked to Randolph," he said, looking at Constantine carefully, out the corner of his eye. "Randolph thinks you've got somethin' going on with Grimes's woman."

"It's my business if I do," Constantine said.

"I'm not gonna tell you to knock it off," Polk said, waving his hand.

Constantine dragged on his cigarette, exhaled. "What *were* you going to tell me, Polk?"

"Just this," Polk said, putting his hand on Constantine's arm. "I passed up on a lot of good things in my life. That's just one of the mistakes I've made along the way, and believe me, I've made plenty. But when you come across something as fine as that woman...you don't let it get away from you, Connie, not for nothin'." Polk lowered his voice, squinted. "If you have to, you take it."

Constantine gently pulled his arm from Polk's grip. "Thanks for the advice," he said.

Polk looked away, then into his drink. He had a sip, had a hit of his smoke. He cocked one eyebrow, shook his head. "Anyway, that's not what I came to tell you. I came to apologize, really. I came to apologize for getting you into all this. I didn't mean for—"

Constantine stopped him. "I let myself in on it, Polk. So forget it."

Polk's expression lightened as he placed his hand back on Constantine's arm. "Well, after tomorrow, there's still Florida. Right, Connie?"

Constantine thought about it, chuckled. "To tell you the truth, I'd forgotten all about it. Florida—that's where we were goin'?"

"It's still on, son. You and me." Polk glanced at his wristwatch, finished his drink in one gulp. "I gotta get goin', pal, Charlotte's waiting."

Polk got off the stool, snapped up his windbreaker to the neck. Constantine put his hand on Polk's shoulder.

"Hold on a second," Constantine said. "There's something I gotta know."

"What?" Polk said.

"In the meeting, you told Grimes that if something happened to you, your share would go to me." Constantine stared into the bright blue of Polk's eyes. "Why?"

Polk smiled. "It's simple, Connie. That day I picked you up hitchhiking—I asked you for a smoke. Well, you probably don't remember, but you gave me your last one. It was a small thing to do, I know. But it's been a long time since someone's done that. It meant something. It meant something, to me." Polk smiled at Constantine.

"Take it easy, Polk."

"You too, kid."

Polk turned, headed for the exit. Constantine watched him limp away.

The bartender, a heavy, slow man with a round, moley face and easy manners, stood in front of Constantine. He wiped the bar with a white rag, emptied Constantine's ashtray, used the rag to clean out the ashtray. He placed the ashtray back on the bar.

"Another?" he said.

"This'll do it," Constantine said. "Thanks."

The bartender went to the register, pulled Constantine's check. Constantine watched him figure out the tab as he mouthed the words to the fat-bottomed funk coming from the deck. Constantine hit his cigarette down to the filter, crushed the cherry in the ashtray. He looked at his face in the barroom mirror through the spaces of the liquor bottles lined on the rack.

So the job, and then Florida. Florida would be next. He had been to Florida, driven there from South Carolina, stayed briefly. He had been most places, it seemed. He supposed it was inevitable that he'd see some of those places again.

"Life is short": he'd heard that overused expression, in bars all over the world. Men used it to explain away everything, from their most recent, foolish purchase, to their next drink, to their last meaningless affair. Life, in fact, seemed very long to Constantine. He could not imagine living another thirty-five, forty years. What would he do?

The thing of it was, Constantine did not fear death. He thought—no, he was *certain*—that death would be exactly the same for him as that time before his birth: a black nothing, a total absence of sensation. The end of his life, though, *that* might be something, as that was something that a man could only experience once. If he was curious about anything, it was to feel those last few seconds of free fall before the blackness. Constantine sat on the bar stool, wondering what it would be like, at the very end.

CHAPTER 19

THE MEN met in the foyer of the Grimes estate at ten o'clock on Friday morning.

Valdez and Gorman stood together next to the entrance to the library, their hands in the pockets of their loose-fitting, zippered jackets. Randolph, Polk, and Constantine stood on the opposite end of the foyer, talking quietly. Jackson dug under his thumbnail with a metal file, and stood alone.

A little past ten, Weiner came down the stairs carrying a large duffel bag in his right hand. Grimes walked from his office, leaned on the rail that ran around the landing, and looked down on the men. Grimes wore a blazer over a salmon-colored polo shirt, with khaki slacks and loafers. His gray hair had been lightly slicked back.

"Good morning, gentlemen," Weiner said, placing the duffel bag in the center of the marbled foyer.

The men formed a semicircle around Weiner and the bag. Weiner crouched down, zipped open the bag. He looked inside it, looked up at Randolph.

"You're okay," Weiner said. "Right, Randolph?"

"I got mine," Randolph said, pulling back the lapel of his jacket to reveal the butt of a holstered .45. Constantine recognized the checkered walnut stock, the raised horse insignia in the middle of the grip.

"Constantine?" Weiner said.

"I won't need—"

"We already went through this, kid."

"The Colt, then," said Constantine.

Weiner pulled a blue-steeled automatic from the bag, handed it, butt out, to Constantine.

"Full clip," Weiner said. "Safety on."

Gorman nudged Valdez as Constantine checked it.

"You know how to use it, driver?" Gorman said.

Constantine ignored Gorman, hefted the gun in his hand.

"Jackson?" Weiner said.

Jackson dropped the file into his pocket, looked down at Weiner. "I got my Walther," he said lazily. "I'm good."

Weiner nodded, pulled another .45 from the bag. "Polk."

Polk took the gun, checked the action, holstered it inside his windbreaker. "Thanks, buddy."

Weiner moved his brown beret back on his head, glanced up at Valdez. Valdez unzipped his jacket, opened it, showed automatics holstered beneath each arm.

"I'll take a revolver," Valdez said, "for insurance. Case one o' these sonofabitches jams."

Weiner drew a snub-nosed .38 from the bag. Valdez took it, dropped to one knee, raised his pant leg, slid the .38 into the empty holster strapped to his ankle. He stood, shook his pant leg down over the holster. Weiner pointed his chin at Gorman.

"I'm holdin' my nine," Gorman said. "You know what else I want. Give it to me."

Weiner reached into the bag, withdrew a 12-gauge pump shotgun with a pistol grip. The skinny man with the gray complexion grabbed it, ran his hand down the barrel.

"This the six- or the eight-shot?" Gorman said.

"The six," Weiner said. "Mossberg makes the barrel shorter by two inches on the six-shot. Thought you'd want the short—"

"It'll do," Gorman said, adding, "Shells."

Weiner tossed a box of shells to Gorman, stood up, faced the men. Gorman put the shells in his jacket.

"Masks are by the door," Weiner said. "Randolph and Constantine, you know the drop for the cars. Any questions, gentlemen?"

None of them spoke.

"That's it, then," Grimes said, from above. He pushed away from the rail, walked back into his office, and closed the door.

THE CAR drop was near Indian Head Highway in Oxon Hill, behind a nondescript commercial strip of rundown brick structures well off the main road. Constantine drove the Super Bee with Polk to the drop. Randolph and Jackson went in Randolph's T-Bird, and Gorman and Valdez took the Caddy. They parked on the side of a closed television repair shop whose windows displayed sun-faded banners, and moved to the rear of the strip. Gorman walked in the middle of the pack, the shotgun tight against his leg.

The Fury and the Road Runner sat together, the only cars in the gravel lot. The sun hung overhead, drying the dew beaded on the cars' hoods. Constantine pointed to the Road Runner, side-glanced Valdez.

"That's us," he said.

Gorman went to it, opened the door, slid the Mossberg behind the buckets onto the floor of the backseat. He walked around the car, opening all the windows. Valdez grunted, got down on his belly, checked beneath the Plymouth for leaks.

Jackson walked to the Fury, ran his hand down the long black hood on his way to the door. He opened the door, got into the shotgun seat, pulled the nail file from his slacks. He pushed the file beneath his thumbnail, stared straight ahead.

Polk, Randolph, and Constantine stood at the edge of the lot and looked out across a weedy field. Beyond the field, a few Cape Cods stood on a dead-end street.

"Hot for April, man." Randolph shifted his shoulders, looked over at Constantine. "You gonna be all right, lover?"

"I'll be all right," Constantine said.

"We best be goin', then. Got to get my ass into work, too. Friday's my day. I *sell* some shoes on Friday, boy." Randolph stared across the field, spoke softly to himself. "Triple dot," he said.

"Go on, Randolph," Polk said. "I'll be along."

Randolph shook Constantine's hand, did not look in his eyes. He walked to the Fury, settled himself in the driver's seat.

Polk said, "Got a smoke, Connie?"

Constantine took the pack from his denim shirt, shook one out for Polk. He lit Polk's, lit one for himself. He took three cigarettes from the pack and slipped them carefully into his breast pocket. He put the remainder of the pack in the pocket of Polk's windbreaker.

"Here," Constantine said

Polk wrinkled his forehead. "You got enough for yourself?"

"Take 'em."

Behind them, they heard the voice of Gorman: "Come on, driver, move it!"

Constantine turned to say good-bye, but the old man was already gone. Polk limped to the car, climbed into the backseat of the Fury. A rumble cut the air as Randolph lit the 440.

Constantine had a drag off his cigarette, followed that with a long hotbox. He pitched the butt, blew smoke in the wind as he walked toward the car. The ugly face of the Mexican gazed out from the shotgun seat.

Constantine opened the door, settled in behind the wheel. He found the key under the seat, fitted it. He looked in the rearview at the gaunt, cadaverous face of Gorman staring out the window. He adjusted the rearview, made an adjustment to the side mirror.

Constantine put his fingers to the key and cooked the ignition.

CHAPTER 20

RANDOLPH PULLED the Fury over to the curb a half-block south of Uptown Liquors on Wisconsin Avenue. He shook his wrist out of his sport jacket, looked at his watch: twelve past eleven.

Jackson took his shades off, folded them, slipped them in the visor over the passenger seat. He pulled his Walther PPK from the holster beneath his jacket, jacked a round into the chamber. He checked the indicator pin on the gun to make sure the round had fallen. He released the safety, slid the Walther back in the holster.

"You ready, old man?" Jackson said.

Polk looked out, past a young couple window-shopping a camping goods store, to the liquor store up the block. A man walked his dalmatian in front of the liquor store, the dog stopping to smell a fast-food wrapper on the sidewalk. Polk touched the grip of the .45 inside his windbreaker. He took a last hit off his smoke, pitched the butt out the window.

"I'm ready," Polk said.

"The old bitch is workin' today," Jackson said. "You see her?" They had driven slowly past the place, one time, around the block. In the spaces between the fluorescent banners hung in the store's plate-glass window, they had seen an elderly woman in a red sweater standing at the front register.

"I saw her."

"All right," Jackson said. "You remember the setup?"

"I was in the place," Polk said, "yesterday."

"The hymie said the money's in three places behind the counter. Two cameras, alarms under—"

"I was in the place."

"We use the masks," Jackson said, speaking rapidly. "In and out."

"Don't kill anybody, Jackson," Polk said.

"In and out, old man," Jackson said. "Nobody dies." Jackson moved his head to a silent rhythm, forward and back. He looked at Randolph behind the wheel, kept the rhythm. The driver was cool— no emotion on his face.

"I'm ready," Randolph said. "Let's get it done."

He engaged the transmission and pulled away from the curb. He drove slowly, past the young couple, past a skateboarder wearing a baseball cap backward, past the man and his dalmatian. Randolph cut in front of a parked Volvo, stopped the Fury in front of the double glass doors of Uptown Liquors.

Jackson had the stocking bunched on the top of his head. Polk had already pulled his down across his face. Randolph looked in the rearview, saw the old man's blue eyes, blue-gray now beneath the mesh, his brush cut spiking through the nylon. From behind the stocking, Polk gave Randolph a wink. Jackson checked his watch.

"Do it, old man," Jackson said. "I'm right behind you."

Polk got out of the car, limped quickly across the sidewalk to the double glass doors. Jackson pushed on the passenger door, leapt out of the car, bumped the door closed, pulled the stocking over his face, ran to the entrance on the heels of Polk. Randolph saw Jackson's hand reach inside his jacket as he followed Polk into the store.

Ten seconds passed. Randolph took his hands off the wheel,

wiped sweat onto his jacket. He put his hands back on the wheel, gripped it.

Randolph heard a woman scream.

POLK DREW the .45, walked to the elderly woman in the red sweater, came behind her, put his arm over her shoulder and across her chest, pulled her against him, put the .45 to her head.

The woman screamed.

Jackson pointed the Walther at the two men behind the counter, his arm straight out. He walked toward them, moving the gun between their open-mouthed faces. The youngest of the men shook his head, did not speak.

"Don't nobody fuckin' move, man!" Jackson shouted. "Arms up, and nobody moves!" He moved the gun quickly to the store's only customer, a man in a Harris tweed, standing by a barrel filled with red wines. "You too, motherfucker"—the man's arms were already raised—"get on the motherfuckin' ground! Kiss it, motherfucker!"

The man dropped to his knees, went flat on his chest.

"I'm not going to hurt you," Polk said quietly in the woman's ear. The wrinkles of her neck folded onto his forearm. He felt her tears, hot on his hand.

"Please," she said.

"Be quiet," Polk said.

"Back the fuck on up!" Jackson screamed, waving the gun at the two older men. They did it, until they touched the wall of seasonal decanters. "All right, Junior"—he put the Walther in young Rosenfeld's face—"the money, motherfucker, not the bullshit in the register, the money beneath the counter, all of it, motherfucker, now!"

"I'll do it," Rosenfeld said quietly, his hands still up, the Rolex sliding down his wrist. "Take it easy."

"The money, man, the money, the got-damn money!"

Jackson touched the barrel of the automatic to Rosenfeld's forehead. Rosenfeld closed his eyes.

"Please," said old man Rosenfeld, a catch in his voice.

Jackson looked quickly toward the darkness of the stockroom, then back to the young man. Jackson made his gun hand shake, shifted his feet, cocked the hammer back on the Walther.

Young Rosenfeld lowered one shaking hand, found a large cloth deposit bag beneath the counter. Jackson could see the rectangular stacks pushing out on the cloth.

"There's more," Jackson said. "Two other spots." He raised his voice again. "The money, motherfucker!"

"Give it to him, Robert," the second old man said.

Polk saw the customer begin to raise his head. "Keep it down," Polk said, out the side of his mouth, and the man complied. Polk blinked sweat from his eyes, loosened his grip around the woman's neck.

"That's right, my man, right here," Jackson said evenly, as young Rosenfeld handed Jackson two more bags.

"Let's go!" Polk yelled, releasing the elderly woman. She fell sobbing to the floor.

"You keep those hands up!" Jackson shouted. He backed up a step, regripped the three bags in his left hand, kept the gun in his right trained on young Rosenfeld. Jackson laughed shortly. "All o' y'all, have a nice day, hear?"

Jackson saw movement in his side vision, turned his head toward the stockroom. Beneath the stocking mask, Jackson smiled.

In the driver's seat of the Fury, Randolph heard two gunshots from inside the store.

ISAAC HAD checked his watch in the stockroom, just as they came in. Eleven-fifteen, on the money, like the hustler had said.

Isaac heard Mrs. Bradley scream, heard the voice of the hustler yelling at the Rosenfelds. So the white man was holding the old lady, up by the front register, and the hustler was up at the counter, getting the money.

Isaac leaned against the cases of cabernet he had stacked that morning by the entrance. He put one hand against the cardboard for support. His other hand held his army .45.

Funny, how it was. When the hustler stopped screaming, there wasn't much sound. He could hear Mrs. Bradley crying softly, but mostly that was it. Funny, how quiet it was.

He heard the hustler cock his piece.

Isaac laid the barrel of the .45 against his own temple. He felt the throb of his pulse, beating from his temple through to the barrel of the gun. He felt a cool line of sweat travel from his brow, down his cheek and over his lip. He tasted the salt of the sweat.

He heard Mrs. Bradley fall to the ground.

"Let's go," he heard the white man say.

"You keep those hands up!" from the hustler, then laughter. And then, "All o' y'all, have a nice day, hear?"

Isaac spun around the corner, out of the darkness of the stockroom into the fluorescence of the store. His eyes passed the hustler—god-*damn* if the motherfucker wasn't smiling—as he turned toward the register, fixed his gun on the little white man in the stocking mask and the blue windbreaker. Beneath the mask, the white man blinked.

Isaac shot him twice, high in the chest.

Isaac dove beneath the counter. Two rounds blew over the counter, above his head. Plaster and glass fell around him. He heard young Rosenfeld fall back against the wall of liquors, heard Rosenfeld's father grunt.

Isaac stood up. The hustler with the muttonchop sideburns downstepped toward the front door, the money bags in his hand.

Isaac aimed carefully, and shot the hustler three times in the back.

Mrs. Bradley was crying loud now, talking to Jesus. Old man Rosenfeld was shouting something out, and youngblood was shouting something too.

Isaac ignored them, kept the gun trained on the hustler, now crawling on his belly toward the door. The hustler was leaving a blood trail on the linoleum behind him, in a wide stroke, like a brush

had put it there. The hustler was gurgling, fighting for air. He man-
aged to get up, grabbed a barrel to do it, looked behind him once at
Isaac, gave Isaac a strange look, his face twisted tight, like all's he
wanted was to ask Isaac that one-word question: *why?*

The hustler made an effort to push through the door.

Isaac shot him twice more, in the back. The shots pushed the hustler out the door.

As Isaac made his way across the store, he passed the little white
man lying on the floor. Dead. The heart shot, most likely. Isaac
kicked the gun out of the little man's hand. He noticed a funny old
shoe, a shoe with newspaper stuffed inside, lying nearby.

He heard the Rosenfelds yelling frantically, almost happily,
yelling behind him, urging him on. He pushed on the door, stepped
out onto the sidewalk. A woman halfway up the block was screaming, and somewhere off—far off, it seemed—he heard a siren.

The hustler was hanging on the door of the Plymouth—looked to
Isaac to be an old Fury—and he was dropping the bags of money
into the window. Blood was streaked all over the sidewalk, and
blood had splashed up on the Plymouth's door. The hustler tried to
breathe one more time, let his grip off the door, fell back onto his
side, kicked some, stopped moving.

Isaac stood back on the sidewalk, raised the gun. He pointed the
.45 into the car. He pointed the gun at the driver of the car.

He looked at the face of the man in the driver's seat. He looked at
the face, and he knew.

The driver hesitated. He stared into Isaac's eyes. He put his hand
into his maroon sport jacket, took the empty hand out, put the hand
on the Fury's shifter.

The Fury caught rubber, smoke pouring from under its wheels.
Isaac watched it scream away from the curb, watched it turn sharply,
crazily right, at the next intersection. Isaac lowered his gun.

He felt the Rosenfelds surround him, heard their thanks, felt their
hands on his shoulders. Isaac smiled dreamily, thought of the man in
the car.

A year ago Easter, he had saved up, taken Nettie downtown to get some shoes—good God, the woman loved shoes. The man driving the Fury, he had waited on them that day, and what the man had done for Nettie, he had made her feel like she was the only woman in that shop.

Afterward, Isaac had taken the salesman aside, said, "Thank you, my man," and the man had shrugged and said, "Ain't no thing," and Isaac knew the man meant it. But it was something, what he did that day for Isaac's woman.

Isaac had shot the white man because that was what he had been paid to do. And the hustler, who knew what he would have done with that gun, right up in the face of the Rosenfelds. The hustler had called him "brother," but he was nothing of the kind. Now, the shoe salesman, the one driving the car? He was something else again. *He* was one down brother.

CHAPTER 21

GORMAN RIPPED open the box of shells, pointed the Mossberg barrel up, thumbed shells into the breech.

Constantine looked in the rearview. "Keep that shotgun down," he said.

"Concentrate on your driving, driver." Gorman stuffed a fistful of shells in the side pocket of his jacket. He dropped the rest of the box to the floor.

"Keep it down, Gorman," Valdez said from the front seat.

Gorman giggled, laid the Mossberg across his lap.

They drove down R, passed the liquor store, saw dim lights, bars on the windows, little else. Constantine turned right on 14th, passed the children's charity outfit, passed the projects, hooked a right on S. The wind from the open window blew back his long black hair.

Gorman reached into his shirt pocket, withdrew the snowseal. He carefully unwrapped it, bent his head down, put his nose very close to the mound of crystal meth. He inhaled sharply through one nostril, then the other.

Constantine looked at Valdez. "What *is* this?" he said.

"This is *it*, driver," Gorman said. "That's what the *fuck* this is." There was white powder specked with blue on the tip of Gorman's nose.

"Take it easy, Gorman," Valdez said quietly.

Constantine turned right on 13th, went south one block, turned right again on R.

"Pull over right here," Valdez said. "Don't cut it."

Constantine took the Road Runner to the curb. Down the block, past row houses, the liquor store looked small standing alone amid the rubble of demolition. On the other side of R stood the Central Union Mission. A group of people—a dozen, maybe—stood on the sidewalk, outside the doors of the mission.

"All right, Gorman," Valdez said. "Three Irishmen, a sawed-off under the left register. They'll be wearin' vests."

"Head shots," Gorman said.

"If we have to," said Valdez.

Gorman took the snowseal, rubbed it on his gums, licked it, tossed it out the window. He put the stocking on his head. His eyes met Constantine's in the rearview. There was chemical color now in the gray man's face, confidence in his smile.

"Constantine," Valdez said, fitting the stocking tightly on his head, then pointing a thick finger down the block. "You curb it right past the liquor store, there. Got it?"

"I got it," Constantine said.

Valdez looked at his watch. "Let's go."

Constantine drove down the street as Valdez rubbed his palms dry on his jacket. Gorman pumped the shotgun.

"No matter what happens," Valdez said evenly, staring ahead, "you don't leave us. You leave us, I'll kill you. You understand that, Constantine? I promise you."

Constantine pulled the Road Runner to the curb where Valdez had pointed. Valdez and Gorman yanked down on their masks.

Just as he stopped, Valdez and Gorman got out of the car, closed the car doors, ran across the sidewalk, Valdez with both guns drawn,

Gorman with the shotgun at his side, and pushed on the door of EZ Time Liquors. Then they were both inside.

Constantine sat alone in the Plymouth, listened to the heavy idle of the 440.

Across the street, on the sidewalk of the mission, a woman with large hoop earrings leaned against a garbage can, talking loudly to another woman who stood nearby. "That motherfucker *dogged* you, girlfriend," she said.

Both women laughed.

A shotgun blast boomed like a bomb from inside the liquor store. The sound of exploding glass came from the store, and then a second explosion from the shotgun, and then more glass.

Some people from outside the mission stopped looking at their shoes and turned their attention across the street. The two women by the garbage can glanced toward the liquor store, and then the one with the hoop earrings pushed playfully on her friend's shoulder.

"He *dogged* you," she repeated.

Someone ran inside the mission. A few people walked slowly across the street, still looking at the liquor store but not nearing it. One of them, a man wearing a Blazers cap, noticed Constantine sitting in the driver's side of the idling black car. The man studied Constantine, turned his head, turned toward 14th, and walked away.

Constantine heard muffled shouts from behind the black bars and glass. He felt a sudden weakness in his knees. Constantine pushed in the lighter, waited for it to pop. He drummed his fingers on the dash.

The lighter popped out. Constantine used it to fire a smoke. He dragged deeply, exhaled through his nose.

The shotgun fired once more in the store, then several gunshots, then two different shotgun sounds, close together. After that, more gunshots.

The people on the sidewalk stepped back. Constantine heard a siren from far away. Steadily, the siren grew louder. Another siren sounded, from a different direction.

The cigarette dangled from Constantine's lips. He kept his left hand on the wheel. His right hand worked the Hurst through the gears. He let up on the clutch, pushed the gas, felt the friction point, felt the Plymouth begin to jump.

The sirens grew louder.

No.

He depressed the clutch, pushed the shifter into neutral. He felt a warm calm, and a sudden wash of power. He had the vague sensation of his hardening sex. The Beat pounded hot, in his chest and his head.

"Come on," he whispered.

He looked into the store. He saw gunsmoke hovering in the dim light. By the door he saw the raised barrel of Gorman's shotgun.

Then, in the rearview, Constantine saw the first cop car, a blue-and-white, coming up behind him on R. He pitched his cigarette out the window.

"Come on," said Constantine. "Come on."

THE FIRST thing Gorman did, as he pushed through the front door of EZ Time Liquors, was shove aside two customers standing near the beer cooler that ran along the rightmost wall. Then Gorman stepped back, squeezed the trigger on the shotgun, and blew the fuck out of the cooler's glass doors.

He pumped the Mossberg, turned, and fired into the vodka bottles shelved on the left wall. He felt a shower of glass and booze. He pumped the shotgun once more, pointed it at the Irishmen behind the counter.

Valdez had made it to the counter, one .45 in the old Irishman's face, the other at his side. Weiner had said there would be three of them, but today there were only two, a father and son, big, square-headed guys, big guts and big hands. Their hands were up, their faces empty of fear.

"You know what this is," Valdez said loudly. "Let's have it!"

The two customers—old juicers wearing blue maintenance uniforms—hit the floor behind Gorman. One of them talked to himself, the other made a steady moaning sound.

Gorman giggled, swung the shotgun around, pointed it at the juicers, heard the talker talk faster, swung the shotgun back at the young Irishman. The crank was fucking good—Gorman wanted to hear the shotgun again, feel the fire surge through his hands.

"Easy," Valdez said, looking at the father, talking to Gorman. "Now the money. The Brinks money, Pops. Come on!"

The old Irishman narrowed his eyes. "There is no fucking money, you—"

"The money!" Gorman screamed, sliding a few feet forward.

Valdez touched the barrel of his .45 to the old man's head.

"Take it easy, friend," said the young Irishman.

"We ain't your fuckin' friends," Gorman said. He snorted the runoff back up into his nose.

"The money," Valdez said, sweat dripping beneath the nylon of his mask. "Now!"

"Okay," the young Irishman said. "Just take it easy."

He kept his eyes on Gorman as he bent down slowly, lowered one arm. He came up with a large cloth bag. He tossed the bag, and it landed at Gorman's feet.

"That's right," Gorman said, nodding his head.

"There's more," Valdez said.

The young Irishman moved a couple of feet to his right, bent down again, came up with a smaller bag. He dropped that over the counter, near the large cloth bag. He stood straight, his arms raised. Above him, on a shelf holding combs, rubbers, and lottery dream books, a rap song played at a low volume from an old clock radio.

"That better be it," Valdez said. The old man took a slow step back, away from the touch of the gun.

"I'll make this motherfucker explode," Gorman said, opening his hand and then wrapping it tight around the barrel of the shotgun.

The young Irishman nodded. "One more," he said. "Just take it easy."

"Come on!" Gorman said.

The young Irishman bent down.

One of the men on the floor behind Gorman had shit his pants, the stench of it cutting the cordite smell that was heavy now in the store. The talking man spoke louder, said, "Please," and then "Lord, no Lord."

Gorman swiveled his hips, pointed the shotgun at the juicers, told them to keep their mouths shut, turned the shotgun back on the young Irishman.

Gorman heard Valdez yell his name, saw the sawed-off swinging up in the young Irishman's hand.

Gorman fired the Mossberg, dove right behind the scotch rack, heard the young Irishman hit the wall behind the counter, heard him grunt, knew he had not killed him, knew he had hit him in the vest. Gorman pumped the shotgun.

The father reached frantically, clumsily beneath the counter.

Valdez had time to take a step back, stiffen his gun arm. Valdez shot the old man three times—gut, neck, face. The face shot took off the jaw on one side. Valdez saw white bone exposed, and a quarter-sized hole spitting blood from the neck as the old man went down.

Gorman stood, saw the young Irishman stand, saw his wild eyes as Gorman took aim above the barrel chest and fired. The young Irishman was thrown back against the wall, his face torn and peppered pink, his sawed-off exploding the plaster ceiling as he fell. Valdez reached over the counter, put another slug into the father, moved the gun, put one into the son.

Valdez said, "Get the money, Gorman."

Gorman grabbed the bags, ignored the juicers spread flat on the floor as he joined Valdez by the front door. Valdez ejected the clip from the .45 in his right hand, palmed a fresh clip into the gun. He looked through the black bars, out onto the street at the idling Plymouth.

"He's there," Valdez said, the sirens growing louder.

"I see 'im," said Gorman.

"They're coming now," Valdez said.

Gorman said, "I know."

Gorman took the shells from his jacket pocket, thumbed them into the Mossberg's breech. Valdez looked left, down the street. He saw the blue-and-white turn the corner.

"What else you holdin'?" Valdez said.

"My nine," Gorman said, wiping his nose on his sleeve.

"How many shots?"

"Fourteen."

"Keep the shotgun and the bags in one hand," Valdez said. "Use the nine."

Gorman drew it from inside his jacket.

The cop car rose and fell on its shocks as it blew down the street. The driver hit the brakes, the tires screaming as the car began its skid.

Valdez said, "Now, Gorman," and put his shoulder to the door.

Valdez and Gorman came from the store, moved quickly across the sidewalk, stopped, and stood straight as the cop car skidded to a halt three feet behind the Plymouth.

Valdez and Gorman fired into the windshield, Valdez moving his gun driver to passenger, repeating with both .45s. The glass spidered crimson, behind it the vague dark shapes of uniformed bodies rocking violently forward and back, jumping, coming to rest.

Valdez and Gorman turned, casings rolling on the sidewalk, crunching beneath their feet. The street was empty now. The siren still wailed from the shot-up cop car and there were more sirens coming from two or three directions.

Gorman got into the backseat of the Plymouth, dropped the shotgun and the bags on the floor. Valdez got into the seat next to Constantine.

"Take off," Valdez said, shutting the door, pulling the stocking off his head.

Constantine's face was pale, tight, stretched back. He worked the gears, stared straight ahead, pumped the gas against the clutch.

"What the fuck's goin' on, man?" Gorman shouted. "Move it, driver!"

The sirens were almost on them now. Valdez put the barrel of his .45 to Constantine's temple. He bared his teeth and put his face close to Constantine's ear.

Valdez said, "Make it fly."

The Beat flashed white in Constantine's head. He let up on the clutch and pushed down on the gas.

The Plymouth laid rubber, screamed into the intersection at 14th and R. Constantine ran the red, skidded into a wide right turn as a blue Chevy sedan three-sixtied, the ass end of it clearing the Plymouth.

Constantine double-clutched the Hurst, headed north on 14th.

"Heat," Valdez said, pointing a finger at a blue-and-white driving head-on in their direction.

Constantine cut the Road Runner across two southbound lanes, jumped the sidewalk at S, heard Gorman's head hit the roof as he put the car back onto the blacktop. In the rearview, he saw the cop car skid into a right, straighten, fall in behind him.

Constantine made a sharp left into the alley, hit the brick side of a row house, saw sparks in his side vision, punched the gas. Pakistanis and Indians scattered ahead, frantically pushing their vending carts out of the way. Constantine landed on the horn, the Road Runner's "beep-beep" sounding in the alley.

"What the fuck is this!" Gorman said, as Valdez side-glanced Constantine.

"Shut up," Constantine said, over the screams of foreign words outside the car.

He blew through a vendor's cart, the cart jumping, tumbling back over the Plymouth's hood and roof. Constantine turned sharply right at the T of the alley, took out a chain-link fence, gave the Plymouth gas, downshifted, got out of the grip of the fence.

Gorman turned, looked out the back window. Through the smoke he could see the cop car, the vendor's cart in pieces on the hood, as it crashed into the ruin of the fenced yard. Sirens still undulated in the air.

"Where you goin', Constantine?" Valdez said.

Constantine raced through Johnson, the Plymouth's four wheels lifting off the ground as it hit the street. The Plymouth came down, threw sparks, reentered the alley.

"Fifteenth," Constantine said.

"Fifteenth's one-way goin' north."

"I know it," said Constantine.

Constantine blew out of the alley, fishtailed left, headed south against the traffic on 15th. A cop car sped toward them.

"Goddamn it, Constantine," Valdez said.

Constantine pushed down on the accelerator, headed straight for the cop car. The front end of the Plymouth went down; Valdez and Gorman pushed back against their seats. Valdez gripped the armrest mounted on his door, his nails digging into the vinyl. Constantine kept the speed, kept the wheel straight. They could see the drawn-back faces of the cops, could see the mouth of the driver screaming.

"Constantine," Valdez said.

Constantine cut it right, nicked the front end of the cop car, turned the wheel into the body of the cop car. There was a heavy collision of metal, the window on Gorman's side imploding, and then the blue-and-white was off its wheels, airborne at the Plymouth's side, rolling twice and landing, then skidding on its roof, stopped by a row of parked cars.

Gorman laughed, screamed "Yeah!," laughed again, rocked back against his seat. Valdez breathed out through his lips.

Constantine turned right at R, drove against the traffic, cleared cars onto the sidewalk with the Road Runner horn. At 16th he cut north, drove to T, went right. Constantine swung left on 15th, headed north again. In his rearview, he saw the overturned car, smoke rising from its hood, a crowd forming around it.

Constantine accelerated, downshifted as he hit the hill at Malcolm X Park. The 440 sang beneath them as they climbed the hill. The park, the people, and the buildings were a bleeding rush of color at their sides.

"You catch Irving up ahead," Valdez said, holstering his .45. "Take that across town, into northeast, catch Michigan Avenue."

Constantine nodded, expressionless.

"Told you he could drive," Gorman said, from the backseat.

"Shut the fuck up, Gorman," said Valdez.

Constantine took a cigarette from his shirt pocket, put it to his lips. He pushed in the lighter on the dash.

CHAPTER 22

THE FLOOR of Mean Feet was filled with customers when Randolph entered a little past one o'clock.

"Thanks for joining us, Randolph," Mr. Rick said from behind the register, where a line of women had formed. Perspiration was beaded across Mr. Rick's brow, his two or three hairs plastered down on his beige head.

Mr. Rick handed a woman her change, kept talking at Randolph as he passed: "You do this to me on Friday, payday to boot. I'm not going to forget this, Randolph."

"I'm here now," Randolph said, as he walked across the floor, headed to the back. He heard a couple of women greet him on the way, but he did not stop to acknowledge them or anything that was happening on the floor. He passed by the speaker that hung next to one of several full-length mirrors—Jorge was playing some Spanish Joe bullshit on the stereo—and entered the back room.

Randolph hung his sport jacket on a nail, went to the water fountain near the stereo. Next to the fountain, two cigarettes burned down in a ceramic ashtray. The smoke curled into his face as he bent down and drank deeply of the ice-cold water. He lowered his face into the arc of water, kept it there.

He stood up, ripped a paper towel off a nearby roll, wiped his face. Above him, in the center aisle of stock, Antoine straddled two shelves, reaching for a shoe box at the top. Antoine looked down, saw Randolph's face buried in the towel.

"Man, what the fuck is wrong with you, man?" Antoine said. "You pick a Friday, not to mention a payday, to stroll on in here at one o'clock? Man, you know these bitches be comin' in here to get all these shoes out of layaway today, and you know whose shoes they be gettin' out. I been runnin' my ass for you all day, man."

"I'm sorry, Antoine, I really am. It couldn't be helped."

Antoine pulled out the box with a deft wrist movement, the boxes above it falling in line. The skinny man jumped down to the worn green carpet. He went to the ashtray, took a drag off the cigarette, exhaled smoke through his nose as he took another. He dropped the cigarette back in the ashtray.

"You owe *me*, Shoedog."

"I said I was sorry."

"Yeah, you sorry." Antoine smiled, let out the last of his smoke. "You be sorrier than a motherfucker when you see the numbers today. Even with all your layaways comin' out, I'll be bustin' a double dot."

Randolph felt heat enter his face. "Double dot? *Any* mother-fucker'd write a double dot today, all those freaks out there on that floor." Randolph tossed the paper towel in the trash. "Shit, Spider-man—"

"Don't call me no Spiderman, man."

"Luther *Van*dross move faster than you. You can't run with me, boy, not on my worst day, hear?"

"Uh-huh." Antoine started walking, his head nodding rapidly. "Well, Shoedog, you just keep on scrubbin' your face and shit. I got work to do."

Antoine jetted out onto the sales floor, and Randolph followed.

Antoine went to his customer by the display, laid the shoe box at her feet. Randolph passed a fine woman in a blue skirt holding a shoe—he knew her, knew the woman never stepped up and bought—and walked straight to Jorge, who was trying to help one of Randolph's regulars.

"You come to get 'em today, darlin'?" Randolph said to the regular.

"Randolph," Jorge said, "we talkin' here, man."

"You talkin' to my *lady*," Randolph said, giving it some teeth, flashing his smile at the woman. "That's right, isn't it, darlin'?"

"I always talk to Randolph," the woman said shortly to Jorge, then looked back at Randolph and smiled. She took an evening shoe off the shelf and held it in her hand.

"It's an eight," Randolph said, "isn't it, baby?"

"Seven and a half," she said.

Randolph said, "I'll be right back."

Jorge followed Randolph toward the back room. He put a hand on Randolph's shoulder. A woman at the register holding a layaway box called Randolph's name.

Randolph smiled, stepped away from Jorge's hand, yelled across the store: "That's a twenty-nine on that one, Mr. Rick." He turned to Jorge. "What you want, man?"

"Man, you just took my lady." Randolph noticed Jorge's thick eyebrows, his thick lips. Even when this one tried to look hard, he just looked pretty.

"No, that's *my* lady." Randolph softened it. "But look here, amigo. You see that freak over there"—Randolph pointed to the woman in the blue skirt, holding up a shoe—"yeah, that one. Well, that's one of my ladies, too. But just so there's no hard feelin's and shit, I'm gonna let you take her. Okay?"

Jorge looked her over, liked what he looked at. He walked to the woman, tapped her on her shoulder. Randolph gave a last look at the floor, saw Antoine talking to an attorney holding a black pump. He studied the woman's feet.

"That's a seven on that pump," Randolph said loudly across the sales floor, and the attorney's head turned. "Am I right?"

"That's right," the attorney said, giving Randolph a smile.

"I'll be right back," said Randolph.

Randolph motored into the back room. He climbed the shelf on the left wall, heard Antoine repeating, "Uh-uh, uh-uh," heard the "uh-uhs" getting louder as Antoine bolted into the stockroom.

Randolph ignored him, reached for the seven—or had she said eight?

"You're disrespectin' me now, Shoedog, you know I don't play that—"

"Relax, Antoine." Randolph jumped down to the carpet, faced Antoine, spoke softly. "You know there's plenty enough for everybody out there, man. Matter of fact, you missin' it right now. Go on, man"—Randolph made a head motion toward the open door to the sales floor—"Go on and get some."

Antoine nodded, turned, went back out to the floor.

Randolph moved quickly down the center aisle, tried to remember the name of that evening shoe—was it the Sweetie?—and the woman's size. He looked blankly at the shoe boxes on the shelf. He thought of the automatic, pointed at his face. He thought of the recognition in the man's eyes.

He climbed up, straddled two shelves, watched his hand shake as he checked a couple of boxes. He found the shoe—it was the Tweetie, not the Sweetie—and pulled an eight. She had said seven and a half—or had she said seven?—but the freak *was* an eight. Randolph jumped down, picked up the pumps, put them on top of the evening shoes. He walked toward the front of the stockroom, feeling suddenly weak. He leaned against the shelf, balanced the shoe boxes with one hand, wiped his forehead with the other.

Randolph laid the shoe boxes on the carpet. He went to the bathroom in the back of the store, vomited in the toilet. He put his hand on the sink, leaned over, finished vomiting. He found some mouthwash in the metal vanity, gargled, and spit into the sink. He splashed some water on his face and rubbed his hands dry on his pressed jeans.

Randolph left the bathroom, picked up the two pairs of shoes, and walked out of the stockroom, onto the sales floor, into the light.

WEINER CHECKED his watch: five minutes past one o'clock. He switched to the left side of the moving steps, felt the ache in his calves as he walked up the long escalator out of the Dupont Metro. Behind him, at the bottom of the escalator, a boy in a white corduroy coat held up a stack of newspapers and repeated, *"Washington Times,* twenty-five cents. It ain't the best, but it ain't the worst." Standing next to the boy, a shirtless man in overalls sang "A Change Is Gonna Come." The richness of the singer's voice resonated in the honeycombed concrete of the well.

At the top of the escalator, Weiner dropped change in the plastic cup of a pleasant, froggish man who stood in the same spot every day, saying "Thank you and have a nice afternoon" to everyone who passed. Weiner headed south on 19th, dodged businesspeople, passed an acoustic guitarist, a food vendor, and a man selling caps and cheap silk ties. He saw the blue neon sign for Olssen's, went to the doors, pushed on one, and walked inside.

Inside, Weiner moved straight through the book section, moved past the sandals-and-eyeglasses crowd. A microphone came on in the store, and then a young woman's tired voice: "I need a manager at the front register, please." Weiner stopped, checked his reflection in a round security mirror hung and angled down above a blind corner of the fiction department.

He looked okay. The mirror added ten pounds, maybe fifteen, that much he knew. The thing was, any extra weight the black shirt would hide. The paisley ascot was a nice touch too. Weiner tipped his brown beret a little off-center, used his thumb and forefinger to groom his goatee. He turned and walked into the music section of the store.

A couple of employees, guys with lavish hair, stood in the back, talked and laughed. A pop song—strings and drum machines and girl-group harmony—played in the shop, and the more willowy of the two employees put his arms up and closed his eyes and swayed back and forth in an approximation of the beat. Weiner did not know the song.

Weiner hit the jazz section, flipped through the CDs. He looked into the back room as he pretended to inspect the titles, absently running his fingers through the pack. He could see Nita back there, talking to a thin young man. Nita held a cup of coffee in her hand, and the young man said something, putting his hands together as in prayer, and Nita laughed. She happened to look out onto the floor, and Weiner caught her eye. She stopped laughing, and just smiled.

Weiner smiled back, put his hand in the pocket of his Sansabelt slacks, and touched the paper wrapped around the small box that held the ring. He straightened his posture, sucked in his gut.

Nita came out onto the floor, a black sweater over black tights, and walked toward Weiner. He checked out her hips, then the rest of her, and he felt a small stab in his chest. Nita had a full, plainish face, and she was on the heavy side—he knew that—but in her own way, the way those hips moved, the youth in her eyes, the freshness of the whole package, God, she was gorgeous. He'd die happy, and with a Cheshire smile on his face, if only he could touch it.

"Hello, Weiner," she said, stopping on the other side of the rack.

"Nita," Weiner said. "You look lovely."

"Thank you," Nita said, bowing her head, her black hair falling across her face. "Can I help you, sir?"

Weiner glanced at the two employees in the rear of the store, joined now by the young man Nita had been laughing with in the back room. The three of them were smiling alternately at Nita and Weiner. When Weiner looked at them, they looked away. So they were her friends, and something was funny. Was this chick putting him on?

"Excuse me, sir," Nita said, getting his attention. "I said, can I *help* you?"

"Possibly," Weiner said, feeling sweat above his lip but not moving to wipe it away. "Yeah, I think you might be able to help me." In his pocket, he put his fingers around the ring.

"Well?" Nita said.

"Well, I've got this itch, see?"

"An itch?"

"That's right. I'm itching—I'm hot, sweetheart, to hear some saxophone. Specifically, some Sonny Rollins–type saxophone. Are you with me?"

"You've got a hot itch," Nita said.

"Like I said," said Weiner.

Nita pulled hair off her face, grinned, pushed her chin out at Weiner. "What else have you got?"

"Well," Weiner said, "by coincidence, I have these two tickets, happen to be to the Sonny Rollins show. Down at One Step—"

"That it?" said Nita.

Weiner shifted his feet, began to withdraw the ring from his pocket. "There *is* something else—"

"We don't need anything else, Weiner." Nita smiled, laughed a little with the smile. He could see in her eyes that the boys in the back of the store were only boys, and that all of this was real.

"The show's really going to cook, sweetheart. I mean, it's *really* going to cook."

"I'm sure the show will be fine," Nita said. "But what I'm really looking forward to is the company."

Weiner loosened his fingers. He let go of the ring, let it drop back into his pocket. The first thing he thought: had he kept the receipt?

Weiner concentrated, tipped his beret back on his head. "You'll go with me, then?"

"Yes," Nita said. "I'd love to go with you, Weiner."

He smiled, getting a picture now, seeing the receipt in the wooden box on the top of his dresser. He'd return the ring, get the three C notes back, maybe take the money to the track. He'd take the money, and he'd parlay it.

"I'll swing by, pick you up at closing time."

"I'll be here," Nita said.

Weiner looked at Nita and said, "Beautiful."

CHAPTER 23

CONSTANTINE TURNED off Indian Head Highway, found the decaying commercial strip at the end of the short road, went behind the strip. The T-Bird and the Fury were gone. Constantine parked the Road Runner between the Super Bee and the Caddy. He cut the engine. In the backseat, Gorman picked chips of glass from his hair.

"Leave the keys in the ignition," Valdez said. "Gorman, you drop the shotgun back there on the floor. Constantine, lay the .45 under your seat."

"It's clean," Constantine said. "I never touched it."

"Leave it anyway," said Valdez.

"What about your guns?" Constantine asked.

"These guns are mine," Valdez said.

Constantine slid the .45 beneath his seat. He looked out across the weedy field. A thin man in a blue zip-up jacket got out of a late-model sedan parked near the row of Cape Cods, and walked toward them, across the field.

"That's Rego's man," said Valdez. "Come on."

"Polk and Randolph," Constantine said. "I guess—"

"They've come and gone," Valdez said. "The Fury's on the way to the chop. You take the Dodge and meet us at the house. Let's go, Gorman. Grab the bags and let's go."

Valdez and Gorman took the money to the Cadillac, drove out of the lot. Constantine got into the Super Bee. He found the key in the ignition, where the old man had left it.

THE BLACK iron gate was open at the Grimes estate. Constantine drove between the squat brick pillars, headed down the asphalt drive, parked the Super Bee next to the Caddy. To the right of the Caddy was the Olds 98. Parked next to that, Delia's Mercedes.

Constantine climbed out of the Dodge, walked toward the house. He looked across the property at the black cage set in the middle of the lawn. The Doberman's head came up, then dropped back down to rest on its paws. The dog's eyes were serene, still, like deep, black water.

Constantine took the steps up, stood beneath the portico, rang the bell. He looked up at the wall of brick, noticed the floodlights hung on both corners of the house. He saw the curtains drawn in Grimes's office, the curtains drawn in the bedroom as well.

The door opened. "Come on," Gorman said.

Constantine stepped into the marble foyer. Valdez was sitting at the bottom of the staircase, rubbing a wet towel across his face. Gorman leaned against the door frame of the library, lighting a smoke. He squinted through the smoke at Constantine, dropped the spent match into an ashtray set on an end table. Constantine looked at Gorman, then at Valdez.

"Where's Polk?" said Constantine.

"He didn't make it," said Valdez. "Neither did Jackson."

Constantine put his hands into the pockets of his jeans, looked at the checkerboard marble floor. He ran the toe of his boot along the line between the black and white of the floor. He listened to Gorman's exhale, listened to the seconds tick off the clock in the library.

Constantine raised his head. "What about Randolph?" he said.

"He did good," Valdez said.

Gorman pushed away from the door frame. "I'm gonna take a fuckin' shower," he said. He walked past Constantine, through a door beneath the bowed staircase. His footsteps echoed in the foyer.

Valdez stood up, folded the towel, and sighed. "Go on up," he said. "Go on up and get your money."

CONSTANTINE KNOCKED twice on the office door, turned the knob, and entered. He closed the door behind him.

Grimes sat behind the cherrywood desk, his blazer hung over the back of his chair. He took his hand away from the mound of magnetic chips on the plastic base, and motioned Constantine into the room. Constantine walked past the chairs upholstered in green leather, went to the window, stood in the sunlight that spilled through the window. He looked out onto the grounds.

"Cigar?" Grimes said.

"No," said Constantine.

Grimes took one from a wooden box on his desk, lighted it slowly. Constantine smelled it, saw the smoke of it creep into the light where he stood.

"You did fine today, Constantine. I knew you would. Valdez said—"

"What happened?" Constantine said. He heard wood creak as Grimes leaned back in his chair.

"The stockman surprised them. Polk never made it out of the store. Jackson got the money to the car. He died on the sidewalk."

Constantine ran his hand through his long black hair. "Gorman. He blew that liquor store *up*. Him and Valdez, they killed a couple of cops."

"I know it," Grimes said.

"We left a lot of bullets, man. People, they saw me. They saw the car."

"I know it." Grimes rolled the end of his cigar on the edge of the tray, dropped a piece of ash. "The cars are being broken down. The guns can't be traced. Nobody on Rego's end will ever talk. Everybody knows not to talk." Grimes pointed his cigar at Constantine's back. "You might want to shave, cut off some of that hair."

Constantine rubbed his face. "You know, Grimes," he said, "you don't seem too shook." His voice was dull, flat. "Those cops, those men in the store. Polk."

"They did their jobs," Grimes said. "All of them."

Constantine closed his eyes slowly. He kept them closed as he spoke. "I know about Korea, Grimes. I know what you did for him. Polk was your friend."

"Yes," Grimes said. "But that was Korea. This is something else." Grimes looked toward the window. "It happens, Constantine. And when it happens, you can't change it. So forget it."

Constantine turned away from the window, walked to the front of the desk, faced Grimes. Constantine's hands gripped the corners of the desk, his jaw set tight. "I'll take mine," he said.

Grimes nodded, reached beneath the desk. He put an imitation leather briefcase on top of the desk, slid it toward Constantine.

"Thirty thousand," Grimes said. "Count it out if you'd like."

Constantine looked at the case, did not touch it. "What about the rest of it?"

"You—"

"The rest of the money, Grimes. Polk's thirty, and the extra twenty, from the old job. That was the deal."

Grimes attempted a smile, made an awkward wave of his hand. "There'll be other jobs, Constantine, and more money. Twice what's in that case."

"No more jobs, Grimes. I'm gone, today." Constantine leaned over the desk. "The money."

They stared at each other for what seemed to be a long time. Grimes looked for something in Constantine's eyes, saw only emptiness. Grimes looked away.

"I don't have the rest of it here," Grimes said.

"Then get it."

"All right," Grimes said quietly. "It's...somewhere else. Go downstairs and meet Valdez in the foyer. I'll have him take you to it."

Constantine nodded, took the briefcase off the desk, walked from the room. When the door shut, Grimes picked the receiver up from the desk phone. He buzzed Valdez and gave him his instructions.

Grimes hung up the phone, sat back in his chair, and drew on his cigar. He looked at his hand and saw that it was shaking.

CHAPTER 24

CONSTANTINE DESCENDED the stairs and met Valdez in the center of the marble foyer. Valdez looked Constantine over slowly, lowered his head, stared blankly at the floor. He shook his head one time, rubbed his finger along the bridge of his nose.

"All right, Constantine," Valdez said. "Let's go ahead and get this done."

Constantine followed Valdez out the front door, down the steps onto the asphalt drive. The sun still came down on the lawn, but the wind had kicked up now, and a slate wall of clouds approached from the northeast. Valdez walked quickly toward the Cadillac. "Where we goin'?" Constantine said to the wide back of Valdez.

"The stable," Valdez said, still walking. "Take the Dodge, meet me there." Valdez stopped at the door of the Caddy, smiled thickly at Constantine. "You know where the stable is, don't you, Constantine?"

"I know where it is."

"I'll see you there," said Valdez.

Constantine got into the Dodge, dropped the briefcase on the passenger seat. He opened the briefcase, ran his fingers through the contents, closed the lid. He put his hand on the ignition key, turned it over, felt the rumble of the 383. He leaned forward, over the wheel. He looked through the windshield, up to the second-story windows. In Grimes's office, the swivel chair moved slowly, back and forth. In the bedroom, he saw the movement of curtains, Delia's slim figure stepping back from the light, nothing else.

Constantine swung the Dodge around, took it down the asphalt drive, passed through the gate, turned left onto the two-lane. He switched on the radio, heard a newscaster's voice, quickly moved the thumb wheel of the dial away from the voice and onto a station playing music. He heard a pedal steel guitar, and a man singing mournfully about a woman, and the solace of drink. He kept the tuner there, gave the Dodge gas.

He drove along the split-rail fence, the woods thick behind it. Up ahead, where the forest broke again to an open field, he saw Valdez turn the Caddy onto the gravel road. For a moment Constantine considered driving on—thirty grand could take him someplace far away, and keep him there—but he flashed on Polk, his blue windbreaker hung loosely on his slight frame, a cigarette locked in his jaw, his flattop, his wrinkled brow. Constantine downshifted into second, followed the Caddy down the gravel road.

Valdez cut the engine by the entrance to the paddock that surrounded the stable. Constantine pulled up beside him. Valdez got out of the car, walked into the paddock. Constantine climbed from the Super Bee, shut the door.

Constantine looked at the suitcase lying on the seat, turned his head, looked at the two-lane a hundred yards back across the field. He could not hear the approach of other vehicles from either direction. The wind blew through the trees, the undersides of leaves flashing white in the last of the sun.

Valdez turned the corner of the stable. Constantine glanced back at the road one more time, then followed Valdez.

He walked across the worn grass of the paddock, walked beside the weathered gray wood of the stable. He heard a snort, a toss of the head, and the clomp of the stallion's hooves behind the wood.

Beyond the paddock, at the tree line, he saw the beginnings of a path cut into the woods. Constantine turned the corner, saw Valdez standing alone behind the stable.

Valdez walked to a post in the split-rail fence, removed his jacket, hung it on the post.

"Where's the money?" Constantine said.

"The money," Valdez muttered, removing his ring and watch, dropping them in his pocket.

"That's right. Me and Grimes, we had a deal." Constantine looked behind him, knew before he looked that the stable blocked a view from the road.

Valdez took both shoulder holsters off, hung the .45s over his jacket. He stepped away from the fence.

"You shoulda kept driving, Constantine. You were a lucky man. That shit today, that was as close as it gets. You shoulda kept driving with that thirty grand, right down the road. You were stone fuckin' free, man." Valdez shook his head. "Stupid," he said. "Stupid."

Valdez walked toward Constantine, moved across the paddock with strong, even strides. Constantine could see that Valdez was not going to stop.

"We can talk," Constantine said.

"Sure," Valdez said, as he reached Constantine. "We'll talk. But first, this."

Constantine saw the blurred flesh of the right almost as he felt it. Valdez connected high in the cheek, knocked Constantine off his feet, sent him down into the dirt.

Constantine got to his knees, looked up, saw the fence and Valdez shooting up at an angle and meeting somewhere in the darkening sky. Constantine leaned back on his elbow, closed his eyes.

"Just sit there," Valdez said.

Constantine swallowed, worked his jaw, tried to focus. After a while, the paddock stopped moving. When it stopped moving, he looked at Valdez and nodded.

"Get up," Valdez said. "You been wantin' to try me. So get up."

Constantine stood. He balled and unballed his fists, sized up the Mexican. He kept his eyes on Valdez, touched his right thumb to his chin, then his left. He knew where his hands were then. He put his weight on the balls of his feet.

"All right," Constantine said, leaving his right hand under his chin. "Come on."

They circled each other in the paddock. The sun fell behind the clouds, and a blanket of shadow settled on the grass. Valdez bobbed, came in.

Valdez threw a roundhouse right and then a left. Constantine covered up, tucked his chin to his chest, breathed evenly, took the blows on his shoulders.

Valdez pulled back for another right. Constantine saw the opening close in, concentrated on the meaty triangle of the fat man's chin. Constantine aimed straight through for the Mexican's skull, exploded an uppercut, connected on his jaw. Valdez's eyes rolled up with the punch.

Constantine combined with a left jab and a right cross, both to the head. Someone's bones cracked in the wind, and Constantine felt a stab of pain in his hand as the Mexican stumbled back, his arms spread wide. Constantine went in.

He put one in the Mexican's gut, buried it there, heard the Mexican grunt. Valdez came back with a head shot that threw Constantine back four steps. Valdez charged, screamed as he charged, pushed Constantine into the back of the stable. Constantine felt his head hit the wood, heard the wood splinter, heard the stallion rear up and come back to the ground behind the wall.

Valdez wrapped his arms tightly around Constantine, squeezed, closed his eyes, made a low moaning sound. Constantine threw his head back, violently butted his forehead down into the Mexican's broad nose, felt the nose give. Constantine butted the nose again, harder this time, felt Valdez's arms loosen, saw the blood shoot from his nose down to his white shirt, saw the fresh blood mix with the blood dried on the shirt.

Constantine saw the black eyes of Valdez, heard the deep howl of his rage. He did not feel the blow that rushed toward him. He did not remember the brown fist hitting him at all.

THE RAIN woke Constantine. He felt it cool and sting his broken face. He knew that he was lying on his side in the worn grass and dirt. He looked straight ahead at the blades of grass, watched the rain fall on the blades. Then he felt the hard barrel of a gun touch his temple.

Constantine stared at the grass. Valdez's face was very close to his. He could hear the Mexican's wheeze, could smell his foul breath. Constantine stared at the grass, feeling neither fear nor anticipation. Feeling nothing, he knew that it was not the end.

"I've done too much killin' today," Valdez said quietly with a sigh, pulling the .45 away from Constantine's head. "Get in the Dodge, driver."

Constantine stayed still, listened to the heavy, slow footsteps of Valdez fade. He heard a car door open and shut, heard the start of the Cadillac engine, heard the wheels spit gravel.

Constantine felt the cool rain, smelled the green of the grass, smelled the lime and urine of the stable. He blinked slowly, breathed evenly. He listened to the Mexican drive away.

CHAPTER 25

CONSTANTINE SLEPT, had a hot shower in his room on Georgia Avenue, then ran a bath. He washed four ibuprofens down with beer, finished the beer while lying in the bath. He stared at the alternating black and beige tiles in the wall of the bathroom, the mildew layered on the grout that ran between them. He thought of Delia, Grimes, and Polk. He thought of them, and the tiles bled white.

The water cooled. Constantine sat up in the bath, reached between his feet, and pulled the rubber plug.

He dried himself with a worn white towel, wiped the steam off the mirror above the sink, and looked into the mirror. Both shoulders carried bruises, the right more painful than the left. There was a deep scrape on his cheek, and the area around his left eye was both purple and black, the lids swollen nearly shut, the eye itself gorged with blood. His forehead was discolored, swollen as well. He looked down at his left hand, thicker now than his right. The forefinger on that hand was twisted oddly at the first joint. Constantine tried to bend it, saw a glimpse of his own ugly wince in the mirror.

Constantine got his shaving kit, taped the broken finger to his middle one, ate two more ibuprofens. He dressed in his denim shirt and jeans, put on a zip-up jacket over the shirt. He laced up his Timberland boots, tied them tightly. He took a hundred in twenties from the briefcase, put the briefcase under the bed, and walked out of the room.

In the lobby, the acne-scarred desk clerk did not look up from his porno mag as Constantine passed. Some breakfast jazz came buoyantly from the lounge at Constantine's back as he moved through the glass doors and stepped out into the Georgia Avenue night. The rain still came down, though the worst of it had passed. Constantine went to the Super Bee beneath the streetlight where he had parked it, got behind the wheel, and drove south.

Constantine pulled the Dodge over at the Shepherd Park library, a couple of miles from the motel. He went inside, walked straight to the computerized index, a screen on a high table set next to a rutted pine card catalog. Constantine put his palm over his swollen eye, focused his good eye as he touched his finger to the alphabetized subjects on the screen. The subject windows became narrower with each touch. Finally he found the one that he was after.

Constantine pulled a book, *The Forgotten War* by Clay Blair, from the shelf. He took the book to a table, had a seat across from a snoring homeless man who slept upright with a magazine stuck in his hand. Constantine sat there for the next hour, carefully reading a long chapter of the book. He barely noticed the smell of the homeless man's soiled car coat, barely heard the laughter of children coming from behind a nearby partition as he read.

When he had finished reading, he sat at the table for a little while longer. The homeless man woke up, asked Constantine for the time. Constantine checked his watch, said, "Seven-thirty." He got up from the table and walked heavily across the carpeted floor. Out on the street, he climbed into the Dodge and headed back to the motel.

CONSTANTINE PACKED his JanSport in the room and slung the backpack over one shoulder. He picked up the briefcase, closed the lights in the room, and went down to the lobby.

Constantine turned in his room key to the desk clerk, then took the backpack out to the Dodge and locked it in the trunk. He returned to the motel lobby carrying the briefcase and walked straight through to the lounge.

The round-faced bartender with the moley face was on duty, standing at the service end, putting up drinks. John Handy's "Hard Work" came through the house speakers. Constantine bought a deck of Marlboros from the machine by the entrance, passed quiet couples in booths, had a seat at the end of the empty bar. He put the briefcase behind the rail, at his feet. The bartender moved slowly, stopped where Constantine sat, wiped the area in front of him, placed a clean ashtray and a coaster on the mahogany.

"Back for more," the bartender said.

Constantine said, "I guess."

The bartender looked squarely at Constantine for the first time, wrinkled his brow. "Hey, man, I know it's none of my business—"

"You're right, it's not." Constantine winked painfully. "I slipped on a wet spot, out on the sidewalk. Tough town."

"Tougher than a *mother*fucker," the bartender said, leaning on one round elbow. "I was listenin' to the radio in my car, on the way into my shift. There was ten killin's today in the District, including a couple of armed robberies, man, uptown and down in Shaw, where these boys just tore it *up*. It's Good Friday today, you know? That's why we're so slow. Anyway, the man on the radio said they'd have to rename it Black Friday in D.C., what with all the—"

"You got a phone I can use?" Constantine said.

The bartender stepped back, stood straight. He wiped the bar rag across his hands. "Pay phone's in the lobby."

"Tell you what," Constantine said. "Put your phone on the bar. I'll make it worth your while."

The bartender thought about it, nodded. "I can do that," he said. "What's it gonna be tonight?"

"Vodka rocks," said Constantine.

"Right."

The bartender served the drink after a few long minutes, and placed the phone on the bar next to the drink. Constantine lighted a cigarette, dragged on it, fitted the cigarette in the notch of the ashtray. He pulled his wallet from the seat of his jeans. In the back of the wallet, he found Randolph's card, the number of Delia's private line at the Grimes estate, and another faded phone number on a folded, thin scrap of paper. He aligned the three numbers on the bar in front of him, and dialed the number penciled in on the scrap of paper.

For the next fifteen minutes, Constantine talked to Willie Hall at the bar in Baton Rouge. He made the arrangements, said goodbye to Hall, got a new tone, and dialed Delia's line. He heard her voice, and felt a drop in his chest.

"Yes?"

"Delia, it's Constantine."

"Constantine."

"I'm fine."

"It went all wrong today, didn't it?"

"Delia, don't talk. Listen, okay?"

"I'm listening," she said.

"I want you to put on something comfortable. Something you can wear for a couple of days. Then I want you to get as much cash as you can carry in your pocketbook, and leave the house. I don't care what you have to tell Grimes, just do it. Understand?"

"Yes."

"Delia, is the Mercedes registered in your name?"

"No."

"Take the Mercedes and drive it down to Union Station." Constantine looked at his watch. "Be at the Amtrak ticket counter at nine-thirty. Can you do that?"

"Yes, I can do it." He listened to Delia breathe in and out. "Constantine, are you going to be there?"

Constantine closed his eyes. "I'll be there," he said.

"It's going to be all right, isn't it?"

"Yes. Delia, it's going to be fine."

"Constantine—"

"Nine-thirty," he said, and placed the receiver back on the cradle.

Constantine lighted a cigarette, signaled the bartender for another drink. He reached into his jacket pocket, shook two more painkillers out of the bottle, and washed them down with the melted ice from his drink. The bartender put a fresh vodka on the coaster and walked away. Constantine dialed the next number, dragged on his cigarette, blew smoke over the bar. Randolph picked up on the third ring.

"Yeah."

"It's Constantine."

"Constantine, man."

"I need your help, Randolph. I need it tonight."

"It's over for me," Randolph said.

"I know it," said Constantine. "It's over for all of us. I'm going to take care of it, understand?"

For a while, neither of them spoke. Then Randolph said, "You in the lounge, man? I can hear that tired-ass funk."

"Uh-huh. I'm sitting at the bar."

Randolph sighed. "I'll be there, all right? Fifteen minutes."

"There's one more thing," Constantine said. "I need you to bring something."

"What's that?" said Randolph.

Constantine told him, and racked the phone.

CONSTANTINE WATCHED Randolph move through the entrance, walk tiredly across the lounge. Randolph wore a loose-fitting sport jacket over a mustard-colored shirt buttoned to the neck. He pulled out a stool at the bar, shook Constantine's hand as he settled on the stool. He studied Constantine's battered face.

"What the fuck happened to you?"

"Me and Valdez," Constantine said.

"You—"

"I'm all right. Thanks for coming, man."

"Ain't no thing," said Randolph.

The bartender came from the service end, stood in front of Randolph. Randolph called him by name, ordered a drink.

"Another one for you?" the bartender said to Constantine.

"Yeah," Constantine said. "Make this one an Absolut."

"Sure thing."

The bartender walked away. Constantine tapped out a beat on the bar, pointed to the speaker hung to the left of the high call rack.

"You remember this one?" Constantine said.

"I remember. It's 'Good to Your Earhole,' right? Funkadelic."

Constantine nodded. "I had the original, with the Pedro Bell cover—"

"On Westbound," Randolph said, giving Constantine skin.

Randolph looked at the bartender's back as he poured the drinks. He turned, checked out the couples sitting in the booths, into each other.

"Nineteen seventy-five." Constantine finished what was left in his glass. "I took my girl to see Funkadelic that year, right over at Carter Barron. You ever see them, man?"

"No," Randolph said, "but I saw Parliament, at the Cap Center, the next year after that. They turned that shit out, man, you know what I'm sayin'? The Mothership came *down*."

"That was the year I left D.C.," Constantine said. "Funny thing, man. After all this time, the only music I remember is the music I was listenin' to when I was here. I can't really give you details about much of anything since then, and I been all over the world. It's like it ended, when I left."

"Here," Randolph said quietly, looking around once more before reaching into his jacket and drawing his .45. He passed it across his lap over to Constantine. Constantine put it under his jacket, moved it around to his back, slid the barrel down behind the belt loop of his jeans, fitted it there. Randolph passed Constantine an extra clip. Constantine slipped that in the pocket of his jacket.

Constantine said, "Thanks," and Randolph nodded.

The bartender put a cognac and a side of ice water in front of Randolph, and an Absolut rocks in front of Constantine. The cocktail waitress with the scarred chin and the bandy legs called the bartender's name, and he walked away.

"All right, man," Randolph said, tapping Constantine's glass with his. The two of them drank.

Constantine smiled weakly, put his glass down on the coaster. "You know, it doesn't taste any different."

"What's that?"

"Nothing," said Constantine.

Randolph squinted. "You okay, man? You drunk?"

"I'm okay." Constantine sipped his drink.

Randolph pulled hard on his cognac, chased it with water, placed the glass back on the bar. He looked into his drink as he spoke. "I'm sorry about Polk. He was a good man."

"He was just a man." Constantine burned a match, put it to the end of a cigarette. "He wasn't what I thought he was. But he was a man."

"You're talkin' crazy, man."

Constantine used his foot to push the briefcase in front of Randolph. Randolph felt it touch his feet, looked down, looked at Constantine.

"One more favor, buddy," Constantine said.

Randolph said, "Go ahead."

"I want you to take this down to Union Station. I want you to take it and meet Delia. She's waiting for me, down at the Amtrak counter. Use some of the money to get her on a train to New Orleans. Get her on a train, tonight. Give her this"—Constantine handed a piece of notepaper with Willie Hall's address and phone number written on it—"and tell her to look this guy up. He's expecting her. He owns a bar and some stables, and he's going to give her some work. Get her started." Constantine dragged on his cigarette. "Tell her I got held up, man, tell her I had one more thing to do. Tell her I'm going to meet her in Baton Rouge."

Randolph hit the cognac, finished it. He put the snifter on the coaster and stared at Constantine. "But you ain't goin' to meet her. Are you, Constantine?"

Constantine looked into his drink, shook the ice around in the drink.

Randolph said, "You love her, man?"

"No," said Constantine.

"What you doin' this for, man?"

Constantine dragged on his cigarette, blew smoke toward the bar mirror. "My whole life, Randolph, I been fuckin' up. Today was the end of it. Some people got killed today"—Constantine closed his eyes, shook his head—"I can't change it, man, but I can't run away from it. I can make it so it doesn't happen again. I can make it so Delia has a chance. I can make it so you and Weiner don't get any more calls." Constantine looked at Randolph. "I just want to do something right. Can you understand that?"

"Sure, Constantine. I understand."

Constantine took Randolph's hand, squeezed it. "You've been a good friend, man."

Randolph nodded, started to speak, did not speak. He bent down, picked up the briefcase from the floor, turned, and walked from the lounge. Constantine watched him go out through the glass doors of the lobby, walk under a streetlight, and disappear.

The bartender placed the tab facedown in front of Constantine. Constantine left thirty on nineteen, pushed away from the bar. He stepped quickly out of the lounge.

In the lobby, he passed the desk clerk, pushed on the double glass doors as the bass-heavy funk pumped and faded at his back. He walked out onto the sidewalk, into the night. The rain had stopped, but a mist still hung in the air. He turned the collar of his jacket up against the chill. Orange and red neon reflected off the puddles in the street.

Constantine stepped off the curb, walked across Georgia Avenue toward the Dodge. He looked down at his feet moving on the wet asphalt, automatic, right before left then right again. He smelled the April air, felt the cool hardness of the gun pressed against the small of his back. And Constantine smiled, feeling as he did, just then, like a dog crossing over a bridge.

CHAPTER 26

CONSTANTINE COPPED a pint of Popov at Mayfair Liquors, then drove to an Amoco station and filled the gas can that he found in the trunk. He rolled the windows down and headed southeast, sipping from the pint as he drove. He found a radio station playing straight-ahead rock and roll—two guitars, a bass, and drums—and turned up the volume. He smoked a cigarette down to the filter, lit another off that one as he caught Pennsylvania Avenue going east.

He took Pennsylvania out of the District, let the 383 unwind as Pennsylvania widened, lost the moniker, became Route 4. He found the turnoff north of Dunkirk, drove to the unlit two-lane road, made the turn, and punched the gas. He tossed the empty bottle over his shoulder onto the backseat, dragged on his cigarette until it was hot against his lips, flicked the cigarette out the window. Up ahead, at the tree line, the split-rail fence began.

Constantine drove by woods, then the Grimes estate. He kept his speed, glanced briefly at the house. The lights were on in the second-story windows; the floodlights that hung on the front of the house burned yellow, illuminating the grounds. He drove past another mile of woods, saw the break in the fence and the gravel road. He turned the Dodge into the gravel road, cutting his lights as he pulled up to the paddock that encircled the stable.

Constantine got out of the Dodge, opened the trunk. He pulled the can from the trunk, poured gas on his backpack, poured some across the roof and on the front and back seats. He walked through the gate, into the paddock, walked through the Dutch doors of the dimly lit stable.

Constantine put the gas can down in the dirt. He found the leather halter hanging on a nail, took it to the stall where the stallion nervously clomped the dirt. Constantine opened the stall gate out and to the left, put his hand on the white diamond between the stallion's eyes, rubbed it there and below, rubbed it gently, as Delia had done.

"All right, Mister," Constantine said.

He held the mane with his right hand, and buckled the crown piece over the horse's head. He patted the stallion on his hindquarters as he talked to him, pulled easily on the rope, walked him out of the stable. He led him through the paddock gate, released him, smacked him sharply on the rump. The stallion trotted away, stopped thirty yards out in the field, bucked his head, and looked back at Constantine. Constantine turned and walked back into the stable.

He picked up the gas can, moved quickly to the corner of the stable, found the green button fixed to the area below the video camera, and pushed the button. The light below the camera burned red.

Constantine stared up into the lens of the camera. He felt a weakness in his knees, an adrenaline surge, and a cleansing wash of power. Constantine held the gas can up to the lens and smiled.

GORMAN WALKED to the kitchen that he and Valdez shared in the back of the house. He had been awakened from his nap by the sound of the Mercedes engine starting up, and he had sat up in bed and spread the curtains, watching the woman drive the car out the front gate. He had rubbed his face, thinking of the woman in the car for only a few seconds, before deciding to pour some glue into the brown bag and have a huff. He had tripped on the glue for a while after that, lying faceup in the bed, and then he had gotten off the bed, put on his shoes, and gone to the kitchen to crack a beer.

He heard the low sound coming from the monitor on the kitchen counter even before he walked into the room. He heard the sound, and then saw the flashing red light as he stood before the screen.

"Valdez," he said, keeping his voice just loud enough for only the Mexican to hear. "Better get in here."

Valdez came from his bedroom wearing his cheap black suit pants and a clean white button-down shirt. He stood next to Gorman and stared at the black-and-white images on the screen.

"What the fuck," Valdez muttered, shaking his head. "What the fuck."

On the monitor, Constantine poured gas around the stable. He poured the gas, and then he returned to the camera, talked to the camera, smiled, talked some more. Valdez looked at the ruined face, the one good eye, the eye that had been empty, now filled with some twisted howl of purpose.

"I thought you killed him."

"I didn't."

Gorman giggled. "You fucked him up real good, though, didn't you?"

"Shut up, Gorman."

"Should we tell Grimes?"

"Shut up and let me think." Valdez watched Constantine light a match, hold it in front of the camera. Then: "Get your gun, Gorman. Get both of mine from my room."

Gorman left the kitchen. Valdez watched Constantine toss the match. Through the white flames that flared across the screen, he saw Constantine's back as he ran away, out of the frame, his long black hair flying wildly about his head.

Gorman came back to the kitchen wearing a jacket, handed both packed shoulder holsters to Valdez. Valdez slipped them on, drew his guns, checked them, reholstered them.

"Come on," Valdez said.

They walked from the kitchen, out to the foyer. Grimes came from the office in his blazer and slacks, stood on the landing, leaned over the rail.

"What is it, Valdez?" Grimes said. "What's the matter?"

"Something at the stable," Valdez said. "We'll take care of it."

"The horse," Grimes said.

"We'll take care of it," Valdez said, looking away from Grimes. He pulled on Gorman's jacket.

Gorman and Valdez went out through the front door, ran to the Cadillac. Gorman got behind the wheel, cooked the ignition. He backed off the circular driveway, onto the grass, pulled down on the column arm, put it in drive. He clipped the bumper of the Olds 98 coming out of the turn. He gave the Cadillac gas.

"You and that fuckin' glue," Valdez said, pulling the rectangular gadget from the visor. "Stop the car."

Gorman braked in the middle of the driveway. Valdez pointed the gadget out the window at the black iron doghouse. He hit the button, and the doghouse gate swung open.

"Move it," Valdez said.

Gorman goosed the accelerator, caught rubber in the driveway, drove through the main gate. He turned left, fishtailed the Caddy onto the two-lane.

"What do you wanna do with the driver?" Gorman said, the dash lights giving a green cast to his gray complexion.

"Shoot him," Valdez said. "When you see him, don't say nothin'. Just shoot, hear? Keep shooting till there's nothing left."

CONSTANTINE WALKED to the path cut in the woods behind the stable. The trees in front of him glowed orange, lit from the fire in the stable behind him. He turned once more before he entered the woods. The stable burned through now, and the Dodge burned as well; the stallion galloped in the field, alternately silhouetted and highlighted by flames. Constantine quickly entered the woods.

It was cooler in the woods, and the coolness felt good. He smelled the carbon on his clothing, the gasoline on his hands, the wet green of the forest. The residual light from the fire gave light to the path, the light dying as he walked. He had clocked the road distance from the house to the stable as a mile, but the road twisted. He was not sure how far he would have to walk to get to the house.

He heard the gas tank go in the Dodge, a muffled surge. The sounds of the fire faded; the woods grew darker, denser. He walked through some brambles, stopped, pulled thorns off his clothes. Moving away from the brambles, he slipped, slid down an embankment, knew he had gone off the path. He saw liquidy movement in the darkness, thought of snakes, panicked briefly, stood, breathed evenly, waited. The moon came from behind a wall of clouds, giving form to the woods. He stared at the ground, saw he was standing at the edge of a narrow creek, put his hand over his blood-gorged eye, stared ahead, saw space between the trees past the creek, saw yellow light beyond the trees. He walked through cold, shallow water, slipped and fell again on the other side of the creek. He got to his feet and headed toward the light.

Constantine found a path, followed it in the moonlight. The light from the house grew brighter, and the woods thinned out. Then he was standing at the tree line, on the edge of the grounds of the Grimes estate.

Constantine pulled the Colt from behind his back, put one in the chamber. He looked at the grounds, half lit by the yellow floodlights, half in shadow and darkness. Delia's Mercedes was gone, as was the Caddy. Grimes's black 98 remained, parked crookedly in the circular driveway. Constantine watched his breath, steady and visible in the light. He stepped out of the woods and walked toward the house.

Across the grounds, on the other side of the house, the black Doberman sprang from out of the shadows.

Constantine stood still, covered his bad eye, extended his gun hand, tried to focus. The Doberman sprinted, head up, pink gums and yellow teeth bared, all black-eyed rage. He moved toward Constantine, moved across the green of the lawn like a crazy shadow. Five feet shy of Constantine, he leapt.

Constantine shot the Doberman in the mouth. The dog yelped, flipped in the air, went down. Constantine put his boot to the Doberman's neck, pinned it to the ground, put another bullet in its head.

Constantine stepped back and vomited in the grass. Empty now, he walked toward the house.

He heard a siren wailing at his back, far away. He gripped the .45 in his hand, flashed on his own image, standing in the road a few days back, his thumb out, his pack by his side. Constantine smiled as he looked at the house, smiled viciously, watched Grimes pace behind the lit square of office window. The Beat pounded white in Constantine's head.

Constantine passed through the yellow floodlights, took the steps up to the door, went through the open door, stood in the marble foyer. He could hear Grimes's shoes pacing the floor above, the tick of the clock from the library, the vague, feline call of the distant siren. Constantine headed for the stairs.

He took the bowed stairs, ran his hand along the cherrywood banister as he ascended. He reached the landing, walked across it, went to the office door, turned the brass knob. Constantine entered the office, his gun down at his side.

Grimes stood at the window, looking out toward the woods.

The fire from beyond the woods reflected in the glass, as if a match had been struck to the window, in front of Grimes's face. Grimes had combed his fine gray hair back; his posture was erect, the crease in his khaki slacks impeccable.

"You've done it now," Grimes said quietly, as if to himself. "Haven't you? The firemen will be coming, and then the police. I figure we've got five, maybe ten minutes." Grimes stared out the window. "It's over."

"No," Constantine said. "Not yet."

Grimes stepped back from the window, looked at Constantine.

"You don't look well, Constantine."

"Valdez," said Constantine.

"He's brutal, isn't he? But no brains. He should have done what I told him to do."

"He didn't." Constantine touched his taped fingers to his face, wiped wet hair and mud away with a shaking hand. He pointed the Colt at Grimes, moved the barrel to the high-backed swivel chair behind the desk, moved it back at Grimes. "Sit down."

Grimes took a seat. He fingered the mound of magnetic chips on the desk, pushed it away, reached into the cigar box.

"No," said Constantine.

Grimes frowned, leaned back in the seat, studied Constantine.

"Delia's gone," Grimes said. "You want the money too, is that it?" Grimes opened his fist, pointed his fingers below the desk. "The rest of it's here. Take it, if that's what you want."

Constantine shifted his feet. "This isn't about money."

Grimes shook his head. "Sentiment, then," he said, with contempt.

Constantine's voice shook. "You set up Polk today, didn't you?"

Grimes looked toward the window. "Yes. He wouldn't go away."

"But I thought that's what you wanted, Grimes. Everybody under you, on a string."

Grimes looked back at Constantine, smiled weakly. "You know, don't you? That's what this is about."

Constantine nodded. "The first time I looked at Delia, there was something in her eyes, something I recognized. I didn't see it then, and I didn't even see it at her mother's apartment, when I saw the patch on her mother's dresser. Twelve twenty-one."

"Hill twelve twenty-one," Grimes said, his eyes gone away. "A bunch of us in Company C who made it over that hill, we had those patches made. So we'd never forget. I carried that son of a bitch across the reservoir, Constantine. Do you know that?"

Constantine stepped slowly to the desk. "You thought that what you did for Polk in Korea, that would make him in debt to you for the rest of his life. But Polk didn't see it that way. When

Delia's mother died, you moved into the picture. You needed something on Polk, something big. Something that would bring him back."

"That's right."

"Polk was Delia's father. Wasn't he, Grimes?"

"Yes," Grimes said.

"After you fell in love with her," Constantine said, "you didn't want Polk around anymore. But he wouldn't go away. That's when you decided to get rid of him."

"Yes." Grimes sat back in the chair. "And he won, didn't he? He beat us all. He dragged you into this, encouraged you to take her away. And it worked. It worked."

Constantine heard tires squeal, heard the dull collision of metal against the brick pillars at the gate, heard the big GM engine as the Cadillac came down the drive.

"That would be Valdez," Grimes said.

"I know it," said Constantine.

Constantine raised the gun, shot Grimes twice in the chest. The slugs threw Grimes and the chair back against the wall. Grimes bucked violently, his hands bent at the wrists. He coughed once, tried to breathe, and then he was dead.

Constantine walked to the window, opened it. The Cadillac braked in the circular drive, skidded to a stop. Valdez and Gorman came out together, Valdez zigzagging combat-style in the yellow light, running across the asphalt, guns drawn, not looking up. Gorman ran straight, slow, his face stretched tight. Constantine squinted painfully, got Gorman in his sights.

Know how to use it, driver?

Constantine squeezed the trigger, saw smoke and cloth tear away from Gorman's knee. Gorman slipped and fell, his automatic thrown to the side. Gorman cried out, reached for the gun, tried to move, could move only in a tight circle. Constantine blew a round into the asphalt, watched the asphalt spark. He aimed again, fired. Blood and smoke sprang from the skinny man's chest.

Constantine heard Valdez yell his name, heard the heavy foot-steps on marble as he charged the stairs. He knew Valdez would come in straight.

Constantine jerked his wrist, ejected the spent clip. He slapped the fresh clip into the Colt. He moved to the middle of the room, centered the gun on the door.

"Come on," Constantine said.

The door swung open.

Constantine heard the shots as he saw the muzzle flash, saw the Mexican's white shirt splash red from the fire of his own gun. Constantine felt the hot stings, like the bee stings from the pear tree in his backyard. He kept his finger on the trigger, squeezed it as his feet left the floor, hearing screams not his own, knowing then that he had killed the Mexican, knowing that the Mexican had killed him.

Constantine fell back, felt his face rip away, saw white, then the brilliant blue cloth of a housecoat. He heard a woman's voice, heard the voice say his name. Black arms encircled him, covered him, closed his eyes.

And Constantine thought: So, this is how it is, at the end.

READING GROUP GUIDE

SHOEDOG

A NOVEL

by

GEORGE PELECANOS

GEORGE PELECANOS ON *SHOEDOG*

I have said many times that I have been blessed with a dream career as a novelist. Though I share with many other writers an early history of low advances, lack of promotional support, few reviews, and repeated non-appearances on the bestseller lists, I never got stressed over it. Instead, I saw all of these supposed hurdles as an opportunity to work on my craft and try different things without intervention. Luckily, I had an editor at the time who believed in what I was doing and a publisher who barely knew I existed. It was kid-in-the-candy-store time for someone who just wanted to write books.

Shoedog was my third novel, a break in the Nick Stefanos trilogy. The switch from first person to third was liberating. My intention was to write a pulp/noir in the tradition of David Goodis with the sensibilities of early seventies film. Or, to put it another way, it would be the literary equivalent of the film version of *The Getaway*, had Peckinpah shot Jim Thompson's mind blowing ending as written.

The novel by design would be relatively short, meant to be read perhaps in one long afternoon, with the reader seated on the subway or on a park bench or in a bar, or simply adrift in the city, lost in the book. It would be a stand-alone, unencumbered by the artificiality of series fiction, so anything could happen. In my mind I saw the construction of the book as a pyramid. The base, the second chapter that describes the worldwide journey of Constantine, was deliberately long. Subsequent chapters get shorter and punchier as we return to

Constantine in the present. The style becomes rhythmic, leaner, and more muscular as the story hurtles toward its climax. The last sentence of the novel "cuts to black." Much like the amped-up cars the book lovingly describes, *Shoedog* is the vehicle for a straight-ahead thriller that means to shock and entertain.

The premise was simple: a drifter returns to Washington, D.C., after a seventeen-year absence, becomes a driver in a dual liquor store heist, and finds the dark center of what he has been unwittingly moving toward his whole life. Its amoral protagonist, typical of the noir antihero, is doomed from the start. With the end certain, as certain as it is for us all, the only thing that matters is the ride.

The book came as quickly as anything I've written. I remember the night I wrote the chapter where Constantine walks into Mean Feet and meets Randolph, the shoe salesman extraordinaire who is the title character of the book. At the time I was living in an un-air-conditioned bungalow with Emily and our then one-year-old son. I worked in the attic, which on that July evening was over one hundred degrees. Typing in boxer shorts and a wife-beater, I wrote the entire chapter of thirteen pages in an hour, the words running behind my eyes faster than I could type them. The prose was clean and went directly to publication as written. It was one of those magic, manic moments that many writers describe. The faucet was full on.

Shoedog incorporated several of my obsessions that would show up in subsequent books. Shoes (and the legs and feet that came with them); American muscle cars; the funk and soul movement of the 1970s; the ritual of drinking and bars; the idea of the workplace as the second home of outcasts, loners, and freaks; work itself as its own reward; and notions of friendship, honor, betrayal, and bloody redemption. I have owned many fast cars and admired the triple holy grail of car-chase films, *Bullitt, The French Connection,* and the relatively unheralded *The Seven-Ups,* all produced by Philip D'Antoni. I always wanted to write a book where the drivers pick out their vehicles. There is a chapter in which they do just that. And a chapter, of course, where Constantine pins the pedal to the floor, takes his

Hurst shifter in hand, and shows us just what kind of driver he can be. The final pages, where Constantine wages a one-man assault on the house of the men who have betrayed him, is as violent and visceral as anything I have written. A reviewer of the book stated that the ending "left him reeling." If that's true, then I did my job.

As was the case for all of my books in the early to mid-nineties, the audience for *Shoedog* was small. It is not an "important" book, but it is one that I am proud of because it accomplishes precisely what it sets out to do. *Shoedog* went quickly out of print and eventually found life overseas, published in France by Gallimard's Série Noire. But up until now it has never been released in trade paperback. For many years it has been the lost book in my canon, fetching ridiculously high sums by dealers and collectors. Now it's available, affordably, in the format and size in which I had always hoped it would be published. Enjoy the ride.

QUESTIONS AND TOPICS FOR DISCUSSION

1. At the opening of the book, Constantine says, "The whole thing started on that road, with the car stopping for his upturned thumb." Looking back, he felt that when Polk stopped to pick him on the side of the road, "things that happened to a man were put in motion by something just that small, that random." Do you think there were opportunities along the way for things to take a different track? If so, when?

2. How does Constantine's relationship with his father affect his decisions later in life? What about his relationship with his mother?

3. George Pelecanos's writing includes many detailed descriptions of things like cars, music, clothes, and food. What do these details add to the story? What do they convey about each character?

4. Constantine and Randolph strike up a camaraderie over the course of the job. What are the similarities between the two characters? What are the differences?

5. Many of the characters have hopes and dreams for their lives after this robbery. Do you think they're realistic? What comes to pass and what doesn't?

6. Discuss the relationship between Polk and Grimes. What do they owe each other? Do any loyalties remain? Who do you think is indebted to whom, and why?

7. What drives Grimes to do what he does? Why did he organize this job with the two liquor stores? What are his regrets and what are his pleasures in life?

8. Why does Randolph call himself a shoedog? What meaning does that have for him? Which other characters ultimately find their "shoedog" focus in the book?

9. How does money drive the story in *Shoedog*? How does it motivate Constantine?

10. Why do you think Polk takes such a liking to Constantine? What do you think Constantine means when he says of Polk, "He was just a man...He wasn't what I thought he was. But he was a man"?

11. What are Constantine and Delia looking for from each other? Do you think each gets what he or she wants or needs from the relationship?

12. What do you think happens to Randolph once Constantine finishes his business at the end of the story? How do you see Randolph's life progressing? Do you think he will remain a shoedog after all that happened?

ABOUT THE AUTHOR

George Pelecanos is the author of several highly praised and best-selling novels, including *The Cut, What It Was, The Way Home, The Turnaround,* and *The Night Gardener.* He is also an independent-film producer, an essayist, and the recipient of numerous international writing awards. He was a producer and Emmy-nominated writer for *The Wire* and currently writes for the acclaimed HBO series *Treme.* He lives in Maryland.

. . . AND HIS NEXT BOOK

In October 2013, Little, Brown will publish *The Double,* featuring Spero Lucas. Following is an excerpt from the novel's opening pages.

ONE

TOM PETERSEN sat tall behind his desk. He wore tailored jeans, zippered boots, an aquamarine Ben Sherman shirt, and an aquamarine tie bearing large white polka dots. His blond hair was carefully disheveled. His hands were folded in his lap.

Spero Lucas, seated in a chair before the desk, was dressed in slim-cut Dickies work pants, a plain white T-shirt, and Nike boots. Lucas, Petersen's investigator, took in the criminal attorney's outfit with curiosity and amusement.

"What is it?" said Petersen.

"Your getup," said Lucas. "There's somethin about it."

"I only wear a tie when I'm in court."

"Something else."

"Think of your father. It'll come to you." Petersen looked down at the contents of a manila file that was open on his desk. Beside it sat other files heaped inside a reinforced hanging folder. The package was thick as a phone book. "Let's get back to this."

They were discussing the case of Calvin Bates, a Petersen client. Bates had been charged with first degree murder in the death of his mistress, Edwina Christian.

"Where was the body found?" said Lucas. He opened the pocket-sized Moleskine notebook he carried and readied his pen.

"I'll give you this short file when we're done."

"You know I like to take notes. The details help me work it out in my head."

"Edwina's body was discovered in Southern Maryland. A wooded spot in Charles County, off the Indian Head Highway. Are you familiar with that area?"

"I put my kayak in down there from time to time."

"Edwina had been missing for a week. Once the police actively began to look into her disappearance, Edwina's mother pointed them in the direction of her lover. Bates was a multiple offender who'd been having an off-and-on extramarital relationship with Edwina for years."

"Both of them were married?"

"Bates was married. Edwina was single."

"How'd the police find Edwina?"

"Bates led them to her in a roundabout way. He was in the High Intensity Supervision Program, run by Pre-trial Services."

"HISP. I'm familiar with it. Bates was already up on charges?"

"Drug charges. Nothing violent, but he'd been violated, and he was looking at return time."

"So he was wearing a GPS bracelet."

"On his ankle. The device records longitude and latitude coordinates every ten seconds and uploads them each minute to a database run by a private company under contract with HISP."

"What company?"

"It's called Satellite Tracking of People. Orwellian, don't you think?"

"*Touch of Evil* is one of my favorite movies."

"Spero, sometimes you work too hard at being an aw-shucks kind of guy."

"It serves me well. So, the company was called STOP."

"You ex-military do love your acronyms."

"And the law went to STOP to collect the data on Bates's whereabouts."

"Correct. The data was plotted onto a satellite-based map, progressed in real time in a video format. The results are accurate to within fifty feet. If the bracelet wearer is in a vehicle, its movement can be tracked as well."

"Let me guess," said Lucas. "The autopsy on Edwina Christian determined a general time of death. The coordinates on Bates put him down in Southern Maryland, where Edwina's body was found, at that same time. Right?"

"It gets more damning. Bates had reported his Jeep as being stolen around the time of Edwina's disappearance."

"Model and year of the Jeep?"

"Two thousand Cherokee. Same as yours."

Lucas drove a 2001, but there wasn't enough difference in the model years to mention. It was the boxy Jeep with the I-6 engine, still seen in great numbers on highways, beaches, and city streets, though the car had not been produced in eleven years.

"The Jeep was found in D.C.," said Petersen. "It had been doused in an accelerant and lit on fire. The Mobile Crime Lab guys had little to work with. No shell casings were found. No prints, no hair follicles. They did find brush and debris lodged in the undercarriage, which suggested that the truck had been recently driven off-road."

"As they're engineered to do. How'd the police find Edwina's body?"

"The GPS coordinates led them to a farm alongside acreage that was heavily forested. They observed tire tracks on a dirt road leading into the woods. The imprints matched the tread patterns on the tires of the burned Jeep."

"How'd they find Edwina *exactly?*"

"Technology got them to the area. Nature led them to the body. The detectives saw buzzards circling over the treetops. They eyeballed the general location of the buzzards and walked into the woods. Edwina had been shot once behind the ear at close range, a small-caliber slug in her brainpan. She'd been picked over by the wildlife pretty thoroughly."

In the file, Petersen found several photographs, original size and blown up, and pushed them across the desk to Lucas. The photos were of the tire tracks found in Charles County. "Notice anything?" said Petersen. When Lucas did not reply, Petersen said, "The tires are kinda fat for that model Jeep, aren't they?"

"Doesn't mean anything. I have eighteens on mine. But I've seen twenty-twos mounted on those lifted Cherokees as well." Lucas stared at one of the photographs. There was something there, but the reveal was yet to come. "Can I walk with these?"

"I made this file for you. I've got the State's discovery material as well if you want to have a look at it here in the office. Three hundred and fifty pages' worth."

"I was gonna grab some lunch."

"Stay here and read some of the material. I'm going over to Carmine's on Seventh. I'll bring you something back."

"Calamari with red sauce, please."

Petersen waved his hand dismissively. "Peasant food."

"Don't sleep on squid," said Lucas. "It sounds like they've got your boy Bates dead to rights."

"Not yet," said Petersen. "But I'm playing an away game. The trial's in La Plata. I've never worked in that courtroom, and I don't know any of the black robes down there. I need your help. Anything you can give me."

"You think Bates murdered her?"

"That's irrelevant to me."

"What would be his motive?"

"Edwina's mother claimed that Edwina was trying to break up with him. That she decided she was done running around with a married man. Possible scenario? Bates couldn't deal with the breakup. If she didn't want to be with him, she wouldn't be with anyone else. Something like that."

Lucas stood. His back was beginning to feel the discomfort of sitting in one of the hard chairs on the uneven planked hardwood floors of Petersen's office. The attorney refused to modernize the rooms of the nineteenth-century row house, set on a corner of 5th and D, near the federal courts. He said he preferred to keep its "integrity" intact.

"*Between the Buttons,*" said Lucas, as it came to him, looking at Petersen's shirt and tie. At Petersen's suggestion, he'd been thinking of his late father, Van Lucas, who had owned an extensive Stones vinyl collection, from their first eponymous release through 1981's *Tattoo You,* which many, Lucas's father included, believed to be the last Rolling Stones record that mattered.

"Very good," said Petersen. "Charlie Watts is wearing an outfit like this in the cover photo. Of course, he's also wearing a double-breasted overcoat in the shot, but it's a bit hot for that today."

"But why are you dressed like him? Do you subscribe to *Teen Beat,* too?"

"I'm partial to *Tiger Beat.*"

"Why that record?"

"Just having fun. It's a very cool cover, and an underrated album, especially the UK version. 'Backstreet Girl' is one of the most beautiful songs the lads ever cut. The Beatles never recorded a song so honest or so real."

Lucas had no skin in the Beatles versus Stones game, and offered no argument. In musical matters, particularly classic rock, he deferred to Petersen, who played no instrument but was a bona fide music freak. A few months back he had taken his annual trip to Jazz Fest, where he typically took in both weekends of the event and crawled back with sunburn, a headache, and ten extra pounds.

"Well, you look real spiffy," said Lucas. "Like a hairstylist on Carnaby Street. Or something."

"And you? Where did you buy that T-shirt? It's not Fruit of the Loom."

"American Apparel."

"And I'm guessing it's a medium, not a large. You're wearing it a size too small."

"For the fit. Your point?"

"Your look is just as studied as mine, in its own way."

"Don't include me in your club. I woke up this morning and threw this on."

At an inch under six feet, Lucas was not particularly tall, and at 175, his summer weight, he was not imposing. Nor was he a strutting peacock. His hair was black, kept short by a Nigerian barber at Afrikutz on Georgia Avenue, and he wore no jewelry, outside of his crucifix and *mati*. He was not stunningly handsome, certainly not in the manner of his brother Leo, who was one year older and looked like a young Denzel. But he had something. When he walked down the street or into a bar, women noticed him. Some of them got damp. He had recently turned thirty-one, and he was as lean, cut, and fit as the day he walked out of boot.

"Which reminds me," said Petersen. "While I'm out getting you lunch, no fraternizing with my interns."

"Right."

"Have you seen Constance lately?"

"No," said Lucas.

"I had planned on promoting her here."

"Guess she had other plans."

"Whatever happened between the two of you, she didn't want to cross paths with you anymore. That's why she left this office. When you have an opportunity to be with a quality young lady like Constance...A woman as choice as her doesn't fall into your hands every day, Spero."

"We had fun," said Lucas. "I liked Constance."

He knew that she was special. But he had been to bed with another woman while he'd been with her. He hadn't promised Constance, directly or implicitly, that he would be faithful. He was a young man, making up for lost time. He was sorry that it hadn't worked out between them, but he had little remorse.

Petersen looked at Lucas, a marine veteran of Iraq who had fought in Fallujah, where the fiercest house-to-house combat of the war, perhaps any war, had occurred. A man who'd left his youth in the Middle East and come back looking for a replication of what he had experienced there every day: a sense of purpose and heightened sensation. Petersen sensed that there were night-black shadows beneath the surface of his investigator's cool facade. He was fond of Lucas, at times close to fatherly, but in personal matters, out of respect, Petersen didn't push him.

"On the Bates thing?" said Petersen. "Get me something."

Lucas said, "I will."

THAT EVENING, Lucas smoked a little weed, then grabbed his newest road bike, put it up on his shoulder, and walked it down the stairs of his crib. Summer nights were his favorite time to ride.

Lucas rented the top floor of a house on Emerson and Piney Branch Road, in Northwest, a four-square backed to a bucolic stretch of alley in 16th Street Heights. His landlord, an elderly fourth-generation Washingtonian named Miss Lee, lived on the first floor. His rent was reasonable and there was ample space for his bikes and kayak, which he hung from hooks on the back porch. When Miss Lee asked, he performed routine maintenance on the house and sometimes he did so unprompted. The setup, a country spot in the city, was perfect for him, though he suspected that his peace would soon be disrupted. A huge Mormon church had been erected across the alley in the past year and was due to open its doors. For now, though, all was quiet.

He had recently bought a used Greg LeMond bike from a friend who was about to leave the country for redeployment to Afghanistan. It was a righteous machine, but he didn't care for its rainbow of colors, and he wasn't into labels. Immediately he degreased, sanded, primed, and painted the tubes and forks a flat black. He kept the red wheels because he found them hot. It was a fast bike, significantly quicker than the one he had been riding for years.

Lucas swung onto his saddle, put his feet in the clips, and took 14th all the way downtown, then cut over into Northeast via K Street, and over to the 400 block of H, where he locked his bike to a post and entered Boundary Road, a restaurant on the edge of the thriving Atlas District. Unlike the riot corridors of U and 7th Streets, which had benefited more quickly from the construction of the Metro and its subway stations, H Street had taken forty years to be reborn after the '68 fires. Lit-up business establishments and the sounds of conversation and laughter on the street said that it was flourishing now.

Boundary Road was an airy two-story space: brick walls, a distinctive chandelier, low-key atmosphere. Lucas had a seat at the bar. The night manager, Dan, frequently played reggae and dub through the house system, an added attraction for Lucas. Plus, he could come as he was—tonight, black mountain-bike shorts and a plain white T-shirt—and not feel out of place. He ordered a Stella from the bartender, a friend named Amanda Brand, who had called and asked to see him. He had silent-bounced for Amanda in other establishments, so they had a history. She also knew of his side work and what he could do.

"You eating tonight, Spero?" said Amanda as she served him his beer.

"I'll have that flank steak, medium rare."

"We'll talk in a little bit, okay? I'm half in the weeds."

"I'm in no hurry," he said.

He listened to the Linton Kwesi Johnson coming through the system and drank from the neck of his cold beer. At the end of the full bar he noticed a nice-looking woman sitting alone. Their eyes met and hers did not cut away. It was he who blinked and lowered his gaze. He was typically a man of confidence, but her bold nature disturbed him. The next time he looked back at her she was getting up off her stool. He watched her walk toward him, heading for the restroom. She wore black jeans, a black tank top, and brown motorcycle boots with a T-strap and buckle. Her chestnut hair was shoulder length with cognac highlights. She had a strong, prominent nose and as she passed he saw her bright blue eyes, brilliant even in the low light of the room. She was tall, curvy, and full-breasted, built like a sixties movie star imported from Sweden or Italy. As she passed he studied her shoulders, her arms, and her back, and Lucas's mouth went dry. He had a long pull off his beer.

Amanda returned with his meal. The bar crowd had thinned out somewhat.

"Eat," she said, nodding at his steak.

Lucas dug in and had his first taste. He swallowed and said, "What's up?"

"I have a friend, a woman named Grace. She's had a little trouble lately. I think you might be able to help her."

"What kind of trouble, exactly?"

"Man trouble. Not unusual for her, actually. Grace seems to attract a certain kind of guy. She's divorced, with a long line of cumsack boyfriends. They don't stick around long."

"Maybe it's her."

"If I didn't know her, I'd say the same thing. Thing is, she's a good person. She works for one of those feed-the-children nonprofits, even though she has a law degree and could be doing a lot better."

"So her flaw is her choice in men."

"This last guy she got tangled up with? If he's not a sociopath, he's in the next zip code."

"I'm no leg breaker."

"This is in your wheelhouse. He stole something from her, and she'd like to have it back. She suspects it wasn't the first time he took her off. But she can't prove it. The police won't do her any good. She needs some private help."

"What'd this gentleman take?"

"A painting. That's all I know. But I think he stole a lot more from her than that."

"Emotionally, you mean."

"You'll get it when you meet her."

"Is she aware of my cut?"

"I told her that you take forty percent."

"And if this turns into something, you'll get a piece of my recovery fee yourself, for the referral."

"Not on this one, Spero. Like I say, she's a friend."

"Give me her contact information," said Lucas. "And the contact information of that woman sitting down there on the end of the bar."

Amanda turned her head and saw the woman, still seated alone, a drink before her. "Does your periscope ever go down?"

"I like to live a full life. Do you know her name?"

"Grey Goose martini, rocks, three olives."

"Maybe I should buy her one."

"That's original."

"I never said I was clever. Just determined."

"Sure you wanna spring for the high shelf?"

"Please ask her if she'd like a drink, on me."

Amanda drifted. Lucas watched her make the pitch to the woman, and shortly thereafter the woman gathered her phone and shoulder bag. She left money and something else on the bar before she got up. Her eyes briefly found his as she passed by, and her lovely mouth turned up in a hint of a smile. And then she was gone.

Amanda returned. "She politely declined your offer."

Lucas spread his hands. "See? I don't always win."

"But the thing is, you pretty much do." Amanda placed a beverage napkin on the bar in front of Lucas. "She left her digits for you, handsome."

He looked at the name and phone number, folded the napkin, and stuffed it into a pocket of his shorts. "Sometimes a fella just gets lucky."

"What is it with you?"

"I don't know." And this was true. He was always somewhat surprised when a woman was interested in him. It wasn't like he was trying.

Lucas stood and reached for his wallet. He left twenty on thirty. If Amanda wasn't going to take a bite of his fee, at least he could treat her right.

"Thanks, Marine."

"My pleasure."

"Do me a favor. I'm going to give you Grace's contact information. Call her."

"I'll hit her up."

On the bike ride uptown, Lucas thought of the woman at the end of the bar, the challenge of a new job, the comfort of a payday, the night of sleep that was to come. Sex, work, money, and a comfortable bed. Everything he dreamed of when he was overseas. A guy didn't need anything else. He shifted into a lower gear and found his groove. It had been a good night, filled with promise.

He couldn't know of the trouble yet to come.